"In this ingenious mess of a novel, with all the bullshit paranormal characters that a superhero-habituated modern audience requires, Jarett Kobek clearly and calmly explains our genocidally idiotic mess of a culture as it plunges enthusiastically into a genuine, non-fictional damnation that Batman isn't going to rescue it from. Brilliantly funny and sociologically terrifying, *Only Americans Burn in Hell* is the best satire of our contemporary nightmare that you will ever see, and very possibly the last. Read it while you're still neurologically capable." **Alan Moore**

"This time Kobek has called all of his own craziest bluffs and rocketed straight over the ionosphere, into sheer blue sky and beyond—this book breathes in outer space. One wishes the phrase 'takes no prisoners' had been saved for when we'd need it. If you don't find yourself busting a gut laughing, then you're probably still in denial of how deeply you feel implicated." **Jonathan Lethem**

"Jarett Kobek's books are an attempt to explode what the novel could still be, as radical as Samuel Richardson or Laurence Sterne's attempts to define what it was in the first place. *Only Americans Burn in Hell* is a fantasy work about mythic Amazons time-travelling to modern America of the type currently clogging multiplexes—but one infected by anxieties about sexual politics, the ethics of the digital world and the horrorshow of the Trump administration. Kobek makes you laugh and think at the same time, engaging both the head and the gut." **Stewart Lee**

"*Only Americans Burn in Hell* is a smoking hot and hilarious dissection of why the world is in such a mess right now. While you watch Jarett Kobek pour gasoline on everything—international politics, Internet culture, the book business, American presidents, Christianity, capitalism, the fantasy genre—you will be so mesmerised and laugh so much that your faith in humanity will be restored by the time he lights the match. Jarett Kobek is one of our most groundbreaking writers." **Dorthe Nors**

"There's a chance that when the dust settles on the cultural and political insanity of the early twenty-first century, only one writer will remain relevant: Jarett Kobek. With scathing wit, shocking insight and brutal honesty Kobek demolishes social media and the publishing industry, introduces us to a Saudi Prince hopped up on DMT, and conjures perhaps the most important and hilarious fairy story ever written." **Ivy Pochoda**

"To think of Jarett Kobek as merely ('merely!') an American Houellebecq would be sorely to miss the point. His energy, intellect, wit, sensibility, erudition, tenderness, and—yes—obnoxiousness add up to something wholly original, and absolutely necessary. *Only Americans Burn in Hell* extends the vibrant, reckless critiques offered by *I Hate the Internet* into our present moment, and perhaps a little bit beyond: one reads it with a sense of elation, gratitude and relief that someone is saying these things out loud. So far as that goes, Kobek may be the only contemporary American novelist who matters." **Matthew Specktor**

# Only
# Americans
# Burn in Hell

*ATTA*
*I Hate the Internet*
*The Future Won't Be Long*
*Do Every Thing Wrong! XXXTentacion Against the World*

# Only Americans Burn in Hell

JARETT KOBEK

First published in Great Britain in 2019 by Serpent's Tail,
an imprint of Profile Books Ltd
3 Holford Yard
Bevin Way
London
WCIX 9HD
*www.serpentstail.com*

10 9 8 7 6 5 4 3 2 1

Typeset in Garamond
Printed and bound in Great Britain by Clays Ltd, Elcograf S.p.A.

A CIP record for this book can be obtained from the British Library.

ISBN 978 1 78816 220 3
eISBN 978 1 78283 534 9

# Introduction

# Thank You for Your Honesty

The last time anyone thanked me for my honesty was in an email sent by the Office of Development and Alumni Relations at New York University, an institution of higher learning centered in New York City's Greenwich Village.

NYU has three distinguishing characteristics.

The first is that it's my alma mater.

I graduated in 2002 AD, after giving the university an absurd amount of money for an undergraduate degree.

This is why the school begs me for money.

It's like a junkie who can't stop.

NYU's second distinction is its inhuman cost.

In 2017 AD, the tuition was $46,170 for a year. Throw in campus housing and administrative fees, and the total was $63,472.

To put this in context: as of 2016 AD, the American median income was $57,617 per person.

You can't charge $63,472 and expect much more than a mixture of the rich and the gullible.

The gullible emerge from NYU in a state of financial ruin, indebted for a substandard education that they could've received for about 1/8th of the price at a state-run university.

Welcome to adulthood!

Time to pay back $253,888!
With compounding interest!

The rich kids come out fine.
The rich kids are always fine.

The third thing that distinguishes NYU is its Abu Dhabi campus, which opened in 2014 AD.

The idea behind the Abu Dhabi campus was to construct a mirror-world NYU that bestowed the same substandard education, and thus conferred the same substandard degree, as the Greenwich Village campus.

The only difference was that the mirror-world campus would be located on Happiness Island in the United Arab Emirates, an absolute monarchy funded by the world's seventh-largest oil reserve.

Nothing says academic freedom like petrol feudalism!

Before the Happiness Island campus had its grand opening, an article appeared in the *New York Times* which detailed the nature of NYU's new venture.

The school's administration had arranged a deal with the government of the United Arab Emirates, in which the oil monarchy would cover the whole expense, and construction, of the mirror-world campus.

Picture this: a repressive regime renowned for its human rights abuses makes a deal with a bunch of very naïve and very greedy American bureaucrats.

What could possibly go wrong?

The oil monarchy sent labor recruiters around the Indian subcontinent.

The recruiters told people that they could make big money if they came to Abu Dhabi and helped build the mirror-world campus on Happiness Island.

When people of the Indian subcontinent arrived in Abu Dhabi, happiness proved elusive.

The workers were stuck in subhuman housing and paid dirt-poor wages.

When they tried to strike for the money they were promised, they had the shit beat out of them by the police.

And the workers couldn't leave Happiness Island.

Their passports had been confiscated.

They were slaves.

And although putting people into human bondage and making them build college campuses was a time-honored tradition, it'd been a very long while since any American institution of higher learning had involved itself in this sort of disgrace.

On August 30th, 2017 AD, I received an email from NYU's Office of Development and Alumni Relations.

The email was from a Senior Annual Giving Officer named Corey, and it informed me that Corey was coming to Los Angeles.

I live in Los Angeles.

Corey wanted to have lunch or get coffee.

For years, I'd received emails from NYU. All of the emails begged for money.

But none of them had extended a personal invitation of food or caffeine.

Corey's email made me wonder if NYU employed a clipping service to search for media mentions of prominent alumni.

In the sixteen months prior to Corey's email, I'd lived as a minor literary sensation off the strength of my novel *I Hate the Internet*. Some of the news stories about my book's unlikely success had mentioned that I was an alumnus.

Whenever someone thanks you for your honesty, what they mean is *shut the fuck up*.

Being thanked for your honesty is like someone tattooing the word SEXY on their upper arm.

If it has to be said aloud, its opposite is sure to be true.

"Your face is very stupid!"
"Thank you for your honesty."

"Madame, everyone in this room knows that your wife is a living grotesque!"
"Thank you for your honesty."

"Never invade Russia in the winter!"
"Thank you for your honesty."

"Your prolonged substance abuse is destroying your body, your employment prospects, and the mental health of your family members!"
"Thank you for your honesty."

I wrote back to Corey.
This is what I wrote:

> **Thu, Aug 31, 2017 at 1:26 AM**
> **From: Jarett Kobek**
> **To: Corey**
> **Subject: RE: Meeting with NYU in LA?**
>
> Dear Corey,
>
> Thanks for the offer, but I've long disconnected myself from NYU.
>
> It's impossible to imagine supporting an institution that allowed slave labor to build an entire campus in Abu Dhabi and has failed, completely, to redress the situation in any meaningful fashion.
>
> Thanks,
>
> Jarett

On the surface, my email would appear to be motivated by a principled stance.

A principled stance is the euphemism that people like myself, who are hopelessly mired in the Looney Left, use to describe those moments when they say or do something that ruins a party by taking exception to a harmless comment or action.

I suppose that it was a principled stance.

It's appalling that I attended an institution which placed a fig leaf atop global evil.

And it's repulsive that the fig leaf was built by slaves.

And, really, I'm sorry how mixed I made that fig-leaf metaphor.

But only a mixed metaphor can contain the existential horror of NYU.

Also: I'm a terrible writer.

But, really, this was why I sent my note to Corey: I just wanted NYU to stop asking for money.

You can't imagine how much email starts coming in after you've been a minor literary sensation.

In the same month that Corey extended his invitation for food or caffeine, a major American publisher issued my follow-up to *I Hate the Internet*. It was a novel that ended up with the title *The Future Won't Be Long*.

It was a massive commercial failure.

Less than 300 copies sold in its first six months!

*I Hate the Internet* sold 300 copies in its first two weeks!

Reader, this was shocking.

If for no other reason than the simple fact that *The Future Won't Be Long* was published by Penguin Random House.

Penguin Random House is the biggest publishing conglomerate in the world. It's a multibillion-dollar multinational corporation owned by another multibillion-dollar multinational corporation called Bertelsmann, which spent much of World War Two producing Nazi propaganda and using Jewish slaves to work in its factories.

My book was backed by Nazi money!

And it still failed!

So what happened?

For decades, everyone who had any pretense to High Culture wasted fathomless hours talking about theorists like Michel Foucault and Jean Baudrillard.

These people with pretenses to High Culture had advanced the idea that reading incomprehensible French books gave them special insight into the way the world works.

Sometimes they expressed this pretense in unreadable texts called master's theses and doctoral dissertations.

One of Baudrillard's ideas was very popular. He'd theorized that there would be a moment when reality collapsed into fiction, at which point it would then be impossible to distinguish the fake from the actual.

He called this the Hyperreal.

But what neither Baudrillard nor his readers could ever locate was the exact moment when the Hyperreal would replace the real.

It was a mystery, floating-point arithmetic without any definitive beginning.

But then it happened.

On November 8/9th, 2016 AD, while I was asleep in London's Little Venice, passed out in someone's former childhood bedroom above Blomfield Road, the real became Hyperreal.

Donald J. Trump, the world's best approximation of living fiction, whose body appears to be constituted of media coverage stitched together with plastic surgery, was elected to the Presidency of the United States of America.

When this happened at around 6AM Greenwich Mean Time, a film crew was on Blomfield Road. They were shooting footage for a film called *Paddington 2*.

The film was about a very fussy bear with a posh accent, its cartoon body generated by computers. The bear goes to prison and makes friends with inmates whose bodies were generated by loveless sexual reproduction.

My smartphone started vibrating.

People were sending me text messages of shock and awe.

They were freaked the fuck out.

*What just happened?* they asked.

It turned out that the people who were the least prepared for the Hyperreal were the same people who'd spent decades talking about the Hyperreal.

They had no special insight into anything!

A fog descended upon them.

Trust me, I know what I'm talking about.

These people are my friends.

And, holy shit, these people did not see this thing coming.

And, double holy shit, did it ever make them annoying.

Only two people have ever thanked Donald J. Trump for his honesty. The Ugandan dictator Yoweri Museveni and David Duke, a former Grand Wizard of the Ku Klux Klan.

Great company!

No one else has ever thanked Donald J. Trump for his honesty.

And with good reason.

The President could not be honest.

This was not because the President went out of his way to exist in a state of perpetual falsehood.

The President could not be honest because he existed in a moral universe where there was no truth and there are no lies.

He was hopelessly insane.
He lived in the Hyperreal.
Ideas floated into his head, ideas floated out.
And the whole world jumped at their utterance.

If the country was bombarded, every day, by a morass of awful noise that displayed at best a partial relationship to the truth, and if the citizens of that country were expected to run around like chickens with their heads cut off in response to this awful noise, then why not empower someone to make a different kind of noise?

Why not get someone who would make noise in a different direction?

To steal a joke from the comedian Stewart Lee: it was like being given a room in a fleabag motel, and, in protest at its unsatisfactory conditions, shitting in the room's bed before realizing that you had nowhere else to sleep.

But people did it anyway.

They shit the bed.

They voted for Donald J. Trump.

A fictitious being with, at best, a tenuous connection to reality ended up at the head of the world's most powerful military and the world's biggest economy.

He was from the fourth branch of American governance: the Celebrity.

And he had taken over the first branch: the Executive.

Reality collapsed into fiction.

And you would think, reader, that the best time to be backed by Nazi money was after a living caricature had inaugurated the Hyperreal.

But you'd be wrong.

Here was the implicit sales pitch behind my book: *The country is collapsing, reality has gone mad, and a White Supremacist just murdered a woman by driving his Dodge Challenger into a crowd of protestors. So please buy my book about drug parties in the 1980s AD!*

No one wanted to read that shit.

And all the Nazi loot in the world couldn't make it otherwise.

This book that you are reading was going to be a cracked attempt at the sorry bullshit that people in the Hyperreal actually want to read, which are mindless tales about supranatural creatures.

I had come up with what I thought was a funny contrast between narrative voice and subject matter.

I was going to write a fantasy novel in the imagined voice of an alcoholic from southeastern New England. It was going to be the *The Hobbit* as told by a gin-room rummy from Fall River, Massachusetts.

It was going to go something like this:

Fuckin' Bilbo the little midget over here, he crawls into the prickers and what does he see but some fuckin' trolls sittin' at a fuckin' fire.

"Wow, I says, wow. You tell me, guy, what the fuck am I gonna do with some trolls?" says Bilbo the Dildo. "Who am I, a fuckin' Terminator? I ain't gettin' myself eaten just cause some big shot Poindexter thinks he's a wizard."

But life kept interrupting.

Things went screwy.

It's possible that I had a nervous breakdown.

Somehow I ended up writing a novel that is not only about whimsical undying characters who live on a magical island called Fairy Land, but is also a book that functions as an accidental allegory for a social media hashtag.

This state of affairs seems like a perfect statement about the present moment.

Corey wrote back about a week after I'd sent my email.

This is what he wrote:

**Thu, Sep 7, 2017 at 11:15 AM**
**From: Corey**
**To: Jarett Kobek**
**Subject: RE: Meeting with NYU in LA?**

Dear Mr. Kobek,

Thank you for your response, your honesty, and your candor.

Best wishes,
Corey

# Chapter One

## Certain Facts about Celia, the Queen of Fairy Land

Here are some things that you should know.

The first of these things: Celia was an immortal and undying being, possessed of supranatural powers.

The second: Celia lived on Fairy Land, which was an island in the sea past the sun.

The third: Celia was Fairy Land's Regnant Queen.

The fourth: Celia had become Queen of Fairy Land when she and the other undying women on the island in the sea past the sun had decided to expel or murder all of the men in Fairy Land.

The fifth: when all of the men were dead or expelled, the women of Fairy Land gathered together and called upon Celia to reign as their Queen.

The sixth: Celia accepted the women's call and wore the crown of Fairy Land.

The seventh: Celia liked to fuck.

Here's another thing that you should know: everything is going to be okay.

It isn't easy living in a world where every device of mass communication has been designed to tell you that you're horrible.

It's no picnic being taunted by a Greek chorus when your only economic future is feudalism.

Take a deep breath.

Make sure your exhale is longer than your inhale.

You're on Planet Earth until you're dead.

Everything between now and then is survival.

And survive is what you'll do until you don't.

Calm down.

For the length of time that it takes you to read this book, everything will be fine.

Despite her status as an immortal and undying being from Fairy Land, Celia was pretty uptight in her understanding of gender and sexual norms.

If Celia had not been so rigid in her embrace of gender and sexual norms, Celia could have just fucked some of the other immortal and undying women on the island past the sun.

It could have been very *Wonder Woman*.

But Celia was a hardliner.

Which meant that Celia was into fucking men.

And Celia lived on an island where all of the men had been expelled or killed.

The construction of Celia's monarchy had screwed up Celia's sex life.

So it wasn't very *Wonder Woman*.

It was very *Game of Thrones*.

*Wonder Woman* and *Game of Thrones* were both literary intellectual properties that had been developed past their humble origins into huge media spectacles.

*Wonder Woman* was about an undying woman named Diana who lived on an island in the sea. Diana left her island of lesbians to kill a bunch of Germans.

*Game of Thrones* was about unpleasant people in a fantasy medieval world.

The unpleasant people in *Game of Thrones* killed and fucked each other while reinforcing a worldwide hegemony that replicated, for no particular reason, the racial, sexual, and cultural prejudices of the British colonial era.

Both media spectacles were pornography about war.

This pornography was very popular with people in the United States of America.

The United States of America was a warrior nation that liked to fuck up the shit of weaker countries through unending battles, through the dropping of bombs, through the wholesale slaughter of the poor.

The huge media spectacle of *Wonder Woman* was released in 2017 AD, by which point the United States of America had been at war with the country of Afghanistan for sixteen years.

It was the longest war in the history of the United States of America.

It was sixteen years of turning illiterate Muslim peasants into bloody red streaks of chalk.

Almost everyone in the United States of America pretended that it wasn't happening.

But they loved *Wonder Woman*.

And they loved *Game of Thrones*.

Celia knew a thing or two about being transformed into a media property.

Back in 1599 AD, a guy from England had written a short book called *The Most Pleasant History of Tom a Lincoln*.

Some of the book was true, in that it recounted events that had happened to Celia.

Most of it was bullshit.

Amongst other nonsense, *Tom a Lincoln* was about how Celia had met Tom a Lincoln, who was also called the Red-Rose Knight. He was King Arthur's bastard son.

*Tom a Lincoln* was about how Celia had allowed the Red-Rose Knight to enter Fairy Land after his boat had washed up on the island in the sea past the sun.

*Tom a Lincoln* was about how Celia had fucked the Red-Rose Knight, and how as a result of that fucking, Celia had birthed a son named the Fairy Knight.

About two years after *Tom a Lincoln* was first published, Celia was given a copy of the book. She discovered something that happens to anyone who becomes the subject of media coverage.

Celia discovered the people who create media coverage are depraved beasts that will say anything for money.

The author of *Tom a Lincoln* was a guy named Richard Johnson. He is described thusly in the *Oxford Dictionary of National Biography*:

> Richard Johnson was in every sense a derivative writer: his romances synthesize a mass of traditional materials along with some more sophisticated modern texts, *The Faerie Queene* among them; he retails familiar ballads, songs, and jests under a light disguise of novelty; and his secondhand pamphlets are aimed at the prides and prejudices of a readership of London citizens and their families. His career is a paradigm of popular commercial writing for the press in his time …

In other words, a total fucking hack.
May they be with us always!

Richard Johnson wrote that Celia had killed herself after King Arthur's bastard son left Fairy Land and didn't return.

This lie was presented in a very dramatic fashion, with the Red-Rose Knight trying to return to Fairy Land but facing ill winds which kept his ship from reaching the island.

Richard Johnson had written out Celia's suicide note, which he said was inked in her own blood.

It was very sad.

It dripped with pathos.

It was stuffed with treacle.

It didn't sound anything like Celia.

No one in Fairy Land had any idea how Richard Johnson had learned about the Red-Rose Knight and his visit to Fairy Land.

So many of the details were wrong. Especially the part about the Red-Rose Knight's valiant resistance to Celia's sexual advances.

Especially the suicide.

How could Celia, an undying being, kill herself?

And why would she do it for a mortal man?

Richard Johnson had written a bit about Celia's son, the Fairy Knight. In Part II of *Tom a Lincoln*, the Fairy Knight performs all manner of great deeds and wins the world.

This was sort of true.

In their sexual congress, Celia and the Red-Rose Knight had indeed created the Fairy Knight. But the Fairy Knight hadn't performed all manner of great deeds or won the esteem of the world.

All that happened to the Fairy Knight was that he lived out his early life in Fairy Land until he was banished in his sixteenth year.

No one from Fairy Land ever saw him again.

Richard Johnson omitted that Celia and the Red-Rose Knight had a second child.

When the Red-Rose Knight arrived on the shores of Fairy Land, he and his shipmates had entered the kingdom and never left.

Why would they?

They were surrounded by supranatural women. Many of these women were like Celia. They were hardliners when it came to gender and sexual norms.

And they hadn't seen any men in a very long time.

The Red-Rose Knight's men lived like princes, fucking their tiny brains out in grottos where the flowers sang songs in time with the sexual thrusting while the trees swept their branches along the rutting lovers' flesh.

While they fucked out their tiny brains, the Red-Rose Knight and his men were enacting the general bullshit con on women that is heterosexuality.

The rules of the game go like this: for every thousand remarkable women, the really beautiful ones, the really smart ones, the really smartly beautiful ones and the really beautiful smart ones, there's about one semi-okay man.

Heterosexuality is a giant joke played on the women of the world.

Here's the punchline: if you're a woman, and you want to experience the biological imperative of sex with a man, you pretty much have to bed down with a sack of worthless crap.

And don't forget: this was back in the early medieval period, so the Red-Rose Knight and his men were no beauties.

They really were sacks of worthless crap.

But they were the only dicks in town.

Richard Johnson wrote that the Red-Rose Knight's men knocked up most of the women of Fairy Land.

This isn't true.

The only person who got knocked up was Celia.

She gave birth to the Fairy Knight.

Then, about a year later, she had her daughter.

Celia named her daughter Fernstuff Wirethorne, Keeper of the Sacred Flame, Fiery Green Horsetender, and Mistress Magical of Fairy Land and Its Environs.

No one on Fairy Land could be bothered saying Celia's daughter's full name.

Everyone called Celia's daughter Fern.

Not long after the birth of this daughter, the Red-Rose Knight keeled over and died of an ailment that had yet to be named.

He was murdered by typhoid fever, which meant that he'd been killed by water filled with human shit.

Unbeknownst to everyone, one of the Red-Rose Knight's men was an asymptomatic carrier of typhoid fever.

The carrier's name was Orson.

Orson's hobbies included skipping rocks across ponds, speaking in a high-pitched voice while imitating his mother's folk wisdom, and pretending that he was a beautiful princess waiting to be rescued by a dashing knight.

Being an asymptomatic carrier of typhoid fever meant that although Orson never showed any signs of having the disease, his body was in a state of constant typhoid production.

Orson was like a factory worker under crony capitalism: he was making something, but he didn't share in the gains of that production.

One night, Orson was corralled into helping prepare a feast. This had happened because one of the usual preparers of food was busy fucking out his brains in a shadowy elm grove by the Ancient Rocks of Forever.

And so Orson helped prepare the feast for the Red-Rose Knight, the Red-Rose Knight's men, and all the women of Fairy Land.

Orson placed the Red-Rose Knight's drinking vessel on the communal table.

Because it was the early medieval period, Orson hadn't washed his hands after using the latrine.

He got his left index finger in the Red-Rose Knight's water.

The women of Fairy Land were immune to typhoid fever.

When the Red-Rose Knight died from drinking too much water filled with Orson's shit, he resolved an ethical dilemma.

The dilemma was this: despite liking to fuck, Celia also believed in and embodied the organizational principles of Fairy Land, and the preeminent organizational principle of the Realm was that all men had to be killed or banished.

Celia had stretched this rule for a very long time. For years, she'd let the Red-Rose Knight and his men stay on Fairy Land.

Her citizenry had started to complain.

At the very moment when the Red-Rose Knight died from consuming too much of Orson's shit, Celia had been trying to figure out how to tell the father of her children that he was to be banished from her island.

After the Red-Rose Knight died, the women of Fairy Land killed all of the Red-Rose Knight's men who'd survived their encounter with Orson's shit.

With one exception.

Rusticano was allowed to live.

Orson was the first to lose his head.

Unlike in his fantasies of being a princess, no one saved him from death.

His hands were filthy.

# Chapter Two

## Some Facts about Fern

A magical bullshit thing had happened when Fern was born. Maybe it was because she was the Queen's daughter, maybe it was because she was King Arthur's granddaughter. Maybe it was because she was the first and only woman born in Fairy Land after the expulsion and murder of its men.

Whatever the cause, the effect of this magical bullshit was that the health of the Realm of Fairy Land was tied, directly, to Fern.

She was its living avatar.

In the times when Fern was happy, Fairy Land was a paradise, full of joy and pleasure. The harvests were incredible, the livestock flourished, and the lesbianism was euphoric and multi-orgasmic.

When Fern was angry, Fairy Land was miserable. The harvests were pathetic, the animals all perished, and the lesbianism drifted into a mythical bed death.

In the times when Fern experienced feelings of vulgar existentialism, wondering about the purpose of her or any other life, the whole of Fairy Land entered a state of paralysis, of grinding malaise without discernible beginning or end.

In the five days before Fern ovulated, Fairy Land was hell on Earth.

One of the ways by which Fern dealt with being the living avatar of Fairy Land was to go on vacation.

Most women on Fairy Land never left the island. There was no rule against travel, but enormous social pressure kept the citizenry from venturing into the wider world.

Some people went on trips, sometimes, but it was always awkward.

No one left as much as Fern.

Fern's first departure from Fairy Land was in the Year of the Silken Cutthroat, which roughly corresponded to 1349 AD, 749 AH, and 5109 AM.

Fern set off on a little boat, with no crew, and sailed across the sea to France.

Once she had landed, she made her way by horse to Paris.

Are you wondering how Fern managed to do all of this?

Don't forget: Fern's mother was Celia, the Queen of Fairy Land. Fern was the daughter of an undying being possessed of supranatural abilities, and Fern herself was the living avatar of a magic realm.

Money and horses and boats and all of that?

Fern waved her hand.

Fern performed magic.

And if you're like the Los Angeles-based artist William E. Jones, when you read about Fern performing her magic, you thought to yourself: "Every time that the supernatural enters fiction, it's a cheap shortcut around the craft of storytelling."

And you're right.

Fern's bullshit magic really was a cheap shortcut around the craft of storytelling.

But take a deep breath.

Calm down.

Everything is going to be fine.

Just remember: this level of unprofessionalism has been positively reviewed by the *New York Times*.

When Fern got to Paris, the French capital was not what she had imagined.

It was 1349 AD.

The Black Death had arrived.

Tumors were sprouting from people's skin and then bursting open into fireworks of wretched fluid.

The Black Death was rotting people's flesh with gangrene until the people died.

They were living beings and they had lives and loves and hates and cares and worries and now they were lifeless matter.

Food for worms.

Trash scattered around the streets of Saint-Germain-des-Prés.

Stinking to high heaven.

It was a pretty shitty vacation.

When she traveled around Paris in 1349 AD, stepping over the bodies of the tortured urban poor, Fern collected news and information about the outside world.

It'd been about a century since the people of Fairy Land had learned much about what men were doing to the planet.

The news was not good.

It never was.

Fern was nothing if not resolute.

When she returned to Fairy Land, she decided to rest, but also decided that she would go again into the wider world.

And so she went on more vacations.

It was the late medieval and early modern periods. Fern saw unfathomable amounts of human suffering, but other than the Lisbon earthquake of 1755 AD, nothing was ever as bad as Paris in 1349 AD.

Fern became a seasoned traveler.

She learned to put up with a lot of crap, as long as she got the manic contact high and psychic relief that comes with being far from home.

And as she moved around the world, she collected more news.

Fern brought back this news in physical formats.

At first it was books, which eventually turned into other forms of media. Newsbooks, broadsides, wire recordings, shellac and vinyl records, audio cassettes, magazines, newspapers, reel-to-reel recordings, LaserDiscs, CDs, VHS tapes, DVDs, HD DVDs, Blu-ray Discs.

This is how Celia learned about Richard Johnson and *Tom a Lincoln*.

Unlike the sojourns of the island's other women, Fern's trips abroad were embraced by the residents of Fairy Land.

There was a simple reason.

As soon as Fern left the island, her mood stopped influencing their lives.

During Fern's seventh trip abroad, which was supposed to be for six months, but lasted about two years, the residents of Fairy Land revised their previous opinion on Fern's forays away from the island.

They had noticed a material change in the quality of their life.

It wasn't anything that anyone could explain.

It wasn't anything that had a definite beginning or end.

But there was a difference in the air, in the very luster of the trees, in the smell of things, in the crispness of life.

It was as if the island had entered into a long, flat period of depression.

People went through the motions, people did what they always did, but something was off. There was a pointlessness that made a mockery of the simplest actions.

Without Fern, the women of Fairy Land had been stripped of magical charm.

They were seeing life as it was.

They were witnessing existence with a dead honest clarity.

And life was brutal.

When Fern returned to the island, the depression lifted.

The magical charm returned.

Here then was Fern's version of the bitter twist in the faery stories and folk tales that mortals used to tell each other before the world anesthetized itself with prescription opioids, anal gangbang pornography, and the illusion of individual freedom in the pyramid of global order.

Without Fern, the taste of the Queen's honey was neither sweet nor bitter.

The sacred oak groves went unkempt.

The birdsong rang hollow.

The lamps burned less bright.

The lesbianism evoked orgasms that offered all the dull-eyed joy of being frigged off inside a stripmall swingers' club.

A deal was struck.

Fern would still leave Fairy Land, but for no period longer than it took for Fairy Land to be stripped of its magical charm.

Which was roughly a year.

All of which brings us to the Year of the Froward Worm, which roughly corresponded to 2017 AD, 1438 AH, and 5777 AM.

Fern had left Fairy Land about eighteen months earlier, during the Year of the Misplaced Butter.

She'd told everyone that she was going to Los Angeles, which was a city on the west coast of the United States of America, the warrior nation that had made a cottage industry of transforming illiterate Muslim peasants into char and bone.

Los Angeles was responsible for a disproportionate amount of the media produced in the United States of America.

The women of Fairy Land were well versed in this media.

They had magicked up an Internet connection and used it to pirate television shows and films produced in Los Angeles, which they then watched on a television they'd magicked up out of some old twigs and a bit of wool.

Fern had visited Los Angeles on several occasions. None of the other women from the island had visited Los Angeles.

In the Year of the Misplaced Butter, Fern announced that she was returning to the city.

It'd been about five years since her last visit.

"You will leave us for the full year?" asked Celia.

"Yes," said Fern. "But worry not, Mother, I shall return as ever."

Fern did not return. She was gone well into the Year of the Froward Worm, which roughly corresponded to 2017 AD, 1438 AH, and 5777 AM.

Flatness settled on Fairy Land.

Celia looked out at her kingdom. All she saw was the citizenry's empty faces and the graying of the flora and fauna. The lesbianism was mega-fallow.

"How long has my daughter been gone?" Celia asked her court advisors.

"By our counts," said the Chieftess of Celia's High Council, "One year, seven months, and six days."

"Have efforts been made to contact her?" asked Celia.

"There has been no response, my queen," said the Chieftess.

"We must go and find her."

## Chapter Three

# How Fairy Land Escaped the
# Clutches of Global Capitalism

The Twenty-First Century AD was full of people who had filthy hands.

In some places, like rural Bangladesh, the filthy-handed people were no different than Orson, the imaginative man who'd used early medieval hygiene to assassinate the Red-Rose Knight.

Their hands were covered with shit.

The exploitive global hierarchy of capitalism had denied them the basic mechanisms of modern life.

They had no plumbing.

The people who exploited the global hierarchy also had filthy hands.

But their hands weren't covered with shit.

Their hands were stained with the blood of the poor, which, like climate change and Islamic-themed terrorism, was a semi-accidental byproduct of exploiting the global hierarchy.

There were a lot of explanations as to why capitalists liked exploiting the global hierarchy.

Some of these explanations were purely psychological.

Some of the explanations were entirely about money.

Some explanations attributed an innate evil to the global capitalists.

But the most logical explanation, really, was that people became global capitalists only after they'd entered a secret contest to see who could own the ugliest house.

Reader, look into your heart.

Pore through your memories.

When was the last time you went to a really rich person's house and found it anything but hideous?

Another reason why global capitalists kept rural Bangladeshis covered in shit is that keeping rural Bangladeshis covered in shit ensured an unequal distribution of the world's wealth and resources, with a disproportionate amount of that wealth going to the global capitalists.

And it was an open secret that the acquisition of vast wealth was the quickest way for a human to become a supranatural being.

It was a documented scientific fact that, after an individual had accumulated vast wealth, then they reached what was called the Cash Horizon.

Beyond the Cash Horizon, the wealth-accumulating individual was transformed into a supranatural being.

In other words: *the rich were not human.*

If you're wondering why the rich felt the need to become supranatural creatures, then good for you!

It's the obvious question.

And here's the answer: there was a sense that by becoming supranatural creatures, the rich could conquer death and thus avoid their certain destination of Hell.

But even with the Cash Horizon, the rich still died.

Death remained unconquered.

And Hell was filled with the rich.

So don't say that this book lacks a happy ending.

In addition to owning unspeakably ugly homes and being able to withstand mephedrone psychosis while attending black-tie galas, those who passed the Cash Horizon were granted the ability to hear the rare Lou Reed outtake "Doin' the Dookie."

Written for the Velvet Underground in 1965 AD but not recorded until sessions for Reed's 1973 AD masterpiece *Berlin*, "Doin' the Dookie" had been sequenced to appear on that album's A-side, but was swapped out at the last minute in favor of "Oh Jim."

The lyrics of "Doin' the Dookie" were what anyone'd expect, Dylanesque nonsense about hip gender-bending junkies punctuated, loosely, by exclamations:

> *Oooohhh, fleet-foot Sam had his can of jam,*
> *Bertha Mason was feeling kinda kooky, huh,*
> *And her girl Will, yeah,*
> *He was looking pretty spooky,*
> *And they was all Doin' the Dookie,*
> *Oh whoa, they was Doin' the Dookie,*
> *For you and me.*
> *Doin' the Dookie!*
> *Oh wee.*

A rogue engineer, stoned beyond belief on Moroccan hash, had misplaced the master tape of "Doin' the Dookie" inside an aquarium.

Ten years later, when the tape was fished out, it was discovered that the aquarium's chemical-soaked water had enacted an alchemical corruption, transforming Reed's recording into high-frequency sound beyond the range of normal human hearing.

The music was still there.

The lyrics were still there.

They simply could not be heard by human beings.

But if a person's net worth had passed the Cash Horizon, then their enhanced senses allowed them to hear "Doin' the Dookie."

And if you're wondering, reader, what it's like to be a superhuman being whose money has pushed you well past the Cash Horizon, you'd do worse than to consider a character who'll show up in later chapters of this book.

This character is named His Royal Highness Mamduh bin Fatih bin Muhammad bin Abdulaziz Al Saud.

HRH was a son of the House of Saud, which was the monarchy that ruled much of the Arabian Peninsula and owned the world's second-largest oil reserve.

HRH was from serious money.

HRH never even had a chance to be human.

HRH came screaming into this world and the money made him into a supranatural creature.

"Doin' the Dookie" was a lot like Fairy Land.

It was both there and not there, invisible to 99.9999 per cent of the world's population.

But Fairy Land hadn't gone invisible by being lost in an aquarium.

Fairy Land had become invisible when the women of Celia's realm used magic to align the island with an unconquered principle of everyday deception.

The principle worked like this: the physical appearance of any given object, be it animal or mineral, arrived with a series of common expectations.

As long as the appearance of that object was maintained, the vast majority of human beings would never notice any deviation from common expectations, and, in fact, people would go out of their way to ignore those deviations.

The most obvious place where this principle operated was within the publishing industry of the United States of America.

Despite decades of effort, and thousands of Internet thinkpieces about the inclusion of marginalized voices, publishing was a dirty business that had done nothing to alleviate a system of ghettoizing its authors based on their physical appearances and socio-economic points of origins.

The books of the publishing industry rested on a cheap short-hand, with each of its marketing demographics defined by the implicit prejudices of the American upper middle class.

And if you think that's an exaggeration, ask yourself this: how many well-received books of Literary Fiction published over the last thirty years do you remember being written by a poor person?

In the unlikely event that a person was allowed to publish a book which spoke beyond the simple facts of their socio-economic origins, then the message of that book was ignored.

Consider *The Women of Brewster Place* by Gloria Naylor, a novel about several African-American women who all live in the same urban development.

The text explicitly states that the titular Brewster Place, the urban development itself, is a machine that manufactures the lives of its women.

The book is an exploration of the way by which the machine crafts, structures, and demolishes its product.

It's a dark, mechanistic text about the nature of urban living, about the secret lines of power, and about the way that Twentieth-Century AD architecture created new perversions and desires.

Remember when J.G. Ballard, a white English colonial, wrote the exact same shit?

You thought it was genius!

You gave him his own adjective!

When Naylor wrote the same thing, no one even noticed.

But *The Women of Brewster Place* was authored by someone whose points of origin fulfilled the paltry expectations of America's upper middle class, a group of people who wanted little more from Black women writers than triumph over individual adversity, folksy homespun wisdom, sexual suffering, and horrible deaths.

And before anyone suggests that this is revisionist thinking about Naylor, cramming some weird bullshit into her work, go and read *1996*.

Read *1996* and then try convincing yourself that Naylor wasn't a writer obsessed with the world of secret persuaders.

And, hey!

Speaking of publishing, let's talk turkey!

It's inevitable that this book will draw comparisons to writings by the late Kurt Vonnegut, who was an American novelist from the Twentieth Century AD.

I couldn't escape the comparisons with *I Hate the Internet*!

At least one question from the audience at every book event!

And I won't escape them with this book!

Total theft from *Breakfast of Champions*!

Even down to Fairy Land!

Most of the comparisons between this book and the writings of the late Kurt Vonnegut will occur in cheap little reviews on Goodreads.com and Amazon.com, which are Internet websites owned by a guy named Jeff Bezos.

These websites are where the American readership makes sure that American authors know their fucking place, and further ensures American authors know that their place is the equivalent to that of a moon-faced kid being shoved into some mud by a bully.

"How do you like that mud, you little shit?" asks the American readership. "This is what happens when you try to do anything! Fucking eat it, you pig!"

"Mgjhasdhashfs fdasmmmppfkjjsad," reply American authors, their pie-holes crushed into a mélange of star-rankings, facile two-sentence comparisons, and moronic assumptions about authorial motivation.

Quick!

Here's how to murder a culture: create a system in which every fucking thing, no matter how small or tedious, is smothered in bullshit instant commentary and hot takes by the stupidest people on the planet.

Good luck.

You're gonna need it.

But who the fuck are the dinosaurs reviewing books on websites?

Losers!

Who reads books?

Nobody!

Who uses a website?

Nobody!

It's all smartphones now.

Here's a text message that a well-known Hollywood screenwriter sent me, unbidden, on December 25th, 2017 AD, while I was trying to watch the 1981 AD film *Christiane F. – Wir Kinder vom Bahnhof Zoo*:

That shit is disgusting.

But it's also brilliant, an entirely new kind of writing that's unfathomable in its complexity and immediacy.

The screenwriter didn't write it.

It comes from nowhere. It's a chaintext that people were sending each other in the days before Christmas. This was how the world talked to itself.

And by any measurable standard, it's much more interesting than reading a book.

Despite the notions thrown about whenever a prestigious novelist gives birth to another tedious narrative bound in paper, the actual function of novels in American society was very different than anyone liked to admit.

Yes, reader, you could shit in some high cotton and talk to your friends about how reading ennobled the human spirit, and how literature connected people to one another, and how the whole enterprise promoted a humanistic understanding of Life in Our Time.

But then, of course, you would be no different from the Xanax-addled Brooklynites who earn small amounts of money by writing crap articles critiquing the implicit racial and gender politics of television dramas about werewolves and vampires.

And, reader, you are many things.

Some good, some bad.

But you're better than the children who pretend, for money, that they're upset about the latest episode of *Supernatural.*

You're not that kind of liar.

I can think of one reason why I can't escape comparisons to Kurt Vonnegut.

And it ain't because my work is so indebted to his own.

It's because Vonnegut was the same as me: another con artist ripping off the French writer Louis-Ferdinand Céline.

A bunch of people have talked shit about Céline.

I don't blame them!

Besides being one of the best writers of the Twentieth Century AD, he was also a rabid anti-Semite who collaborated with the Nazis.

But I can't judge!

I too have collaborated with Nazis!

I was published by Penguin Random House!

But the real reason why I can't escape the Vonnegut comparisons is not because our books are rip-offs of the same anti-Semite, but rather that the entire conception of the Serious Novel is a hideous stew of baked-in prejudices.

These prejudices are so omnipresent that they're invisible.

Whenever someone writes a work of incandescent prose about privileged people whose artistic, cultural, and familial foibles result in a plot-and-character-driven catharsis, no one goes on Goodreads.com and accuses them of ripping off Henry James.

But they should!

All of that crap, all of the good writing, the well-structured paragraphs, the emphasis on plot, the unexpected quirks of prose, the pretend lives of pretend people which resolve into a reflection of Our Time and Our Selves!

It's all technique!

Henry James was doing that shit before your parents were fertilized zygotes!

It's older than old hat.

Ancient technology!

And that's how we've defined the Serious Novel.

By pretending that technique from the Nineteenth Century AD can encompass the horror of the Twenty-First Century AD.

And because of that definition, most Serious Novels are so fucking boring that they have zero hope of competing with smartphones.

Imagine a very cranky human being who, while riding public transit, gets upset when they witness other people using smartphones.

"No one reads anymore," laments the very cranky human being. "Look at all these kids using smartphones!"

And you nod your head in agreement, don't you, reader?

You think it's ever such a shame that the public is no longer willing to engage with long tedious narratives bound in paper. How terrible you find it that smartphones have killed literacy!

You agree with that crank!

But the problem isn't the smartphone!

It isn't the people using their smartphones!

It's that books got defined down!

There's one working standard for judging quality!

*Is this tedious narrative bound in paper less boring than watching peoples' slack faces as they ride a crosstown bus?*

I don't blame anyone for using a smartphone to alleviate boredom while riding public transit. I know that pictographic messages about sexual encounters with Santa Claus are slightly less boring than reading novels about Life in Our Time.

So, no, reader, I'm not like that crank.

I don't blame anyone for getting addicted to their smartphones.

I only blame people for their terrible attempts at reviewing my work.

Vonnegut, Vonnegut, Vonnegut!

He invented the short sentence!

He invented the short paragraph!

He invented jokes!

## Chapter Four

# Child, Be Strange

Before going to Los Angeles, Celia had left Fairy Land on one previous occasion.

This was when she went to the city of London on the island of Great Britain.

She traveled in the Year of the Sulky Octopus, which roughly corresponded to 1608 AD, 1017 AH, and 5369 AM.

Celia had arrived in the middle of the Little Ice Age, which was a long period of freezing winters and terrible cold.

Celia went to London a few days after Christmas, which was a holiday that celebrated the birth of an itinerant preacher from Galilee who'd promulgated an ideology of love, non-violence, and forgiveness.

Somehow this ideology of love and forgiveness, which was called Christianity, had been transformed into a religion responsible for tens of millions of deaths.

History is so fucking weird.

More Vonnegut!

He invented Jesus!

Prior to Celia's first departure, Fern had returned with news from a peregrination abroad: *Tom a Lincoln*, the book by Richard Johnson, had been adapted into a play.

"A play?" asked Celia. "Whatever is a play?"

"Some people are chosen to embody roles around a theme. The chosen people speak words as if they themselves were their embodied roles."

"You say that they have made a play of my life?" asked Celia.

"Yes," said Fern.

"Someone will speak as me?" asked Celia.

"Yes," said Fern.

"I must attend," said Celia.

Fern could not go to England with her mother.

She'd been away from Fairy Land for about a year.

Whenever Fern returned from a vacation, she'd stay on Fairy Land for at least two years, which was long enough to chase away even the slightest hint of the island's collective depression.

One of Fairy Land's more aggressive women was drafted into service as Celia's escort.

Her name was Rose Byrne.

When the women of Fairy Land had banished or murdered all of the island's men, Rose had been one of the more violent and vocal agitators.

Rose had argued against banishment. She wanted to kill all the men.

She hadn't killed all the men, but she had murdered more men than anyone else on the island.

She'd cut off their heads.

She'd hung them from gibbets.

She'd boiled them in oil.

She'd drowned them in ale.

She'd crushed them with rocks.

She'd buried them in sand, covered their heads with honey, and let their skulls be picked clean by ants.

About two centuries before Fern first left the island, Rose began taking her own trips away from Fairy Land.

Rose's trips abroad were very short affairs.

She only left long enough to sail a skiff to a distant land, get blotto stinking drunk, and then brutalize unsuspecting men in dirty taverns.

But the violence tourism had taught Rose how to travel, which made her useful as Celia's companion.

Celia was the Regnant Queen.

She wasn't traveling by boat.

She did some faery bullshit and opened a magic window to London.

The magic window opened in Southwark, on the south side of the river, between the bear-baiting ring and St. Saviour's church.

A bunch of awful London people stood around, gaping at Celia and Rose Byrne.

The awful London people had seen a lot of things in their miserable London lives, but they'd never witnessed the spontaneous materialization of a fairy queen and her disagreeable companion.

One of the awful Londoners was a drunken scoundrel.

He only had one eye.

The scoundrel began dancing like a chicken, in the hopes that Celia or Rose would give him coin for alcohol.

"Let us anon, lady," said Rose. "Before I rip this one's arms from his shoulders and beat him about the head with his own appendages."

"Come on, missus," said the scoundrel. "Come on, I'm a righteous chicken and I'm a-dancing for you!"

Before Fern left England, she'd put a faery glamor on the location where the play of Celia's life would be performed, which was the Hall at Gray's Inn.

Gray's Inn was one of the four Inns of Court, which were places where upper-class families sent their sons to train as barristers.

A barrister was a fancy lawyer.

The inmates of Gray's Inn were learning to exploit England's ad hoc legal system.

This training helped the inmates' families abuse the poor and retain an iron hold over the country's unjust social structure.

It was good work if you could get it.

Which you couldn't.

Because you were poor.

Celia cast a spell.

The spell created a long thin tendril of magical light, like a ropey strand of saliva, that led from the faery glamor on Gray's Inn to Celia's location in Southwark. The tendril snaked through the streets of London, creating the most effective route to Gray's Inn.

It was a little like getting directions from a smartphone, but without supplying every stupid fucking detail of your sad little life to the sociopaths who operate megalithic American corporations.

Celia and Rose left the Londoners and followed the tendril.

"Come on, missus," cried the one-eyed scoundrel after Celia and Rose. "Come on, don't you want to pluck me old feathers? Don't you want to tug on the old beak? I've got some nice meat on me old chicken bones!"

The tendril led Celia and Rose over London Bridge.

There were human heads on spikes attached to the bridge's southern gate.

Celia and Rose passed through the gate, taking no notice of the human heads, which were in various stages of decomposition. It was nighttime, so the heads weren't very visible, and, anyway, a bunch of men's heads on spikes was nothing new to the women of Fairy Land.

London Bridge was lined with buildings and shops on either side, and the passage was narrow, and as Celia and Rose followed the tendril, they often found themselves in darkness illuminated only by the tendril's light.

The tendril brought Celia and Rose into Holborn, which was mostly countryside in the greeny northwest of the city.

The tendril brought Celia and Rose through the Holborn gate of Gray's Inn.

There was a crowd of people, all headed in the same direction as Celia and Rose.

"What a great number have come to see this play of my life," said Celia.

"Why would they not?" asked Rose. "What else would the dogs do? Bark at sparrows, chase cats up trees, and, by the smell of them, shit themselves every other Tuesday."

Just past the gate, there was a little bookshop under the sign of a white bear. It was tended by a man named Henry Thomes.

Henry Thomes stood in front of his shop, crying out at passersby.

"Books, books, books," he shouted. "Books of the Red-Rose Knight. Parts one and two. Books of the Red-Rose Knight. Read about the Red-Rose Knight in *Tom a Lincoln*!"

Celia stopped.

"The book has two parts?" she asked.

"The writer published the second but last year."

"I will have this second part," said Celia.

"For you, the cost is but four pence."

"Pence?" asked Celia.

"Pennies," said Henry Thomes.

"The swine asks for money," said Rose. "We have spoken of money, lady. Do you remember?"

"Money," said Celia. "I have no money."

"No money, no book," said Thomes.

"Would you take some ham?" asked Celia. "I believe Rose is carrying cured ham on her person. We could share it with you."

"What am I to do with your old hog?" asked Thomes. "What I need is coin."

Celia and Rose followed the crowd into the Hall at Gray's Inn. They entered into a temporary autonomous zone called the Kingdom of Purpoole.

Almost every Christmas season, the young men of bleeding privilege who studied at Gray's Inn would throw a huge party, creating a pseudo-monarchy of Purpoole, in which one of their number would be made Prince.

The Prince would rule for the season with his own courts, ministers, and government.

He was expected to put on masks, revels, plays, and dances.

The current Kingdom had been established on the 12th of December.

A pupil named Thomas Rudde, of Higham Ferrers near Northampton, was made the Kingdom's prince.

As the two women entered the Hall, the subjects of the Kingdom of Purpoole were escorting guests to their seats.

Prince Thomas was watching over his court.

Prince Thomas was drunk as a skunk. He'd been drunk for sixteen days.

He saw Celia.

Some of the tendril's magic light had rubbed off on Celia. She glowed with the power of Fairy Land.

"How now," Prince Thomas cried from his throne. "Who is this that comes amongst us? See how her face and bosom glow with light of the waxing crescent! Why, I shall avail myself of her company."

The Prince leapt from his throne and took Celia's arm in his own.

Prince Thomas was too drunk to notice that Rose Byrne had taken out her sword and was about to murder him.

Celia raised her hand, staying Rose's assault.

"Sweetest creature," said Prince Thomas. "Who art thou with thy fiery raiment?"

"I am Celia, Regnant Queen of Fairy Land."

Prince Thomas laughed and laughed and laughed.

"What a jape!" he cried. "Which man of Gray's Inn has architected such a jest?"

"Why are you laughing at my lady?" asked Rose.

"Many jibes arise throughout a Christmas Revel, but I know not of any previous happenstance when a character from imagination has come to life and presented herself at our court."

"My lady is no product of imagination," said Rose. "She is the Regnant Queen of Fairy Land. She has come to see the play."

"Tell me," said Celia. "What is your name?"

"I am Prince Thomas of this, the Kingdom of Purpoole."

"I thought us in the Kingdom of England," said Celia.

"In these walls, I am the true prince. All that happens within is for my benefit and by my leave."

"As we are both monarchs," said Celia, "shall we not watch the play together?"

"Excellent," said Prince Thomas. "I have no throne for a queen, but my minions will find you some grand chair upon which to rest your bones and flesh."

"Who whispered to you that my flesh wanted rest?"

Prince Thomas roared with laughter.

The play was presented by the Queen Anne's Men.

The audience sat around three sides of the great hall. The fourth side was kept behind a curtain, which was used for scene changes during the play.

Celia watched.

Celia watched.

Celia watched.

At first the play was pretty fucking boring, some old shit about whether or not King Arthur could fuck the Red-Rose Knight's mother. Then the living incarnation of Time came out and showed a bunch of other shit that happened, none of which was that interesting, and then an abbess put King Arthur's bastard son, who was a baby called Tom a Lincoln, into the hands of a shepherd. Then Time came out again and Tom a Lincoln was much older and he and his fellow shepherds took up weapons and abandoned their sheep. Tom's friends crowned him with a laurel of roses, thereby making him the Red-Rose Knight, and then all of the former shepherds camped out on a heath and robbed people, and then they ended up dragged to the court of King Arthur.

King Arthur and the Red-Rose Knight fought each other until their sublimated incestuous homoeroticism convinced King Arthur to accept the Red-Rose Knight as his son, and then the Red-Rose Knight and King Arthur kicked the shit out of the French, and then the Red-Rose Knight took some of Arthur's men on boats and they went sailing around the world. Time came back on stage and said some shit. And then finally, the Red-Rose Knight and his men turned up on Fairy Land.

And Celia was there, watching herself, watching a man dressed up as Celia, watching as the man dressed up as Celia spoke words that Celia had never said and acted out deeds that Celia had never done.

The sexual morality of Fairy Land wasn't prudish, but it was an out-of-body experience to watch a fictional iteration of yourself bed down with a makeshift knight.

In its many lies, Richard Johnson's *Tom a Lincoln* had contained no mention of Rusticano.

But in the play at Gray's Inn, Rusticano was about 30 per cent of the action.

A musical intermission occurred after the Red-Rose Knight left Fairy

Land. There was a great amount of social mingling, with young rakes talking to women, and an outrageous amount of drinking.

"You are far more fair than the one who acts out your story," said Prince Thomas.

"I am not a man," said Celia. "Of course I am more fair."

"You would be surprised," said Prince Thomas. "Many of the boys who play as ladies are very comely, and it is said that most are paid catamites. I promise you, my queen, that the Celia of our drama shall find himself enveloped by one of Gray's brutes before the night is through."

"The lust of men can be overpowering. It was not the case with the true Red-Rose Knight. He mewled like a kitten."

"Some men, often those who are princes, are known to roar like lions."

"A sound that I am certain could shake my bones," said Celia.

Celia didn't pay attention to the rest of the play, which was claptrap about the Red-Rose Knight leaving Fairy Land and getting another girl pregnant and then Celia killing herself by jumping off a rock.

It wasn't much different from *Tom a Lincoln*.

After the applause died down, Prince Thomas turned to Celia and asked, "How then, my fair elf queen, did you like the play of your own life?"

"It was very strange," she said. "But was it a good play? We have no such entertainments in Fairy Land."

"It was passable," said Prince Thomas. "I have seen better, I have seen worse. But look at you, still your dusky skin is illuminated by the light of moon. My word, lady, what kind of woman are you?"

"I have told you," said Celia. "I am the Queen of Fairy Land."

"A queen of Clerkenwell, more like, a sister of Luce," said Prince Thomas. "What a jest! Dressed as a queen! Did they send you here to inquire of me, my girl, as you inquired of the Red-Rose Knight? Are you this prince's tribute? Is it my bed that next you target?"

"Where do you sleep?" asked Celia.

"I keep a chamber in the south court. Beyond this door and a small walk."

"Is it fit for a queen to consort with a prince?"

"Our two kingdoms, my queen, are not as of other kingdoms," said Prince Thomas. "So why should our congress be ruled by their practices? My lady, you arise in me the sacred demon of ungovernableness!"

Celia followed Prince Thomas to his chamber in the south court.

It was tepid British sex with the chinless scion of an upper-class family.

But it'd been almost a thousand years since Celia had fucked.

She took what she could get.

When Celia emerged from Prince Thomas's chambers, she found Rose Byrne standing outside of the building.

"My lady," said Rose Byrne. "Have you finished with your antics?"

"I believe so," said Celia.

"Let us anon. Fairy Land is waiting."

"A word," said Celia.

"Yes, my lady?" asked Rose Byrne.

"You saw the false Rusticano."

"Who could miss the spectacle?"

"When we return to Fairy Land," said Celia, "you are free to speak of the play in any fashion that you might wish. My one request is that you not inform anyone of the false Rusticano."

"I do as you command," said Rose Byrne.

"I would not have him know of the insult," said Celia. "For the peace of us all."

As they walked towards the Holborn gate, Rose handed Celia a small book.

"Part II," said Rose, "of *Tom a Lincoln*."

"How did you come by this?" asked Celia.

"I had some time while you were at your frolic," said Rose. "I convinced the little man that he wanted my cured ham."

"Was there any violence?"

"Only a bit," said Rose.

# Chapter Five

## Wonder Women

Then about four hundred years happened.

The industrial revolution poisoned the Earth's atmosphere, the United States of America was founded on the dual principles of genocide and human slavery, and soccer became very popular.

And Fern lost herself in Los Angeles.
Which meant that Celia had, once more, to leave Fairy Land.
She took Rose Byrne with her.

Those four hundred years, by the way, were some of the most monumental in the planetary existence of homo sapiens.
Fern had warned Celia about the changes, back before her disappearance, and Celia had caught some glimpses on Fairy Land's woolen television.

If you asked people living in Los Angeles during the Year of the Froward Worm about the last four hundred years, they'd almost certainly talk about things like the Internet, smartphones, and air travel.
But the women of Fairy Land were immortal and undying beings, and they viewed the previous four hundred years in a very different light than the people living in Los Angeles.
The women of Fairy Land knew that most of the technological

developments of the previous four hundred years were about as impressive as an old dog learning a new trick, only to discover that the dog's new trick was something useless like shelling pumpkin seeds, translating the *Apocalypse of the Pseudo-Methodius* out of Syriac, or building a career in the American recording industry by performing parodies of popular songs.

Smartphones, the Internet, and air travel were only refinements of a principle that had governed human behavior from its very beginnings.

All the technology really did was create new ways for a person to be annoyed by the neighbors.

Fern and Celia knew where the real change had been.

They knew what the real difference was between Los Angeles in the Year of the Froward Worm and, say, the early medieval period or the Ancient Hellenic era.

Fern and Celia knew that the real change had come with the development of indoor plumbing and, specifically, the management of sewage.

Celia and Fern were more sensitive than usual to the problem of human waste and its effective management.

After all, they'd both watched the Red-Rose Knight be assassinated by Orson's shit.

The effective management of human sewage had been developed about one hundred years prior to the Year of the Froward Worm.

Homo sapiens had been on Earth for about two hundred thousand years, which means that it took the planet's dominant species roughly one hundred and ninety-nine thousand nine hundred years before someone realized that people shouldn't do a poo on the living-room floor.

So don't get your hopes up.

When Celia and Rose Byrne went to Los Angeles, they had difficulty in figuring out where they should arrive.

It wasn't like London in the Seventeenth Century AD.

Fern hadn't left any magical beacons hanging around to guide her mother through the landscape.

Los Angeles County was four thousand square miles.

When Celia cast her spell that opened a magic window onto Los Angeles, she had to do a little faery fudging, asking that the window open on the place which would be the most hospitable to their arrival.

She didn't specify the exact nature of this hospitality.

The magical window opened in the lobby of the Vista Theater, which was a movie house in the neighborhood of Los Feliz.

The Vista, which was a giant single-screen theater, had been built in 1923 AD.

The exterior façade of the building was Spanish Colonial Revival, but its interior décor was early Twentieth-Century AD Egyptian kitsch, which meant that the theater was filled with Pharaonic heads and hieroglyphics.

Celia and Rose Byrne arrived on the evening of Thursday, June 2nd, 2017 AD.

This evening hosted the Vista's first screening of *Wonder Woman*, the huge media spectacle in which a lesbian named Diana left her magical island with the intention of beating the shit out of some Germans.

For decades, the Vista had been managed by a man named Victor Martinez.

A curious feature of Victor's tenure was his delight in dressing up as characters from the films that showed at the Vista.

Victor's appearances in these outfits were always more enjoyable than the films themselves.

When the Vista had shown *Iron Man*, which was about a war

profiteer who learned that war profiteering could be more profitable if the war profiteer built a suit of armor and personally killed Muslims with his own mechanical hands, Victor Martinez wore a version of the war profiteer's suit of armor.

When the Vista had shown *The Hobbit: An Unexpected Journey*, which was about a fussy midget drawn into an unlikely adventure by a slightly pompous wizard, Victor Martinez dressed as the wizard.

When the Vista had shown *Pirates of the Caribbean 3*, which was a film about a pirate rapist with a charming accent, Victor Martinez dressed as the pirate rapist.

Because *Wonder Woman* was about a female character, Victor Martinez did not dress as the film's lead role on June 2nd, 2017 AD.

Instead, he dressed as the film's male sidekick, an indistinct American soldier during World War One.

Another of the Vista's employees, who was a woman, dressed as the lead character of *Wonder Woman*.

They stood outside the theater, greeting attendees.

Victor Martinez and his fellow employee were not the only people dressed in costumes on June 2nd, 2017 AD.

A curious feature of early Twenty-First-Century AD life was that fans of media spectacles liked to dress up as characters which appeared within those media spectacles.

In the case of the Vista's premiere screening of *Wonder Woman*, this was really weird.

No one had seen the film!

It could have been a total piece of shit!

Unlike Victor and his fellow employee, who had a vested economic interest in the film's success, the people who dressed in costume at *Wonder Woman* had no stake in the property.

*Wonder Woman* had arrived at the Vista anointed in a sold-out madness emblematic of the United States of America in the Twenty-First Century.

This madness was long-brewing and the result of multiple historical occurrences and tendencies.

Some of these historical occurrences and tendencies had been running for decades.

Some had been running for centuries.

The culmination of these historical occurrences and tendencies was the recent election of Donald J. Trump to the Presidency of the United States of America.

The Presidency was the highest office in the country, to which individuals were elected every four years through an arcane process that had been designed, originally, to make sure the United States was cool with enslaving people from Africa.

Enslaving people from Africa was great business, and it was the economic bedrock of the fledgling nation, and it involved owning human beings who would be forced into labor and receive no benefits from that labor.

About seventy years after its founding, the country held a big debate as to whether or not it was cool to enslave people from Africa.

After this debate had killed about 716,000 poor White people fighting for the economic masters, and 36,000 Black people fighting for their freedom, everyone decided that enslaving people from Africa probably wasn't too cool.

Because it was no longer too cool to enslave people from Africa, which was the country's explicit purpose, the United States entered a malaise.

It had lost its demon.

The purpose of the Presidency shifted.

If its original function no longer existed, then surely some new purpose could be found.

It turned out that the Presidency was really good at making war.

After all, it had overseen about seventy years of war on Africa.

So new wars were made.

Decades and decades and decades of war.

By the time that Donald J. Trump was elected to the Presidency, the elections which chose the President had transformed from referendums about who would best administer the international slave trade into contests about who'd get the chance to reduce illiterate Muslims into pulpy masses of intestines.

Even by the dubious standards of candidates for the United States Presidency, Donald J. Trump was a wretched specimen.

He was the most famous person who had ever lived.

He was the most famous person who would ever live.

He was orange, he wore a stupid wig, and he was a pawn of multinational corporations.

He was hella racist.

By any honest account, he was into sexually assaulting women.

It was rumored that he was a speed freak, which would explain the difference between his public appearances as President and his public appearances in the 1980s AD and 1990s AD, when he'd been a fixture of New York City's tabloid culture.

In the early days, the President had been, if not especially bright, then at the very least coherent.

By the time that he won the right to turn Muslims into shattered masses of agony, the President could barely speak.

Amphetamine abuse has a terrible effect on the brain.

For decades, the political liberals of the Celebrity branch of American governance had profited off Donald J. Trump's crass public persona.

They'd given him deals for books that he hadn't written and stuck him on television whenever they thought it'd turn a buck.

Trump, who pretended on television that he was a billionaire, was big entertainment dollars.

His media persona was this: he was a total fucking jerk!

And he was rich!

He was great entertainment in a country that fostered a delusion in its poor that they too, someday, would be rich enough to treat other poor people like shit.

Donald J. Trump ran for the Presidency, and won, by embracing political viewpoints in direct opposition to the very people who had created him.

The liberals in the Celebrity branch of American governance had made a beast which they could not control.

It was like Mary Shelley's *Frankenstein, or, The Modern Prometheus*, a novel about a scientist who creates a monster out of spare human body parts that he's dug up from graves. The monster gets angry. Things go badly.

There were some differences.

The monster in *Frankenstein*, made of rotten human remains, had a body that was slightly less disturbing than the body of the President, which was made of media coverage stitched together with plastic surgery.

The monster in *Frankenstein* didn't have a speed habit.

And the monster in *Frankenstein* had a more honest relationship to literacy.

The monster in *Frankenstein* was into reading Milton, Plutarch, and Goethe.

By contrast, the monster who was the President just put his name on books that other people had written and then took money from political liberals in the publishing industry.

*What's the harm?* asked the publishing industry.

*It's all just business,* said the publishing industry.

199,900 years of shitting in the living room.

Anyway, the election of Donald J. Trump made America go nuts.

To be fair, the country had always been pretty crazy.

War, genocide, and slavery aren't good for anyone's mental health.

But after Trump assumed the Presidency, the madness got worse.

The people who'd voted for Trump went nuts because they'd won and had no idea what to do with their impossible victory.

The country's political liberals went nuts because Trump put them in the position of facing an undeniable and yet unpalatable truth.

This was the truth that the political liberals could not deny and could not face: beyond making English Comp courses at community colleges very annoying, forty years of rhetorical progress had achieved little, and it turned out that feeling good about gay marriage did not alleviate the taint of being warmongers whose taxes had killed more Muslims than the Black Death.

You can't make evil disappear by being a reasonably nice person who mouths platitudes at dinner parties. Social media confessions do not alleviate suffering. You can't talk the world into being a decent place while sacrificing nothing.

The socialists didn't go nuts.

They were the people who'd thought about the complex problems facing the nation and decided that an honest solution to these problems could be achieved with applied Leftism.

But don't get your hopes up.

Despite being correct in their thinking, the socialists were the most annoying people in America. When they spoke, it was like bamboo slivers shoved under a fingernail.

I don't know why.

It was the single biggest American tragedy of the last one hundred years.

By the Year of the Froward Worm, too much warmongering had splintered the national psyche into a series of tribes.

The most obvious schism was between the public voices of the liberal warmongers and the public voices of the tribe that had helped Donald J. Trump win his impossible victory.

For the sake of clarity, let's call this second tribe the Fucking Assholes.

The noise from the public voices of the liberal warmongers had become the dominant voice of the haute bourgeoisie. This contingent was represented by a mixture of high-grade celebrities, op-ed writers, Democratic party apparatchiks, and the mentally ill. A great number of these public voices had passed the Cash Horizon.

For varied reasons, the public voices of the liberal warmongers had devised an idea that was extraordinarily profitable for the arch-capitalist class: that the Celebrity branch of American governance, and its products, could be read as a proxy for the struggles and strife of the great American unwashed.

The public voices of the Fucking Assholes were represented by a mixture of low-rent celebrities, op-ed writers, Republican party apparatchiks, and the mentally ill. A great number of people in these public voices had passed the Cash Horizon.

The public voices of the Fucking Assholes agreed with the public voices of the liberal warmongers: the Celebrity branch of American governance, and its products, could be read as a proxy for the struggles and strife of the great American unwashed.

The only difference of opinion was about the interpretation of this proxy.

Both sides accepted the unchallenged underlying thesis.

The argument proved to be very profitable for the arch-capitalist class who actually owned the Celebrity branch of American governance.

Everything was an advertisement.

And if you're wondering about the opinions of the non-public voices, then go and fuck off back to the Dark Ages.

You're revealing a thinking that's very Twentieth Century AD, with atavistic tendencies towards logic and dreams of a populace that hasn't been preyed upon by the mind-altering substances of the pharmaceutical industry. That shit is ancient news.

You either agreed with the country's priestly castes, and their apparatuses of sycophants, novitiate aspirants and true believers, or you found yourself on the receiving end of a barrage of hatred and death threats.

Here was the difference between the priestly castes, many of whom had opinions on deadline for money, and everyone else: sane people shut the fuck up, nodded their heads, and did what they needed to survive in a toxic political landscape.

In an era when public discourse was the bought-and-paid property of roughly twenty companies, and the airing of an opinion could subject a person to unfathomable amounts of abuse and recrimination, the only reasonable option was to be quiet.

So when you next fawn over someone's brave public thoughts, repeat the following: *The contours of discourse are so horrendous that one thing has become certain. Any individual offering up a public opinion necessarily must be either hopelessly stupid or insane. I am engaging with a product of madness and idiocy.*

Regarding the public opinions offered up in this book, they are the products of both idiocy and bad craziness.

But at least I have some justification for engaging with the stupidity and insanity of this book.

I wrote the thing.

Reader, what's your excuse?

Here was one thing that all the priestly castes agreed upon in the run-up to the election in the Year of the Misplaced Butter: Donald J. Trump could not, should not, and would not be President.

It was impossible.

But Donald J. Trump won anyway.

A creature created by the Celebrity branch of American governance had taken over the Executive branch, the conflation of entertainment into political life was complete, and it had happened without the blessing of the high clergy, and it shut out the vast majority of people who were from the Celebrity branch of American governance.

By the way, all of this is why one's political tools should probably be comprised of effective organization, decent arguments, an understanding of the actual political landscape, as opposed to an imaginary map built as a reflection of one's own virtue.

If the only tool in your political arsenal is shame, don't be surprised what happens when you meet a shameless man.

Enter *Wonder Woman* in 2017 AD.

There'd been about fifteen years of films about superheroes, which were intellectual properties about supranatural beings like Celia.

These films were all the same: a supranatural being reenacted American foreign policy by responding to an existential threat through exaggerated violence, generally after another supranatural being reenacted 9/11, which was when some Muslims blew up two ugly buildings in New York and facefucked reality into a cartoon.

What differentiated *Wonder Woman* from the rest of the superhero films was that its lead character was female.

Because the country was run by a monster created by liberals in the Celebrity branch of American governance, and because liberals were totally disconnected from the political structure of their country, and because the film mapped to easy marketing demographics, *Wonder Woman* was freighted with a swollen ideology.

It arrived as a place where the unexamined ideologies of American life could belong to women as easily as men.

If you think this is an exaggeration, please read the following quotes from "Want to Take Political Action This Weekend? Go to the Movies", an article written by Melissa Goodman for the website of the Southern California branch of the American Civil Liberties Union:

> Political action doesn't always have to take the form of marching, holding a house party or calling your local representative. You can make a bold and necessary political statement just by buying a movie ticket.
>
> Go see *Wonder Woman* ...*

That was politics at the mid-point of 2017 AD.

It arrived in an article on the website of an organization dedicated to civil liberties which suggested that an alternative to applied Leftist action was to patronize media produced by a massive multinational corporation owned by the same old shits who'd been ruining the world for centuries.

This was the madness of the moment.

People had lost the ability to tell the difference between the Celebrity and the other three branches of American governance.

Because the world has gone stupid and elected a rogue member of the Celebrity branch of American governance into the Executive, allow me to point out the difference: representation in the traditional three branches of government really does matter, because the people who end up in the government are the people who make policy and laws.

In other words, these are the people who determine whether or not you will be able to make a living wage.

These are the people who shape your lives.

People who end up in the Celebrity branch of American governance are the people who make movies and television and huge profits for the same old shits who rule the world.

In other words, these are the people who are taking your money.

---

* https://www.aclusocal.org/en/news/want-take-political-action-weekend-go-movies

I know of what I speak.

I'm one of them.

I've duped you into buying my turgid work.

Unless you've pirated this book.

If you have, then good for you!

Do me a favor. Steal *The Future Won't Be Long*!

And, yes, reader, I know the arguments about why it's important to see diverse faces in television and in films.

And, yes, I realize that no one agrees with me on this topic.

But I'm sorry, arguing about the shadow theater of the entertainment industry is not politics.

What did everyone at the Vista Theater see when they made a bold political statement by giving money to the people who'd ruined the world?

*Wonder Woman* was a film made by people baptized in the primordial ooze of unconscious American life.

The attendees saw a story about the unexamined glory of American foreign policy, of the meaningfulness of war and violence, and a story about how a woman could be like a man in her ability to simulate genocide.

A woman named Diana lives on an island full of lesbians. Her mother is the Queen of the island. Everyone lives in paradise, doing what everyone who's ever met a lesbian knows that all the world's lesbians do, which is train for perpetual war. This goes on for millennia until one day an American in an airplane crashes on the island. Diana rescues the American, only to find that the reason he crashed is because a bunch of Germans were firing materiel at the plane. The Germans invade the lesbian paradise. The lesbians murder all the Germans. The Germans murder some of the lesbians. The American gets naked and feels insecure about the size of his penis on an island full of lesbians and then confesses that he's working as a spy against the Germans, who have developed biological weaponry. Some nonsense happens where Diana gets convinced that Ares, the Greek god of war, is responsible for the chaos. Diana and the American go out into the world with the intention of murdering a bunch of Germans and stopping Ares from developing biological weapons. Then Diana goes to London where, as Celia once discovered, English shit is widely acknowledged as Europe's most toxic. Then she goes to France with a motley crew of drunkards, and for some reason only the dark-skinned drunkards are capable of belief in the supranatural. Then Diana kicks the shit out of some Germans for about forty minutes, performing ritualistic genocide that saves the fictional world while adhering to an unspoken embrace of American foreign policy. Somewhere in here, weirder members of the audience cheer and cry because they've imbibed enough primordial ooze that they believe the appropriate solution to the horror of men is to adopt the tactics of men. In other words, the committing of genocide has become so ingrained and unexamined in the American psyche that there is no longer any purpose in questioning whether or not one should commit genocide. The real question is who gets to kill. And for some reason it's important that women have opportunities to butcher their fellow living beings. Just ask the ACLU. Then Diana kills Ares, who turns out to be an Englishman in a bowler hat, which is probably the only realistic thing in the entire film, and then the war ends and everyone is happy because Diana has committed genocide against the right people at the right time and there's no way that the roman numeral at the end of World War One could possibly predicate a sequel.

At least the genocide simulator of *Wonder Woman* gave some people at the Vista an opportunity to dress in goofy costumes.

And it was those costumes that brought Celia and Rose Byrne to the premiere.

The magic bullshit window had chosen well.

Celia and Rose Byrne were clothed in Fairy Land's haute couture, which over the last season had moved into animal pelts.

Had they arrived anywhere else in Los Angeles, their outfits would have drawn a lot of attention.

At *Wonder Woman*, they were just making a political statement.

They arrived through the magic bullshit faery window, popping dead center into the lobby of the Vista, right in front of the concessions counter.

They saw a lot of people going into the twin double doors of the theater.

They both remembered *Tom a Lincoln* at Gray's Inn.

They knew what it looked like when people went to a show.

Celia and Rose followed the crowd inside.

They found two seats to the back right of the theater.

They watched the movie.

# Chapter Six

## Willkommen im Dschungel

Around the time when I started writing Chapter Twelve of this book, right between two paragraphs in which I insult George R.R. Martin and *Game of Thrones*, I underwent an unexpected religious experience.

To make sense of this: at the beginning of June 2017 AD, I decided that I should go see the band Guns N' Roses perform live at the Staples Center.

What can you say about Guns N' Roses?

Back in the 1980s AD, they were total Hollywood scumbags, the dregs of the dregs, homeless trash who became the most famous people in the world.

It's the greatest faery story ever told.

The band carried on for about five years before flaming out.

Lead vocalist Axl Rose was left in control of the name, but all of the other original members quit or were fired. A period of twelve years followed.

This period included the album *Chinese Democracy*, mocked because it took forever to be released, but which is actually pretty good.

Anyway, they were a great band, and their iconography haunted my childhood and is about 70 per cent of the reason why I live in Los Angeles.

In 2016 AD, three of the original members reformed the band and ventured out on a reunion tour.

I saw their August 19th, 2016 AD show at Dodger Stadium.

Because 2016 AD was a year in which I had made a significant, but not substantial, amount of money, I bought a General Admission ticket to the pit.

It cost about $280.

I was way in front.

I was next to the stage.

The whole thing was filmed by a professional camera crew.

If there's ever a live DVD, you'll see me. I'm the guy with no hair looking very uncomfortable as he stands next to a group of models who are younger than the songs being performed.

When a second American leg of the tour was announced for 2017 AD, with the Los Angeles dates in late November, I decided that I should buy another ticket.

Because 2017 AD was a year in which I earned an even more significant, bordering on substantial, amount of money, I bought a General Admission ticket to the pit.

It cost about $550.

Which is manifestly insane.

But I have a lot of disposable income.

This is because I don't spend any money.

In the twenty-two months following the release of my novel *I Hate the Internet*, I made just under $200,000, net, pre-tax, pre-agents' commissions, and the only things I bought were a cemetery plot and two tickets to see Guns N' Roses.

On June 30th, 2017 AD, I purchased a General Admission pit ticket to see the Guns N' Roses show at the Staples Center.

The show was scheduled to occur on November 24th, 2017 AD.

Because I like useless ephemera, I paid an extra $5 to have a physical ticket.

The ticket arrived about a week later.

It was sent via postal mail.

Then, in August of 2017 AD, right around when my novel

*The Future Won't Be Long* was published by Penguin Random House, ensuring that I made significantly less money in 2018 AD than I did in 2017 AD, I found a surprise in my postal mail.

I'd been sent a second ticket.

I compared the two tickets.

Except for the barcodes, they were identical.

Barcodes are bits of black ink and numbers printed on every ticket. Whenever you try to enter an event, someone's there with a device that scans the barcode and ascertains the ticket's validity.

The tickets had different barcodes.

There were two options: (1) believe that the second ticket supplanted the first or (2) believe that both tickets were valid.

I opted for a soft belief in the second option.

I now had two tickets to see Guns N' Roses at the Staples Center.

Which meant that I had to find someone to come with me.

I called Arafat Kazi.

Arafat Kazi is my best friend.

He used to be the fattest man in Bangladesh.

Now he's an American citizen and had recent gastric bypass surgery. Hundreds of pounds of fat have melted off his body, but their absence has draped him in a suit of empty skin.

He's also a drummer.

We met in 2001 AD, when he was an undergrad at Boston University.

One of the very first things that we talked about was his taste in music, which in those days was almost entirely Heavy Metal.

He was into Iron Maiden and Judas Priest.

The worst bands of all time!

One of our few overlaps in taste was Guns N' Roses.

We built a friendship talking about the band.

"Dude," I said into the telephone. "I have this extra ticket to see

63

Guns N' Roses that was mailed to me by mistake. You've got to come to Los Angeles for Thanksgiving."

"Okay, dude," he said. "I'll do it. Can you pay my plane fare?"

Fast forward to November 23rd, 2017 AD.

Thanksgiving Day! Celebration of genocide with disgusting food!

Around 9PM, I picked Arafat up at the airport and brought him to my apartment.

I suggested that he sleep on the pull-out, but he insisted on taking the floor.

He passed out around midnight.

About twenty hours before Arafat's arrival, an astonishing thing happened: somehow *The Future Won't Be Long* was shortlisted for the *Literary Review*'s Bad Sex in Fiction Award.

The *Literary Review* was a London magazine for, quote, People Who Devour Books, unquote.

The Bad Sex in Fiction Award was an award that, quote, honoured an author who has produced an outstandingly bad scene of sexual description in an otherwise good novel. The purpose of the prize is to draw attention to poorly written, perfunctory or redundant passages of sexual description in modern fiction, unquote.

The shortlisting of *The Future Won't Be Long* generated more emails than any other thing that had happened in my life.

When I woke up that morning and examined my inbox, it was flooded.

Draw your own lesson, reader.

Here was mine: people remain unbelievably primitive.

The emails had a 50/50 split.

Half of the people felt bad for me and wanted to make sure that I was okay.

The other half understood the shortlisting for what it was:

absolutely fucking awesome, even if it did produce a moral compromise.

The moral compromise emerged from the fact that I am a hopeless case.

I loathe human attempts at establishing status.

I object to the general idea of awards and literary awards in specific. But.

The Bad Sex in Fiction Award?

For the first time in my life, there was something that I wanted to win.

I knew that I wouldn't.

The shortlisted passage wasn't a sex scene.

It was an absurd, pretentious character describing her reaction to sex in a manner that was absurd and pretentious.

There was no way that it fit the bill.

My novel does, in fact, contain an actual sex scene.

It's two pages long. It's disgusting. It's redundant. It's perfunctory. It's so pretentious that at the moment of climax, it mentions James Boswell, a writer from the Eighteenth Century AD.

So why wasn't it nominated?

Here's my theory: the actual sex scene in *The Future Won't Be Long* is the description of a down-and-dirty homosexual encounter.

Major league assfucking!

And all of the passages shortlisted for the Bad Sex in Fiction Award were exclusively heterosexual.

Clearly, the pretentious passage for which I had been nominated was a stand-in for the pretentious passage which contained a description of actual sex.

I was weighing this in my mind while I waited for Arafat Kazi to get off his plane.

Everyone else in the airport terminal waited with anticipation for the arrival of their friends, lovers, and family.

And I was there too, and I was trying to decide if the liberal intelligentsia believed homosexuals are incapable of having bad sex.

With Arafat crashed out, I fell asleep around 3AM after beginning to write Chapter Twelve.

When I woke up at 10AM, he wasn't in the apartment.

I checked my email and found the following:

**Fri, Nov 24, 2017 at 9:18 AM**
**From: Arafat Kazi**
**To: Jarett Kobek**
**Subject:**

Hey dude, I couldn't sleep from friction of excess skin on floor, so I got a hotel. About to go to sleep for a couple of hours. It's 9:18 am.

Sent from Arafat's iPhone.

We met for a late lunch at Musso & Frank, which is the oldest restaurant in Hollywood, and also the setting for a short story that I wrote about the film director Wes Anderson using a urinal. The story is titled "Wes Anderson Uses a Urinal." You can find it in a recently published anthology called *Mixed Up: Cocktail Recipes (and Flash Fiction) for the Discerning Drinker (and Reader)*.

Before I left for lunch, I checked my ticket on the website from which I'd ordered it, and discovered something that I hadn't noticed before.

Despite tickets to the pit being General Admission, my purchase had been assigned a seat.

The reason I'd adopted a soft belief in both tickets' validity was on the basis of General Admission. Why would any General Admission ticket be assigned a seat number?

Ipso facto, one ticket couldn't replace the other.

But now my belief was shattered. It was clear that there was only one seat.

Ergo, one ticket.

A sensation of dread crashed on me.

I'd made Arafat Kazi fly out to Los Angeles and bought his plane ticket and we'd been talking about this stupid concert for months and now he was staying in a hotel because the empty skin which draped his body had made it impossible to sleep on my apartment floor.

And he wasn't getting inside.

Before I left, I made a vow to the universe: if Arafat Kazi got into the pit to see Guns N' Roses at the Staples Center, then I would stop worrying about the outcome of my life.

I would take it as a sign that everything would be fine, even if my last novel had commanded a high advance and turned out to be a commercial failure.

I'm not sure why I made this vow.

It happened while I was urinating.

Shades of Wes Anderson.

I went to Musso & Frank. I ordered a hot turkey sandwich. Arafat got a French Dip sandwich. Then we ordered dessert.

I had a piece of key lime pie.

Arafat had something called the Diplomat Pudding.

I had, and have, no idea what's in a Diplomat Pudding.

It looked disgusting.

We left the restaurant and walked for a few blocks.

Arafat used his smartphone to hail an Uber, which was a private car operated by a company that's single-handedly set back the American labor movement by about seventy years.

The car brought us to his hotel. We sat around his room for an hour and a half, talking about Muslims in America.

Arafat's a Muslim.

I'm half a Muslim.

Break out the misspelled placards!

"Dude, I know people, you know," he said, "who have jobs as bank managers, who are nice when you see them, and then you go back home and see that ten minutes after you parted, they've posted about Sharia law on Facebook."

"I read about this poll a few months ago," I said. "They asked people of every possible demographic how they felt about people from every other demographic. And, dude, Muslims polled worse than anyone else in America. With every single demographic. When they asked Muslims about other Muslims, dude, they still polled worse than everyone else."

"Well, dude," he said, "I think you've got to realize that even though people express a public opposition to the rhetoric, when that rhetoric comes from the top, it still seeps in."

Then I convinced him to change his clothes.

He'd packed an outfit that he wanted to wear to the concert, but earlier that afternoon, he'd decided against it.

We argued, but I won the day with the following thought: "If you're dressed like a circus performer, there's a better chance of them letting you inside."

This was the outfit: hot pink pants and a striped multi-colored psychedelic shirt.

Arafat also had a cap which matched the shirt.

He changed his clothes.

It was incredible.

He really did look like a circus performer.

We took another Uber to the Staples Center, which is a circular-shaped venue where the Los Angeles Lakers play basketball and imbue the city's cocaine addicts with a sense of regional superiority.

The driver parked across the street from the venue.

We got out of the Uber.

We walked over to the Staples Center and discovered that there was a special line for people with General Admission tickets. It was much shorter than the normal line, which was full of sane people who hadn't paid $550 to see middle-aged men perform thirty-year-old songs.

I gave Arafat one of my tickets.

"Let's see how it goes," I said.

At the front of the line, a pleasant woman tried to scan the barcode on my ticket.

It didn't work.

"What about his?" I asked.

She scanned Arafat's ticket.

It worked.

We tried to convince her that she should let us both in. She said that she couldn't. We'd have to talk with the box office manager.

We walked away and then she called us back.

Because she'd scanned Arafat's ticket, and it worked, one of us would have to go inside.

I took Arafat's ticket.

I went inside.

He said he'd go talk to the manager.

When I got inside, there was a table for General Admission tickets, and the young woman working at the table was checking barcodes and names against a list of people authorized to be in the pit. If your barcode matched an entry on the list, then she'd put a purple leopard-spotted paper bracelet on your left wrist.

The bracelet was your pass into the pit, and even with that, you still had to get through about four more security checks.

I got down to the pit, which was about five feet from the stage.

*Arafat would have loved this*, I thought.

*It's awful that he isn't here*, I thought.

*Everything's ruined*, I thought.

There were fifteen other people in the pit. They were pressed up against a railing that separated the pit from the stage.

I was the only person standing in the middle, not pressed up against anything.

It felt awkward.

I went back to the round concourse of the Staples Center.

And then I did what all pathetic writers do.

I found the bar.

With a bloodstream full of overpriced vodka, I texted Arafat.

I wrote that he shouldn't worry, that he should just get a scalped ticket on his smartphone, and I'd pay him back.

At the very least, I thought, he could get a ticket in the cheapseats. It'd be a shared memory even if we were apart.

But he didn't respond.

Showtime was at 7:30PM.

Around 7:20PM, I decided that I should go back to the pit.

I again went through the phalanx of security.

When I got into the arena, I saw only one thing.

Arafat Kazi, standing in the pit, his circus performer costume as bright as the sun.

He'd talked his way in!

I was so happy that I insisted we pose for a picture where I was kissing his greasy fucking head.

The show was amazing. Guns N' Roses was the best band I'd ever seen.

They were so good that they were even better than when I saw them at Dodger Stadium, where they'd been brilliant. They were good in the way that people are good only when they hate the alternative so much they'll do anything to avoid it.

And in the case of Guns N' Roses, this was the alternative: go home and lead a normal life.

The next day, Arafat Kazi woke up and took a train to San Diego.

He sent me a series of text messages:

My head is still spinning

Nothing makes sense

I think it was a capstone moment in our friendship

That's what the final scene in the movie about us would be

This is as formative as anything we've shared

There are two options here.

You can believe that Arafat Kazi getting into the pit to see Guns N' Roses at the Staples Center was the byproduct of a random universe acting out in its mechanistic complexity.

But to believe this, you have to accept a chain of events so unlikely as to be incalculable in their probability.

You have to accept a universe so random in its possibilities that it was able to produce the unlikelihood that Arafat Kazi, the only person alive who could talk his way into a $550 ticket, would have a best friend who would be mailed, by accident, two tickets to the same concert after stumbling into the impossibility of making a bunch of money from writing a novel, and that this best friend would see the second ticket and know exactly how it should be used.

And you would have to accept that all of this would happen while someone was dressed like a circus performer.

The other option is to do what I've done.

You can accept that the universe, for whatever reason, wanted Arafat Kazi and myself to be in the pit to see Guns N' Roses at the Staples Center. It wanted us to have that formative experience. It wanted to write that last scene in the movie about our lives.

You can accept that a divine hand was involved in the whole process, easing our path, guiding the journey.

You can accept that I saw the face of God.

And you're going to have to forgive me, because the worst possible time to see the face of God is in the middle of writing a novel.

It's going to make a mess of everything.

The last few chapters of this book are going to dissolve into a hectoring lecture about Jesus Christ.

Sorry about that.

Don't say you weren't warned.

Anyway, here I am, the author, Jarett Kobek, and I say to you, reader, that I was in the Staples Center, I was in the pit, I was at Guns N' Roses, I was with Arafat Kazi, I was shortlisted for the Bad Sex in Fiction Award, and I saw the face of God.

And it looked like this:

And this:

# Chapter Seven

## The House on the Hill

And while Celia and Rose Byrne were seeing *Wonder Woman* at the Vista, another attendee at the same screening was a man named Francis Fuller. He'd been a director of films and television for about thirty years between 1950 AD and 1980 AD.

Fuller began his filmmaking career as a young native Angelino who was queerer than a three-dollar bill and made short experimental films on 8MM and 16MM.

These films were more expressionistic than narrative, featured aggressive editing, and were shown at makeshift cinemas for audiences of people who smoked too much marijuana and had too much sex with strangers.

Embarrassed as he later would be by his works of youth, Fuller admitted that they'd helped earn him admission to the film school at USC, where he'd gained a fundamental understanding of the craft.

After graduation, he'd bummed around Hollywood until 1963 AD, when his life had changed through a meeting at a cultural salon hosted by the former actor Samson de Brier.

It was a night when everyone'd been smoking too much tea, and too many people'd been talking about Thelonious Monk. Everyone was crammed into a little house in the backyard of de Brier's property on Barton Avenue.

Fuller was bored. He didn't know fuck all about jazz.

He looked around de Brier's tiny cottage and saw an exceedingly corpulent man pressed up against a Venetian mural.

Fuller went over and said hello to the corpulent man.

The man turned out to be a lush named Aram Menechian, who'd come to Hollywood with the intention of laundering some of his brother's ill-gotten money.

Fuller said that he had a screenplay. Fuller said that he'd gone to USC. Fuller mentioned that *Time* magazine had sneered at his short films.

Fuller walked out of de Brier's salon with an offer from Menechian to produce the screenplay.

The screenplay was entitled *Handspun Roses* and for two years, it'd been sitting in Fuller's bedroom at his parents' house in Riverside County.

*Handspun Roses* was a loose adaptation of Elizabeth Gaskell's "The Poor Clare." The action was transposed to the San Fernando Valley.

Despite its reliance on narrative, the finished film exhibited the same qualities as Fuller's experimental work, this time exercised in service of the horror genre.

*Handspun Roses* caught the attention of Roger Corman, who gave Fuller work directing several more feature-length films, including a black-and-white psycho-biddy starring Myrna Loy.

As the 1960s AD wore on and became the 1970s AD, Fuller found himself working in television. He directed bonecheap made-for-TV films and countless episodes of sitcoms and evening soap operas.

He missed the old days of handheld 16MM cameras, when you could tell ultra-butch straight boys that you were making a movie and watch as they put themselves into homoerotic situations for the sake of maybe kinda getting famous.

But the TV money was good.

And Fuller retained a certain silverback-daddy sex appeal.

And he'd bought his own home on Glendower Avenue in

Los Feliz, which was an upper-middle-class neighborhood north of the Vista Theater.

Fuller grew old.

Work dried up, but he'd managed his investments, and he drew a pension, and thanks to Proposition 13, the taxes on his property were almost non-existent. He'd never reached the Cash Horizon, but he'd gotten pretty close.

Fuller lived on, a lonely geriatric in the pink house where once he'd thrown lavish parties full of rent boys and rough trade.

Some fans wrote to him, and there'd been one last non-union effort with a crowdfunded adaptation of "Young Goodman Brown" by Nathaniel Hawthorne, and there were always emails to be answered.

By 2017 AD, Francis Fuller knew that he was nearing the end and that very little excitement would come again.

He'd returned to the primary activity of his youth, when the world seemed full of promise: he went to the movies.

The films had changed.

The glamor and the glitz were gone. Most movies were parables about American foreign policy and had an intended audience of bloodthirsty men.

That's why he was at *Wonder Woman*.

He saw everything that played the Vista.

When *Wonder Woman* finished simulating genocide, Francis Fuller went to the lobby and thought about using the bathroom.

There was a line of young men who needed to urinate. Fuller was too old to be pushed about in the queue. He decided to wait until the bathroom was empty.

And it was while he waited that he saw the two most astonishing women.

They were dressed a bit like Diana, the hero of *Wonder Woman*, but instead of wearing bondage-themed body armor, they were wearing animal pelts. Real fur!

And they were so muscular.

But not at all.

And so femme.

And yet not.

He couldn't determine their ages.

Were they very old?

Or were they very young?

Francis Fuller couldn't help himself.

He had to talk to them.

The conversation turned into Francis Fuller giving Celia and Rose Byrne a ride in his vintage Jaguar. He drove them to his house on Glendower Avenue.

Celia and Rose Byrne ended up in Francis Fuller's living room, where, because of effective sewage management, only one person had ever voided their bowels.

The house was high enough on the hill that Celia and Rose could look through Fuller's picture window and see the whole of the city.

It was infinite lines of car headlights, the north–south avenues intersecting with the east–west boulevards, a fathomless grid of industrial pollution and greenhouse gases.

"We are in a new world," said Celia to Rose Byrne.

"It is much worse than on our television," said Rose Byrne.

"One does not expect much," said Celia. "But one maintains hope. The mortals I have known in my life have been pleasant enough. How can they have created such a nightmare?"

"The human condition, my dears," said Francis Fuller as he came from his kitchen, holding a tray with three cups of black Darjeeling tea.

There were many things that Francis Fuller couldn't imagine.

He'd spent most of his professional life making films about supranatural entities and now he had brought supranatural entities into his own home.

And he had no idea.

Fuller couldn't imagine the level of danger implicit in the women's presence.

If *Wonder Woman* was a genocide simulator, then Rose Byrne was genocide.

Other than individuals in the military arm of the United States of America and former Presidents of the United States of America, she'd killed more human beings than anyone on Earth.

They sat in Fuller's living room, drinking his tea.

Celia looked at the décor.

It was shabby old furniture surrounded by vintage framed movie posters, all of which were advertisements for 1940s AD films produced at RKO by Val Lewton.

*Cat People, I Walked With a Zombie, The Leopard Man, The Seventh Victim,* and *Isle of the Dead.*

"You have a wonderful eye," Francis Fuller said to Celia. "Not many people pay attention."

"My queen is a rare being," said Rose Byrne.

"I've known some rare queens," said Francis Fuller. "They're all dead now. Except Ken Anger. I heard he was still down on Hollywood Boulevard, you know, screaming at anyone who'll pretend he's interesting. The last time I saw him was at Curtis Harrington's funeral. Poor Curtis, he and Ken had a thing back in the '40s. The funeral was ghastly. Ken was even worse than usual and spent the whole time heckling anyone stupid enough to speak from the podium. He made a whole show over Curtis's body, kissing the corpse. But that's Hollywood. It's always been like this."

Like most readers of this book, Celia and Rose Byrne had absolutely no idea what Francis Fuller was talking about.

"There's something I have wondered," asked Celia. "How do people hear the stories that they put into films and plays?"

"Hear them?" asked Francis Fuller.

"Yes," said Celia. "How did the actors in *Wonder Woman* hear about Diana and her island and her journey into the world and her queen mother?"

"Honey," said Francis Fuller, "that answer is too long. We live in the era of the mega-franchise."

"But where did the story come from?" asked Rose Byrne.

"Comic books," said Francis Fuller. "These days, all of the movies come from the funny papers."

Celia and Rose Byrne had never seen comic books, which were cheap little periodicals that contained American power fantasies.

But Fern had brought home many a newspaper and the women of Fairy Island had pored over them, paying especial attention to the comic strips that arrived printed in full color in the Sunday editions.

"You mean that the story of Diana came from *Krazy Kat*?" asked Celia. "Or *Blondie*?"

*Krazy Kat* was an old newspaper comic strip about a cat struck with love for a mouse that liked throwing bricks at the cat's head. The cat was named Krazy. The mouse was named Ignatz.

*Blondie* was an old newspaper comic strip about a Jazz Age flapper who married a man with an insatiable appetite for sandwiches. The flapper was named Blondie. The husband was named Dagwood.

Celia had seen both strips in the early 1940s, when Fern had brought home copies of the *New York Journal-American*.

"Something like that," said Francis Fuller. "Recycled old pap. That's what the flickers are these days. When I was in the business, things were different."

"You made films?" asked Rose Byrne.

The doorbell rang.

Francis Fuller jumped up. His octogenarian bones buckled under the sudden thrust of his mass.

Fuller answered the front door, which was in a foyer off the living room.

Standing on his doorstep was Adam Leroux.

Leroux was Fuller's makeshift assistant.

He was twenty-eight years old.

Leroux had first shown up in Fuller's life after Leroux sent an email asking about *Handspun Roses*. A correspondence ensued, wherein many topics about old Hollywood were discussed. This led to Fuller's discovery that Leroux lived in Los Feliz. An invitation was extended for Leroux to visit Fuller's home.

When Leroux arrived for the first time, Fuller was delighted.

The young man was so handsome and butch.

Fuller was fascinated by the short story of Leroux's life, which had included a few military years in Iraq, where Leroux, who was poor, had shot Muslims at the behest of rich people.

For his part, Leroux was drunk on proximity to someone who'd directed films and known people like Anaïs Nin, James Whale, Susan Sontag, Dorothy Dean, and Orson Welles.

It wasn't long before Leroux was coming over every day and helping Fuller with his memoir.

They were a Hollywood odd couple of the Twenty-First Century AD.

The old man, decaying in his earth-tone suits, and his young assistant, body covered in tattoos, head pierced with metal, dressed in black T-shirts and jeans.

"Adam," said Fuller. "You'll never believe who's here."

Fuller brought Leroux into the living room.

Leroux had a sixth sense.

He'd killed enough Muslims, and had enough Muslims try to kill him, that he knew when he was in danger. One look at Rose Byrne, broadsword dangling against her exposed thigh, and he understood that he was staring at death.

Leroux had a seventh sense.

He was a Hollywood assistant with no future who'd attached himself like a barnacle to an old ship. Fuller was his one shot.

Leroux had an almost preternatural sensitivity to moments when his hold on the old man was threatened.

There'd been other guests who pinged off Leroux's seventh sense.

The ones who wouldn't leave.

The ones who'd stolen memorabilia.

The ones who'd take advantage of Fuller for the sake of social media.

Leroux knew that Fuller was a man who collected stray dogs.

But none of the others had carried a sharpened sword forged in the fires of Fairy Land.

Fuller made introductions between his guests and Leroux.

"They were just asking me the most wonderful question," said Fuller. "They asked me how the people who made *Wonder Woman* had heard the story of Princess Diana and the island of the Amazons."

"I haven't seen it," said Leroux.

"We just came from a screening at the Vista," said Fuller.

"How was it?" asked Leroux.

"Moronic," said Fuller. "But you know, at my age, and in this town, I don't expect much."

There was more small talk, with Fuller and Leroux explaining the magic of moviemaking to Celia and Rose Byrne.

These efforts failed, as both men relied on the expectation that the women were conversant with Hollywood's shared cultural history, which was an American religious mythos that had penetrated every recess of the globe except Fairy Land and some remote tribes in South America.

Fuller's bladder, which had dogged him for several years, again demanded voiding. He excused himself and went to the bathroom at the back end of the house.

"Francis is older than he looks," said Adam. "He gets tired very easily. People don't realize how much these conversations take out of him."

"It is said that aging past usefulness is the worst thing that can befall a person," said Celia.

"He's still useful," said Adam Leroux. "He's working on his memoirs."

"What is a memoir?" asked Rose Byrne.

"His personal history," said Adam Leroux. "He's known some very interesting people. There's a whole chapter about Joanna Cassidy."

The women of Fairy Land didn't respond.

"Francis is too kind to say it himself," said Adam Leroux, "but you should probably get on your way. It's close to his bedtime."

"We have nowhere to go," said Celia. "We are newly arrived in Los Angeles."

"I don't see how that's Francis's problem," said Adam Leroux.

"Are you telling us that my queen should leave?" asked Rose Byrne.

"That's exactly what I'm suggesting."

Rose Byrne stood up from Francis Fuller's shabby couch, took out her sword, and chopped off Adam Leroux's head.

He tried to defend himself but he was a mortal and Rose Byrne was an old hand.

All his military training and killing of Muslims were for naught.

He didn't stand a chance.

His head rolled around the living room.

His body twitched out its last bioelectric moments of life.

Rose Byrne stormed to the bathroom, where Fuller was sitting on the toilet with his penis tucked between his legs, struggling against age to void his bladder.

She drove her sword into his chest.

"Oh," said Francis Fuller.

## Chapter Eight

# Gentlemen Prefer Blood

On the very same day that Rose Byrne chopped off the head of Adam Leroux, HRH Mamduh bin Fatih bin Muhammad bin Abdulaziz Al Saud was guest speaker at the Lunch Series put on by Harvard University's Program for Constitutional Government.

The title of the talk was this: "Teaching Foundational Classics to the Mid-East: What It Means and Why It Matters."

It was held in room K354 of the CGIS Knafel Building on Harvard's campus in Cambridge, Massachusetts, which was a satellite city across the Charles River from Boston.

Harvard University was a hedge fund that masqueraded as an institution of higher learning. It was one of the places where the world's upper classes enjoyed grade inflation as they became economic warlords of the technocratic elite who mouthed platitudes about equality while crushing the global poor.

The political philosopher Harvey Mansfield introduced HRH.

Mansfield explained that HRH was an alumnus of Harvard, having received a Master's in Public Policy at the Kennedy School before earning his Doctorate of Philosophy from the London School of Economics.

Mansfield explained an initiative funded by HRH's non-profit wing.

It was a multi-disciplinary program that brought promising students from the Middle East and funded their undergraduate

84

education at Harvard, with a focus on a broad liberal arts education and exposure to the foundational influences of Western thought.

After Harvey Mansfield finished speaking, HRH addressed the room.

HRH talked about education being the cornerstone of liberal democracy.

HRH talked about the paucity of books in Arabic translation.

HRH said that while a great many students from the Middle East were receiving educations in America, their focus was on STEM, and that this had left them disconnected from ideas underpinning the basic political philosophies of the Twentieth Century AD and Twenty-First Century AD.

HRH talked about how it was impossible to expect events like the Arab Spring to resolve productively if people in the Middle East weren't exposed, in advance, to a diversity of ideas about governance.

HRH finished with this: "I am not an expert like some of the people in this room, but I am resolute in my belief that if human rights are to emerge, we must first educate humans, and then teach them what is right."

The audience applauded.

Harvey Mansfield opened the event to questions from the audience.

The first question was familiar.

The questioner told HRH that she had Googled him and found his interviews refreshing and unexpected. Then she asked: "I was wondering if you could speak about the reaction of the Saudi government to your more provocative statements?"

HRH smiled.

His bridgework was fucking fantastic.

"Madame," said HRH, "I was raised in the hotels of Europe and America. I hold citizenship in Malta. I do not speak as a member of my family. I speak as an inhabitant of the world."

The next question was also familiar.

It was being asked on every American campus by people who were terrified of college students.

"I don't know if you've followed any stories," said a man in a suit. "There's been a thing happening where the students at our universities have been asking for safe spaces. If you're not familiar with the term, and I wasn't until a few months ago, a safe space is a place where the students can be coddled away from hearing ideas that they don't like, and it's disguised under the idea of oppression. You're from a region beset by conflict. I tell my students that there are no safe spaces in Aleppo. Do you have an opinion on this phenomenon?"

HRH smiled.

His bridgework was fucking fantastic.

"I always err on the side of generosity. If people require safe spaces, then I see nothing wrong with providing them, as long as the institution tempers their presence with a robust environment of educational rigor."

When the questions were over, pleasantries were exchanged.

HRH texted his manservant Dmitri Huda.

"HEY NONNY HEY, ARE THINGS IN ORDER?????" asked HRH.

"Yes, Dennis," texted Dmitri Huda. "I'm downstairs."

HRH's father Fatih bin Muhammad bin Abdulaziz Al Saud was the second-richest man in the Middle East. He built a fortune after being exiled from the Kingdom.

This exile followed the parking-lot execution of Misha'al bint Fahd bin Muhammad bin Abdulaziz Al Saud.

Fatih bin Muhammad was a convenient scapegoat for the assassination.

It was said that he encouraged delusions of romance in Misha'al.

He was given the riyal equivalent of $200,000.

He was kicked the fuck out.

He traded off the family name, got into construction and

concrete, and used that money to diversify his holdings. When he had established his fortune, he decided to do what all people do when they want to legitimate their place in the hierarchy of global evil.

He wrote a book.

First published in French as *Le chemin du conquérant arabe: les leçons d'un prince saoudien*, an English translation appeared in 1999 AD under the title *The Conqueror's Path: Business Lessons from a Saudi Prince.*

It was a CEO-style autobiography married, awkwardly, with Fifteen Lessons that Fatih bin Muhammad had learned through the ups and downs of doing business on an international scale. Each lesson was expanded with historical parallel and floating anecdote.

*Il Principe* meets *Trump: The Art of the Deal.*

It sold in small numbers until references began appearing in the songs of well-known hip-hop artists, who adopted the book's maxims of worldly success into anthems of global capitalism.

Sales exploded.

Fatih bin Muhammad became The Conqueror.

One of The Conqueror's Fifteen Lessons, present in *Le chemin du conquérant arabe*, was the idea that a successful businessman, particularly if he comes from a place unfamiliar to his potential financial partners, must take up stratagems to evoke comfort in others.

Following this advice, HRH had adopted many names in different languages.

In Chinese, HRH was called 野生花卉, which meant Wild Flower.

In Spanish, HRH was called *el Diablo árabe*, which meant The Arabic Devil.

In Turkish, HRH was called *Küçükkutsaldağ*, which meant The Little Holy Mountain.

In German, HRH was called *Der Meister der Weltschmerzes*, which meant Master of the World's Sorrows.

In English, HRH was called Dennis, which meant Dennis.

Dmitri Huda had commandeered a surface parking spot on Cambridge Street.

HRH came out of the Knafel Building.

HRH walked towards the car.

Dmitri Huda jumped out of the driver's seat and rushed to the rear passenger door of the gun-metal 2016 AD Bentley Mulsanne.

"Dmitri! Play not the dogsbody!" cried HRH. "What do you take me for? Have I too lost the ability to walk? Must I next crawl?"

Dmitri Huda returned to the driver's side door.

"Do you behold this complex, Dmitri?"

HRH pointed to a series of drab buildings on the other side of Cambridge Street.

"This august institution is the Cambridge Rindge and Latin School."

"I see," said Dmitri.

"It is notable for its alumni," said HRH. "Most prominent are the actors Matt Damon and Ben Affleck. Followed only by Dzhokhar Tsarnaev and his brother Tamerlan, who together orchestrated the bombing of the Boston Marathon. When news of the blasts reached my ears, it evoked salad days misspent in Cambridge. I sensed in my inner heart that the perpetrators would be revealed as local yokels. Only the trite provincialism of a Bostonian would suggest the Marathon as a target. Dmitri, if you wish to further your spiritual development, you should consider the occult principles of this complex. It always produces its monstrosities in pairs."

HRH climbed into the back seat.

Dmitri Huda returned to the driver's seat and started the engine.

"You know the location?" asked HRH.

"It's in satnav."

HRH opened the refrigerated bar.

Inside there was a vaporizer and a bag of marijuana.

"Is this indica or sativa?" asked HRH. "I will not suffer the mellow vibes of indica. Not tonight. I must invigorate with the lush and vibrant caress of sativa."

"It's sativa," said Dmitri.

HRH vaped sativa.

HRH pressed a button, which deployed a bespoke Android tablet embedded in the reverse of the front passenger seat.

HRH engaged with the bespoke Android tablet.

HRH opened the YouTube app.

HRH streamed "Dark Avenger" by the American heavy metal band Manowar.

"Dark Avenger" played through the Naim audio system.

"Drive on, Dmitri," shouted HRH over the 1,100 watts of pulsing metal power. "Bring me to my destiny!"

HRH's destiny was an old factory in Waltham that had been gentrified into offices and loft apartments.

For a solid century, the building had manufactured watches. Now it crafted the aspirant lives of the haute bourgeoisie.

Dmitri Huda navigated the Bentley from Cambridge to West Cambridge to Watertown and through the other suburbs. It was that New England experience: the transition between multiple disparate landscapes in less than forty minutes of travel. Dense urbanity giving way to small-town life to post-industrial decay.

When they arrived at the old factory, Dmitri Huda idled in the parking lot.

"Remain here," said HRH. "I am sure to stride forth, triumphant in my victory."

HRH emerged from the 2016 AD Bentley Mulsanne with a rattle-snake suitcase under his arm.

Here's something that Harvey Mansfield didn't explain in the CGIS Knafel Building: HRH had been hipped to the possibility of a Doctorate in Philosophy at the LSE by Saif al-Islam Gaddafi.

Saif al-Islam Gaddafi, famous for being the son of a lunatic dictator who blew up a passenger plane over Scotland and was beaten to death after hiding in a drainage pipe, had demonstrated how this possibility worked.

The vampire of the LSE sucked blood money.

Its conscience was soothed with paid holidays for the administrative staff and faculty, all the better to generate white papers and editorials in the *Telegraph*.

In terms of education, the metropolitan area was lousy with debauched Eton boys who would handle your coursework and dissertation.

They only asked what anyone asked.

Lucre, filthy lucre.

One needn't spend much time in the Old Smoke, but it did help to make the occasional appearance. Besides, as Dr. Johnson had told Mr. Boswell, when a man tires of London, he tires of life.

And if, during his salad days, the stout erections of HRH's penis had carried any information, it was that his corporeal form had yet to tire of life.


HRH managed his way through the old factory until he came to the fourth-floor apartment.

HRH knocked on the door.

A sex worker, who held a lease on the apartment, opened the door.

"You must be Dennis."

"Madame," said HRH. "You have identified me with utter precision and laser focus."

The sex worker moved from the doorway.

HRH passed into the apartment.

The sex worker led HRH down a small staircase to the apartment's lower level, which housed a bedroom, a kitchen, and a living/dining space.

"You will please to remind me," said HRH. "Did my assistant forward the funds through Venmo? Or must I be discreet in my placement of the requisite white envelope on your granite countertop?"

"We got the money," said a male voice from the living/dining space.

It was the sex worker's bodyguard.

He was a large man. He was wearing a blue-and-silver sports jersey advertising his avowed fandom of the New England Patriots and the team's star quarterback Tom Brady.

The bodyguard was sitting in front of a television. The bodyguard was watching the television with its speaker muted.

He was reading the closed-captioned subtitles, which conveyed the story of an attack on a casino resort in Manila. Thirty-seven people had been shot and killed.

"I was unaware that another soul would be present," said HRH.

"Is that a problem?" asked the bodyguard.

"My dear fellow," said HRH. "I flourish on company. What a stout, robust lad you seem! Shall you too join us in our deluge of flesh and avarice? I should like very much to see and feel that frame of yours in its bounding action. What thighs you have, my liege!"

"I'll pass," said the bodyguard.

Above the bodyguard's head, there were three clusters of helium-inflated balloons, tied together in a haphazard fashion to create letters from the Roman alphabet.

The balloons said:

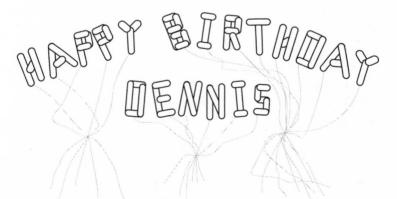

HRH walked over to the exterior wall of the apartment, placing his hand on its exposed brick. Its windows looked out over the Charles River.

"Fear death by water," said HRH. "As my manservant drove me towards this monolithic structure, it occurred to me that perhaps my father had some hand in its conversion. The Conqueror is consumed with a smothering love for Boston and its environs. The redevelopment of Boylston in the Fenway was his own initiative."

"Let's get going?" asked the sex worker.

"Wunderbar, my dear lady!" cried HRH. "To the stables!"

In the bedroom, two other sex workers were waiting.

HRH and the original sex worker entered.

Each of the sex workers had been picked by Dmitri Huda via an arcane process that began with The Erotic Review, which was the Internet's top community of escorts, hobbyists, and service providers.

The Erotic Review's vast userbase was comprised of people who fucked sex workers and then went on The Erotic Review and reviewed the performance, looks, and personalities of recently fucked sex workers.

The Erotic Review offered its reviewers the option to confirm whether or not a recently fucked sex worker provided specific sexual activities during the recent fucking. These included: (1) cum in mouth (2) touch pussy (3) lick pussy (4) two-girl action (5) more than one guy at a time (6) multiple pops allowed.

After Harvard University invited HRH to be a guest speaker, Dmitri Huda had contacted a sex worker whom he'd procured several years earlier using The Erotic Review.

The sex worker wrote back. She wasn't available. She was working in Dallas.

She recommended a friend, who got Dmitri Huda in touch with an agency that sometimes did cross-over work with people from FetLife.

The agency said that it could satisfy HRH's demands: three

girls, athletic, Ivy League educated, very bi, 420-friendly, unafraid of BDSM, and willing to go anal.

Dmitri asked the agency to procure helium-inflated balloons.

The balloons were HRH's way of making sure that his requests had been fulfilled to the utmost. Past experience had demonstrated that if the balloons were not present, then other requests would also be ignored.

HRH had learned this trick by reading about Van Halen's tour rider.

HRH put his rattlesnake suitcase on the bed.

"Good day, ladies," HRH said. "We meet now in this temporality but I believe that we have known each other always."

HRH opened the rattlesnake suitcase and extracted a vaporizer and a small, clear plastic bag that contained an off-white powder.

"First, mes chères amies," said HRH, "You shall watch as I consume dimethyltryptamine. Fear nothing, my sweets, for the effects are not long lasting. This ease of use has earned the substance a wonderful soubriquet. They call it The Businessman's Trip."

HRH sat in a plush chair purchased from IKEA in Stoughton.

HRH vaped DMT.

HRH's eyes went blank.

HRH's breathing became labored.

One of the sex workers got up from the bed and waved her hand in front of HRH's face.

HRH didn't respond.

"He's out," said one sex worker to the other sex workers. "Don't worry. These guys are the easy ones. We give them what they can't get in Dubai."

"What's that?"

"The kissing and the cuddling."

HRH went on an inner trip.

There was a psychedelic tunnel.

HRH went through the psychedelic tunnel.

Everything looked like a Mandelbrot set transformed into quivering nerves.

HRH turned back and saw himself in the IKEA chair, surrounded by sex workers.

HRH continued through the psychedelic tunnel.

HRH came through on the other side.

HRH found himself in a mystical land, surrounded by elfin creatures, with fractal trees sprouting forth from the earth. The elfin creatures spoke a strange language that sounded more like buzzing than words.

HRH tried to talk but his words came out as shattered glass.

HRH didn't know it, but the dimethyltryptamine had sent an astral projection of his soul to Fairy Land.

This happened to every user of dimethyltryptamine, leading to endless reports on Erowid.org and Reddit.com. And some very bad writing by Terence McKenna and Tao Lin.

Terence McKenna, Tao Lin, and the users of Erowid.org and Reddit.com thought that they had traveled in fourth-dimensional space and held forth with cybernetic elves.

But really, they were just in Fairy Land, and the astral projection was creating a perceptual filter that prevented full comprehension of the experience.

The women of Fairy Land could see the spiritual projections of dimethyltryptamine users.

The souls appeared like flickering lights.

The women of Fairy Land thought that these lights were ghosts of the People Who Came Before.

They didn't know that the flickering lights were just some old assholes on drugs.

The trip wore off.

HRH came back into consciousness, back to the watch factory.

HRH jumped out of the IKEA plush chair.

"Another entheogenic experience!" said HRH. "Further communion with the divine! I seek knowledge! Soon I shall have the answer!"

"That wasn't very long," said one of the sex workers.

"As I said, madame," said HRH. "It is the trip of a businessman."

"You must inform me," said HRH to the sex worker who leased the apartment. "What is your WiFi network and its password?"

"The network is arcticmonkeys," said the sex worker. "The password is doiwannaknow. All lower case, no spaces."

HRH opened his rattlesnake suitcase and removed an Amazon Echo Dot.

It was the shape and size of a hockey puck.

HRH put his hands into his pantaloons.

HRH fished out his smartphone.

HRH engaged with his smartphone.

HRH opened the Amazon Alexa app.

HRH plugged in the Amazon Echo Dot.

HRH used the Amazon Alexa app to get the Amazon Echo Dot on the sex worker's WiFi network.

Perhaps you are wondering about the exact nature of the Amazon Echo Dot.

Reader, its nature was two-fold.

The Amazon Echo Dot was a device that connected to the Internet and responded to voice command. Its users could ask the Amazon Echo Dot to play music, which would emerge from its onboard speaker. If the Amazon Echo Dot was networked with a television, it could be used to play films and television. It could be used to order products through Amazon.com, which was a website dedicated to the destruction of the publishing industry. And the Amazon Echo Dot could be used to relay information.

To achieve these tasks, users would say the word, "Alexa," which was the magic phrase that alerted the Amazon Echo Dot that an instruction was forthcoming. Then the user would say an instruction, which would be something like, "Play *Jersey Shore*" or "I want to shop for cat food."

The Amazon Echo Dot would then respond with the synthesized voice of a woman and attempt to follow the user's command. This synthesized voice was the personality of the device. It was the ghost in the machine. Its name was Alexa.

The Amazon Echo Dot was one in a line of Echo products offered by Amazon.com, each offering some variation in shape and size, but retaining the same core functionality.

Reader, this was the surface nature of the Amazon Echo Dot.

Its true nature was this: it represented concrete evidence of the disconnect between issues that journalists believed were of public importance and the swells of indifference that these issues produced in the public.

Following the election of Donald J. Trump to the Presidency, there was a clamor about the manner in which his campaign may have misappropriated the private information of millions of Americans.

This was all of the media coverage distilled: the users of social media had provided their private information with no intention of it being deployed for anything other than their banal self-expression on platforms owned by megalithic corporations. Its unauthorized use in a political campaign represented a grievous breach of ethics and corporate governance.

If you took this media coverage at face value, reader, you would believe that most people were outraged about turning their private information over to megalithic corporations.

But listen to someone who became a minor literary sensation on the basis of a book that critiqued turning over one's personal information to megalithic American corporations.

Enthusiastic journalists wrote twenty-seven thousand articles about *I Hate the Internet.*

It gave the impression of a book that was all dominant, all powerful, all consuming.

But I've read the only writing about *I Hate the Internet* that matters.

Royalty statements.

And so I speak with the authority of someone who managed to get an obscene amount of press coverage for what was, ultimately, an obscure book: most people do not give a fuck or a tuppence about what happens to their private information.

A hockey puck that was always listening.

It was indistinguishable from espionage devices. It sent the inner workings of private homes to a corporation with one of the largest market caps in the world.

There was no illusion about its purpose.

Its nature was both its virtue and its advertising hook.

And at a moment when journalists were producing hundreds of thousands of words about privacy on social media networks, millions of people were buying the Amazon Echo Dot.

By the end of the Year of the Froward Worm, it was a necessary accoutrement of every middle-class American home.

HRH disrobed.

"Please, please, my sweets, you too must remove your store-bought modesty."

The sex workers disrobed.

"I have requested you because of your academic pedigrees. For this evening of transcendence, I want no Masshole curs trapped in the amber of ignorance. Is it true that each of you has received an Ivy League education?"

"Yes," said the sex worker with the lease on the apartment.

"Yes," said the second sex worker, who was lying. She had an undergraduate degree from Babson.

"Yes," said the third sex worker.

"I believe you to possess what is necessary," said HRH. "Tonight I demand that you address me only as Enver Hoxha, the former Albanian head of state. Cast back your imaginations to that glorious moment when Hoxha rejected the reforms of Khrushchev as revisionist Leninist–Marxism and took up the cause with Red China. Imagine it! An isolated European country, surrounded by its enemies and the sea, aligning itself with Maoist principles!"

HRH opened up his rattlesnake suitcase.

"As I do not doubt that you learned while earning your Ivy League degrees," said HRH, "a key difference between Stalinist Marxist–Leninism and Maoism is the Maoist belief in reeducation. The Stalinists would excommunicate the unwanted, while the Maoists enacted programs of reeducation. Why else did the Symbionese Liberation Army bring Patty Hearst into the fold? They demonstrated her to be a fascist insect preying upon the life of the people and through class consciousness reformed her into a revolutionary."

HRH removed a device from the suitcase.

The sex workers couldn't see what HRH was holding.

"Tonight," said HRH, "we shall query Alexa and discover what she knows about the People's Republic of Albania. When Alexa fails in her knowledge, then your acres of skin will be reeducated. Tonight, the fleshzone is a labor camp and you are its prisoners. Arbeit macht frei, meine Mädchen."

One of the sex workers caught a glimpse of what HRH was holding.

It was a rhino-hide chicotte, restored and recovered from the Congo Free State.

"Before we embark upon our merriment," said HRH, "I suggest that we test the ability of Alexa to provide us with information."

HRH stood over the Amazon Echo Dot.

"Alexa," said HRH. "Why does the caged bird sing?"

"The caged bird sings," said the Amazon Echo Dot, "because its heart is still free and using song is an efficient way for birds to communicate over distance."

"That's actually kind of cool," said one of the sex workers.

"Schnell! Schnell!" said HRH. "It is time to make a great leap forward."

"Alexa," said HRH, "who was Enver Hoxha?"

HRH pronounced *Enver Hoxha* properly: En-ver Ho-dja.

"Hmm," said the Amazon Echo Dot. "I don't know that one."

"Alexa," said HRH, "who was Enver Hoxha?"

HRH pronounced *Enver Hoxha* in phonetic English: En-ver Hox-ha.

"Here's something I found on Wikipedia," said the Amazon Echo Dot. "The Rwandan Genocide also known as the genocide against the Tutsi was a genocide of mass slaughter of Tutsi in Rwanda by members of the Hutu majority government."

"Alexa," said HRH, "who was Enver Hoxha?"

HRH again pronounced *Enver Hoxha* in phonetic English: En-ver Hox-ha.

"I'm not quite sure how to help you with that," said the Amazon Echo Dot.

"It should be rather clear that we have long hours of Maoism ahead," said HRH.

There was a moment when the labor camp screaming grew so loud that the bodyguard burst into the room.

He found two of the sex workers on the bed, crying, bleeding.

The chicotte had offered bitter instruction.

The third was being forced to hold the Amazon Echo Dot over her head for as long as her arms would allow. She'd been instructed to address the Amazon Echo Dot only as Aten, after the Egyptian Sun disc.

"What the fuck is going on in here?" asked the bodyguard. "What the fuck is this shit?"

"My darling patriot," said HRH. "You have joined us at last. I have waited for your flesh all these long hours. Would you care to act the Gomorrhean? I am your willing receptacle, and if you like, I can ease the path towards priapism with a surfeit of cocaine. Snow is general all over Ireland. It is a dead certainty that a man with your thighs must ache with a clutched need to relieve the vital center. Let rain down your frothing spittle like Agent Orange upon the Vietnamese peasantry!"

The orgasm occurred.

The Amazon Echo Dot was playing "Blood of My Enemies."

"Blood of My Enemies" was a song by Manowar.

HRH threw back his head and cried out, "All of my foes shall perish before me! To Asgard the Valkyries fly! 诉苦!"

The fleshzone decommenced.

HRH unplugged the Amazon Echo Dot.

HRH repacked his rattlesnake suitcase.

HRH left a white envelope on the kitchen granite countertop.

The white envelope contained a very generous tip.

Dmitri Huda was waiting in the Bentley.

HRH climbed into the rear passenger seat.

"Was it everything you'd hoped?" asked Dmitri Huda.

"I met a charming fellow named Steve," said HRH. "He informs me that he was raised in Lowell."

"That's what everyone loves about you, Dennis," said Dmitri Huda. "You always make friends in new places."

HRH vaped sativa.

"What is my agenda for the morrow, Dmitri?" asked HRH.

"You're doing a TEDx at Brandeis," said Dmitri Huda. "Have you forgotten?"

"I never forget," said HRH. "I remember everything."

# Chapter Nine

## Cleaning up the Mess

So there was Francis Fuller's house on Glendower Avenue, with its low property taxes and its grand view of Los Angeles. It was full of blood and bodies.

Celia examined the headless corpse of Adam Leroux and wondered about the wisdom of bringing Rose Byrne to Los Angeles.

A psychotic sidekick made sense amongst the lawless stupidity of Jacobean London, but in a world dominated by a professionalized police force, it could prove problematic to be accompanied by the supranatural embodiment of genocide.

"You might have waited," said Celia to Rose Byrne. "I am certain I would have persuaded him with my charms."

"He was a warrior, lady," said Rose Byrne. "I could see it in his eyes."

"I have not bedded with a man in four centuries."

"We have concerns beyond the bowers of pleasure," said Rose Byrne.

"As you say."

Celia walked to the bathroom.

Francis Fuller's body, impaled on Rose Byrne's sword, sat on the toilet.

Blood was everywhere.

Because Celia had engaged with the woolen television of Fairy Land, a sense of *déjà vu* washed over her.

She remembered, vaguely, a scene from the television adaptation of *Game of Thrones*. It was from the end of Season Four, when the mad dwarf Tyrion Lannister assassinated his own father while the latter sat above a latrine.

Celia's *déjà vu* was a common feeling. The world was saturated with media. The memory of unreal things had imposed themselves upon the real. The President was a creation of television. The appearances of things were more important than the things themselves.

Celia returned to the living room and stood above Adam Leroux's unliving body. She stared out at the forever infinity headlights of Los Angeles.

She cast a spell.

It was a 1970s AD neutron bomb sort of magic, erasing all traces of both Francis Fuller and Adam Leroux while leaving Fuller's personal property intact.

Celia had no idea how long she would be in Los Angeles.

She needed a place to crash.

Why not keep the house on the hill?

It was the darkest of faery magic, the ancient stuff where children would walk the ferny path and never be seen again, lingering only as memories, leaving behind crying peasant mothers who talked about lost daughters wandering over green hills with the seely folk, until the mother herself died and the missing girl became nothing but a legend, just a name sung in a ballad that had been corrupted by endless performances over decades and then centuries.

It was the total effacement of humanity.

Goodbye, Francis Fuller.

You lasted for one of this book's longer chapters.

Goodbye, Adam Leroux.

You managed about a thousand words.

An entire segment of obscure film history was rewritten. Fuller's early experimental efforts disappeared. *Handspun Roses* never happened. The films produced by Roger Corman evaporated. Myrna Loy's filmography lost one of its stronger late entries.

The television stuff didn't change much, because television was the result of an industrialized process in which the people behind the camera were interchangeable. Francis Fuller's name was struck from the collective credits of *Charlie's Angels* and *Dynasty*, but the episodes themselves were unaltered and lingered in the unpopular consciousness.

Almost all of Fuller's friends and family were dead, so there were hardly any gaps in individual memories.

Paragraphs disappeared from a few books. Alterations occurred in a handful of sad men's underwhelming master's theses. Some very old webpages evaporated. A few torrents stopped being listed on Cinemaggedon and Karagarga.

If he were alive, Francis Fuller would have been astonished at how small his life had been, at how easily the hole was patched.

He was like everyone else.

He thought that he was more important than he actually was.

But no one was any more or any less important than anyone else.

You can beg the Earth to stop turning, but it never listens.

And, please, reader, don't get amped up on this statement of your relative position of egalitarian non-importance.

You're still not qualified to review this book on Amazon.com.

The same thing happened with Adam Leroux.

His memory went out.

His family forgot him.

His friends forgot him.

He was struck from the computerized databases of surveillance and corporate marketing that dominated modern life.

Someone else got his car.

Someone else got his apartment.

Someone else got his French bulldog.

Someone else got his vintage 45 Grave T-shirt.

All of the Muslims that Adam Leroux had killed were like the episodes of television directed by Francis Fuller.

Their corpses were the end result of an industrialized process. The person pulling the trigger wasn't a big deal.

The Muslims were still dead.

The one place where the faery magic didn't have any effect was Adam Leroux's Instagram account.

Instagram was a social media platform that existed on telephones and computers. Its users shared pictures of their squalid lives, which fostered the illusion of a human connection while generating revenue for Facebook, which was a publicly traded company headquartered near San Francisco.

Instagram was also history's single most successful terrorist attack on the self-esteem of women.

Adam Leroux had managed to avoid most of social media.

Facebook, the company that owned Instagram, had another social media platform which was also called Facebook.

The company was named for the platform, which had started out as a student project at Harvard University.

Harvard was where HRH had received his Master's in Public Policy.

The Harvard version of Facebook, the ur-Facebook, had been designed to rate whether or not the hedge fund's female students were sexually attractive.

The ur-Facebook evolved into actual Facebook, spreading beyond the hedge fund's campus, and conquered the world.

Adam Leroux only logged into his Facebook account about once every three years, which gave him a slightly unique perspective when he checked it in the year 2016 AD.

He'd last been a heavy user of Facebook in 2008 AD, when the most annoying thing on the social media platform was people insisting that they were so happy and so in love with their latest semi-monogamous partner.

Things had changed.

By 2016 AD, no one was boasting about how their latest semi-monogamous partner made them so much happier than their previous semi-monogamous partners.

Now Adam Leroux's friends were bombarding each other with images of murdered bodies and shrieking about the corruptible nature of human beings while they apologized for social privilege which derived from their relative position in the global hierarchy.

"Fuck this shit," said Adam Leroux, logging out of Facebook for what would be the last time.

Another social media platform called Twitter held even less appeal.

Twitter was a place where people practiced bumper-sticker morality while other people threatened to rape and murder each other for expressing simple sentiments about banal objects.

"I like cats," a user typed into Twitter.

*I will fucking rip your ugly fucking shit face off you fucking jew cuck jew*, replied Twitter.

"Crayons are good," a user typed into Twitter.

*Your soul will be mine in hell as you suck molten fire from my demonic warted prick*, replied Twitter.

"My grandma wears a knitted hat," a user typed into Twitter.

*I am coming to kill and rape you until you are dead and raped you assfucked pussy*, replied Twitter.

Twitter was also where Donald J. Trump ruled over America.

Donald J. Trump on Twitter was the ultimate tool of distraction.

Each day of Donald J. Trump's Presidency, his administration dismantled some aspect of the federal government, terraforming America into a dystopian misery, but no one talked about it and very few media outlets gave it any coverage.

All anyone paid attention to was Donald J. Trump's activity on Twitter, where he issued mean-spirited and stupid opinions about nonsense.

Concerned about Donald J. Trump stacking the federal bench with crypto-conservatives who believe that dinosaurs were made of chocolate pudding?

Shut the fuck up!

The President is upset about professional sports!

On Twitter!

Worried about nuclear war?

Who fucking cares?

The President called an actress ugly!

On Twitter!

Adam Leroux stayed away from Twitter.

But the multi-tentacled hivemind of global capitalism was nothing if not adaptable.

It had become necessary to enchain every human being with some form of social media. New platforms were being developed every minute of every day, attempting to unlock each individual mind.

In Adam Leroux's case, it turned out that Instagram was the key.

And I could easily write some very long and possibly pithy descriptions of Instagram's terrorist attack on female self-esteem, explaining how it had become the #1 destination on the Internet for plastic surgery disasters, for a plethora of fake asses, fake tits, hair removal, skin lightening, lip enhancements and Botox, and how female celebrities with certain physical features used their Instagram followers to advertise products that they'd been paid to hawk, and how the products were inevitably chemical warfare on the natural beauty of women, and how all of this was a sustained spiritual attack and how I myself know a handful of amazing people who'd gone haywire with plastic surgery inspired by Instagram.

But why bother with that?

Here is the simplest way to describe how awful Instagram was for women: it had weaponized yoga.

Instagram had created an environment where ridiculously blonde women from the ridiculous upper classes could flaunt their ridiculous lifestyles comprised of samosas and endless Caribbean vacations and could, somehow, wrap this excess of capitalism in a blanket of spirituality, photographs of Downward Dogs and Warrior Poses, the language of body-positive affirmation, and cloying truisms about the ability of anyone to achieve their dreams if they put enough effort and faith into the achievement of those dreams.

Yoga was one of the many weapons of mass destruction employed in Instagram's terrorist war on women's self-esteem.

A tool to bludgeon people with the things that they couldn't have.

Impossible bodies, impossible wealth, impossible life.

If anything could have resisted, it was yoga.

Yoga was as old as the hills.

It was ancient technology. It was almost as old as Fairy Land.

And it too had fallen.

It was like everything else on Instagram.

Just another weapon in a long war.

So don't even ask about the fucking Kardashians.

Because heterosexuality is a bullshit con on women, the accidental byproduct of Instagram's remorseless terrorist war was the even more remorseless arousal of Adam Leroux's sexual desire.

His particular demesne was Instagram accounts belonging to women who were strippers in the city of Philadelphia.

Adam Leroux liked their fake asses, he liked their fake tits, he liked their fake lips, he liked their fake hair.

Say what you will about the strippers of Philadelphia, but they had a leg up when it came to Instagram. They'd done something nearly impossible.

They'd monetized their participation in Instagram's terrorist war on women's self-esteem.

Their primary motivation for using Instagram was to advertise to potential customers.

They posted pictures of themselves and alerted the world about which nights they'd be working the clubs.

Adam Leroux's attention was an accidental byproduct of this monetization.

Adam Leroux had discovered these women in 2015 AD.

Using his own Instagram account, he had spent almost two years commenting on their photos.

Here are some of the choicer comments that Adam Leroux had posted to Instagram:

(1) *bae i wanna crawl up in that a$$ like a small wood land animal and die*
(2) *would lick that pussy until u exploded just one taste its all im asking*
(3) *beautiful face bootiful body y wont u let me touch*
(4) *girl u got wot i need and wot i need is a$$ lol*
(5) *wont u let me show u a good time my hand to god above ill come to philly and teach u bout brotherly love and u can buy whatever u like*

Adam Leroux had left thousands of these comments.

For some inexplicable reason, the dark magic of Fairly Land had left them unaffected.

The comments remained long after Leroux's death.

He'd spent the last year of his life imagining that his literary output would be as the co-writer of Fuller's memoir.

But the old man's life and memory was gone.

This was Adam Leroux's legacy.

Comments on Instagram that expressed his infinite and endless thirst for the surgically inflated buttocks of Philadelphia's strippers.

Welcome to the future.

## Chapter Ten

## On the Streets of Los Angeles, There the Wild Beast Slumbers

Being a serial killer, Rose Byrne was in her post-murder cool-down phase.

She was sleeping in the master bedroom.

Celia watched television.

The content that she saw was different than what had played on the woolen television of Fairy Land, where all of the programs had been pre-selected and pirated by the island's more knowledgeable women.

The television on Fairy Land had focused on what the American liberal intelligentsia suggested was worth watching: shows from Netflix, from HBO, a select peppering of BBC, the Amazon.com adaptation of Chris Kraus's *I Love Dick*, and some basic cable like *Mad Men* or *Breaking Bad*.

By contrast, sitting in the living room of the former Francis Fuller, there was no pre-selection. There was only what aired on television in the middle of an average day.

It was what Los Angeles produced for the 99.5 per cent of Americans who weren't part of the country's liberal intelligentsia.

Celia saw an episode of *Judge Judy*, in which a multimillionaire fake judge ritually abused the poor while adjudicating their small claims court cases.

She saw an episode of *Dr. Phil*, in which a multimillionaire fake therapist ritually abused the poor while oozing a synthetic variant of empathy.

She saw an episode of *Family Feud*, in which a multimillionaire comedian asked the poor to produce sexual innuendo in exchange for the promise of money.

She saw an episode of *Laura Luke's Paternity Court*, in which a multimillionaire fake judge humiliated poor African-American women for engaging in the biological imperative of sex.

She saw an episode of *Divorce Court*, in which a multimillionaire fake judge convinced poor African-Americans that they should embrace the global hegemony by creating two consumer households where there had originally been one.

She saw an episode of *Dr. Oz*, in which a multimillionaire Turkish-American doctor hawked pseudoscience to the poor while embarrassing the fuck out of the five other Turkish people who lived in America.

She saw an episode of *The Real*, in which a group of multimillionaire women from marginalized backgrounds pretended that their money hadn't taken them past the Cash Horizon.

She saw an episode of *TMZ Live*, in which a multimillionaire lawyer/feudal lord encouraged his cow-eyed millennial vassals to explain the sexual dysfunction of Twitter celebrities.

She saw an episode of *Keeping Up with the Kardashians*, in which a family of multimillionaires proved that the biggest existential threat to the African-American male was not the Ku Klux Klan or the organized brutality of law enforcement or the school-to-prison pipeline but, in fact, the family themselves.

She saw an episode of *The Ellen DeGeneres Show*, in which a multimillionaire comedian excreted a synthetic variant of sisterhood.

She saw an episode of *My 600-lb Life*, in which a multimillionaire doctor ritualistically abused poor people who'd destroyed their bodies with a toxic diet of repressed homosexuality, junk food, and prescription painkillers.

She watched CNN, MSNBC, and Fox News, which were 24-hour news channels dedicated to obsessive, and non-stop, coverage of Donald J. Trump.

These television networks were watched by the elderly and the insane.

These networks served a valuable social function.

They were voluntary euthanasia through informational poison.

Celia shut off the television.

She wanted to go home.

The next day, Celia stood in the living room of the house on the hill.

She looked out over the infinite vastness of Los Angeles.

She cast a spell.

It was some bullshit magic that was intended to solve an intra-narrative problem while moving forward the storytelling.

The spell was supposed to create a direct line of smartphone navigation to Fern. It was supposed to be another bullshit tendril of ropey saliva.

But Celia's spell did nothing.

It fizzled.

Here is why Celia's spell fizzled: Fern was nobody's fool.

Fern knew that her mother would try to find her.

Months before Celia took possession of the house on the hill, Fern had cast her own spell, which blocked any attempts to establish a ropey strand of smartphone navigation.

As Celia's spell fizzled, Rose Byrne watched from the alpine-blue couch. She looked like a teenager who's been told by her parents that the whole family is going on a sea cruise themed around an intellectual property geared towards children.

Celia tried to recast her magical bullshit spell.

It fizzled for a second time.

The two women from Fairy Land conferenced as to what was wrong.

Neither of them suspected Fern of blocking Celia's spells.

Rose Byrne said that perhaps Fern was no longer in Los Angeles, but it was pointed out that this wouldn't block the ropey smartphone navigation.

Besides, Celia could sense Fern's presence in Los Angeles. It was one of those fucked-up faery things, just a green feeling that her daughter was present in the same rough geographical locale.

Rose Byrne suggested that as they were in the United States, they could emulate the practices of the American security apparatus.

She proposed that they track where Fern had spent her money and then triangulate her location based on clusters of purchases in a localized region.

Celia cast a spell.

It did nothing.

Fern was from Fairy Land.

She was using an older, weirder form of magical bullshit than money.

Rose Byrne suggested summoning Rusticano.

But no one wanted that.

The women of Fairy Land were stumped.

Then Celia remembered something Maeveen Licksweet had told her.

There'd been a period, back in the Nineteenth Century AD, when Maeveen Licksweet had spent a great deal of time away from Fairy Land. She'd traveled around the world for reasons that she never shared with anyone.

But she did talk about something that she'd noticed in Udine, where she'd spent three weeks.

Maeveen's landlady in Udine was a widow who'd convinced herself that whenever she slept, she went on a spiritual journey into barren fields where she did battle with witches.

In her dreams, the widow would beat the witches with bundles of fennel and the witches would beat the widow with stalks of sorghum.

One day, after Maeveen returned to her lodgings, the widow asked if Maeveen's room had been painted.

*Of course not*, said Maeveen. *Why would I paint a room? And what is paint, really?*

*Then why is the room the color of wolves?* asked the widow.

Maeveen thought this was more witch nonsense, but she followed the landlady into the room.

At first, Maeveen couldn't see what the widow was talking about. But then she caught it out of the corner of her eye. A faint glow permeated everything.

If Maeveen acknowledged the glow, the widow would chatter on for ages about the color of wolves.

Maeveen cast a spell that messed up her landlady's mind.

The widow shut the fuck up.

The rest of Maeveen's time in Udine was quiet.

As Maeveen traveled throughout the Italian peninsula, she kept looking out of the corner of her eye. In each of her quarters, in each new city, the glow appeared after she'd been in residence for roughly a week.

Maeveen spent some time thinking about the glow's cause.

She realized that it was herself, in her magical puissance, having an effect on her lodgings.

It was a byproduct of being a citizen of Fairy Land in the mortal world.

After Maeveen reported this story to the women of Fairy Land, the few who did leave the island noticed that they too had the same effect on their lodgings.

Celia recalled Maeveen's story and realized that although she was unable to find Fern, she could seek out the radiation traces of her daughter's puissance.

Celia cast a spell, with as broad a mandate as possible, to look for sources of preternatural power in Los Angeles.

But Los Angeles was as bad as Fairy Land.

It was full of magical bullshit.

It had been built on magical bullshit.

It was nothing but magical bullshit.

About fifty ropes of smartphone navigation saliva emerged from the living room of the house on the hill and stretched out into Los Angeles County.

"We have little choice," said Celia. "We shall follow each until we find the one that brings us to Fern."

Two practical matters arose.

Celia pointed out that their clothes, the haute couture of Fairy Land, were going to attract attention.

She cast a spell.

Celia wasn't well versed enough in contemporary American fashion to pick clothes, so she let the magic do the work of a personal stylist.

The magic made the women look like recent transplants to Echo Park, which was a traditionally Latino neighborhood that had gentrified into a fashionable enclave of upscale dining and high-level annoyance.

The women's fur-clad haute couture transformed into designer denim, vintage metal T-shirts, Balenciaga sneakers, and Marni handbags.

Rose Byrne's T-shirt said: EMPEROR.

Celia's T-shirt said: SAVATAGE.

Neither of the women knew it, but the magic had failed in its job as a personal stylist.

Vintage metal T-shirts were the hot look of the previous summer.

The other practical matter was one of transportation.

Los Angeles was too big for the women to walk, and the smart-phone saliva didn't interface with magic windows, so teleportation was prevented.

Celia remembered the former Francis Fuller's vintage black Jaguar XJ-S, which was parked in the driveway.

The women went outside and looked at the car.

Neither of them knew how to drive.

Celia suggested that she cast a bullshit spell of knowledge which would teach Rose Byrne how to drive.

For the first time in her life, Rose Byrne was about to find a natural place for her ingrained psychosis. She had become a driver in the hellscape of Los Angeles, just another murderous freak steering several thousand pounds of death machine.

Celia got in on the passenger's side.

Rose Byrne got behind the wheel.

Her bullshit magical training took over. Her psychosis flowed into the machine and then back into her own body. She was ready.

She backed out of the driveway.

She followed one of the ropey strands of smartphone navigation.

Celia fiddled with the Jaguar's radio until sound came through the car's paltry speakers. The radio was tuned to 89.9FM, KCRW, one of Los Angeles County's several stations affiliated with National Public Radio.

National Public Radio was, in part, radio sponsored by the American state. It was a relic of another era, which is to say the mid-1960s AD, when there was still currency in the idea that civic institutions could serve, and enrich, the lives of the citizenry.

What a jest!

What a jape!

KCRW was broadcasting the afternoon NPR news show, which was called *All Things Considered.*

As Rose Byrne followed her saliva-based smartphone navigation, the women heard the stories of the day.

The lead story was of some interest to both Celia and Rose Byrne, as it was about a recent Islamic-themed terror attack on London Bridge.

Like all terror attacks, the London Bridge incident had evoked a general aura of stupidity, and like all terror attacks in London, it had produced a plethora of people with silly accents waiting to give interviews to the vultures called reporters.

"Oi, guv, I tell you what, terrorism is bad stuff, innit, hey, guvvy?" said KCRW.

NPR dedicated thirty seconds to the importance of Donald J. Trump's tweet about the terror attack. He'd insulted the Mayor of London.

What an asshole.

Rose Byrne drove the Jaguar into Hollywood.

# Chapter Eleven

## Let Slip the Dogs of War

The only good advice that anyone ever gave me about writing came from the author Stephen Prothero.

He said something like this: "If there's an obvious comment about your book, don't run from it. Just include the comment in the book itself and make it part of the text. Get there first."

In the spirit of those words, let's address the big fat elephant in the room.

Let's talk about how you can't write a novel about an island of women who banish and murder all of their male co-citizens and not have everyone think that you're writing an allegory about #MeToo.

#MeToo was a hashtag.

Hashtags were a method for a bunch of people on social media to comment on the same topic, roughly at the same time.

You took an alphanumeric phrase and put the # symbol in front of that phrase and appended the phrase to a comment on social media.

#FuckTrump was a popular hashtag.

So was #NotMyPresident.

This book is not an allegory.

It was begun in August of 2017 AD.

#MeToo didn't start until October of 2017 AD.

The first 12,000 words of this book were written before October of 2017 AD.

#MeToo kicked off with an article in the *New York Times* and a follow-up in the *New Yorker*. Both articles were about a film producer named Harvey Weinstein.

He had produced nearly every middlebrow American film of the last twenty years, he was a bully, he was a braggart, he was physically repulsive, and he was in deep with the Democratic Party.

And he was also a serial sexual abuser of women and a rapist.

With every news story there is a visible layer, the one that plays out in media coverage, and then there is an unconscious layer, the story serving as a medium through which unspoken social undercurrents are made manifest.

And the unconscious layer of the Harvey Weinstein story was all about Donald J. Trump.

They were both disgusting fat slobs from New York City, they were both from the Celebrity branch of American governance, they were both deep into politics, and it was a barely kept secret that both of them were pigs with women.

Had Donald J. Trump not won the election, #MeToo would not have happened.

The psyche of the haute bourgeoisie would not have bruised.

There would have been no waves of outrage.

And no one would have scrutinized Harvey Weinstein, who had decades of extraordinary access to Donald J. Trump's opponent.

He would have been on the winning side.

And everyone always falls in line behind a winner.

The election of 2016 AD produced a problem: Donald J. Trump had both won and lost.

He was a beneficiary of the Electoral College, which was a system

119

of proportional representation designed by America's founders to ensure that no one would ever outlaw owning slaves from Africa.

The Electoral College didn't stop America from outlawing slavery, but it did seriously screw up the Twenty-First Century AD.

Here's how the Electoral College worked: the general election, in which the will of the people was expressed, meant nothing.

A candidate could win a majority of votes and still lose the election.

This is exactly what happened in 2016 AD.

Donald J. Trump lost the popular vote and won the Electoral College.

Millions more people voted for Donald J. Trump's opponent than voted for Donald J. Trump. Way more Americans had decided that his opponent was the appropriate person to turn Muslims into garam masala.

Which made sense.

Under the previous President, Donald J. Trump's opponent had been the Secretary of State, which meant that she'd been intimately, and professionally, involved with the obliteration of Muslims.

And say what you will of Donald J. Trump, but for all of the endless accusations hurled in his direction during the Year of the Misplaced Butter, no one ever suggested that he'd killed a Muslim.

Experience matters!

It wasn't as if Donald J. Trump's victory was unprecedented. Recent history had contained another split between the Electoral College and the popular vote.

2000 AD!

Everyone forgot.

But not me.

Here are three emails between me and a woman who shall remain nameless:

**Sat, Nov 5, 2016 at 11:26 AM**
**From: XXXXX (xxxx@xxxx.com)**
**To: Jarett Kobek**
**Subject: quick**

election prediction in 1, 2, go!

**Sat, Nov 5, 2016 at 12:42 PM**
**From: Jarett Kobek**
**To: XXXXX (xxxx@xxxx.com)**
**Subject: Re: quick**

TRUMP
possible popular/electoral split

**Sat, Nov 5, 2016 at 1:26 PM**
**From: XXXXX (xxxx@xxxx.com)**
**To: Jarett Kobek**
**Subject: Re: quick**

Omg not again. Not again. I cannot take another popular/electoral split. I will lose my goddamned mind.

She didn't lose her goddamned mind.

But everyone else did.

The Weinstein story exploded and went metastatic in a way that stories don't go in an era of media fragmentation and a politically divided citizenry.

It was all-consuming, a black hole at the center of a depraved galaxy.

It opened two floodgates.

The first floodgate had held back a torrent of stories about men who worked in the Celebrity branch of American governance and their proclivities towards sexual assault.

The second floodgate was ancient magic.

It'd been there for a very long time, holding back all of women's awful experiences with men from the dawn of civilization.

And now it was open.

There was an organic outpouring of stories.

These appeared on social media under the hashtag of #MeToo.

Women wrote about being sexually harassed, about being raped, about being treated like idiots. It amounted to a profound discomfort with the way that sexual politics worked in the post-industrial civilized world.

And let's be clear.

Whatever the merit of any individual statement, the general intent of #MeToo was undeniable. It was people saying that a society built around the whims of men is a recipe for a disaster.

And if you disagree with that, go and look out the fucking window.

Or inside your smartphone.

And, reader, don't mistake me for one of your dopey male acquaintances who, after #MeToo broke, went and posted statements on Facebook about how they were learning to be better people, when all they were really saying was this: *Please don't get me fired because I tried to fuck you when I was drunk at the office holiday party.*

I wrote an entire book about the horror of a society built around the whims of men, and I did it long before there was any obvious reward for performing this particular piety.

It's called *I Hate the Internet*.

It made me famous in Serbia.

Serbia!

Despite its obvious virtues, #MeToo demonstrated why the Twenty-First Century AD may preclude the possibility of meaningful political protest.

In August of 2017 AD, Donald J. Trump returned to Trump Tower, which was a giant golden skyscraper that he'd built over Manhattan's Fifth Avenue.

This was where Donald J. Trump had lived before he moved into the White House.

This was where he had staged his bid for the Presidency.

He hadn't been back since he'd become President and earned the right to bomb the living fuck shit out of Muslim peasants in the name of American freedom.

A few days before his return, there'd been a White Supremacist rally in Virginia where a young woman was killed when a Neo-Nazi drove his car into a crowd of counter-protestors.

On the very same day as Donald J. Trump's return, I happened to be staying on the eleventh floor of the Warwick Hotel, which is about two blocks south and one block west from Trump Tower.

From my hotel room, I could hear the protests outside of Donald J. Trump's former home.

I walked over to Trump Tower, where the NYPD had blocked off Fifth Avenue.

Donald J. Trump still hadn't arrived.

Like the novel *The Life and Opinions of Tristram Shandy*, Trump Tower was empty of its eponymous hero.

About two thousand people were barricaded on both the west and east sidewalks.

People were holding signs.

People were wearing T-shirts relevant to their political protests.

People were using their cellphones to record video of the protests.

People were chanting.

They were screaming: THIS IS WHAT DEMOCRACY LOOKS LIKE!

When they screamed THIS IS WHAT DEMOCRACY LOOKS LIKE, I think what they meant was this: *Donald J. Trump, here is the face of the American public, and we oppose you in all of your manifold perversions. We repudiate you in your evil. A change is gonna come, Bubba.*

The scene was straight out of Tolkien.

A few thousand people, restrained by the Orcish Host of the NYPD, had been corralled into pre-approved places from where they shouted impotent chants at an impregnable empty golden tower.

The protestors were right.

It really was what democracy looked like.

In an era when significant amounts of social protest occurs on the Internet, it necessarily means that all of that social protest is monetized.

And not by the protestors.

#MeToo generated unbelievable amounts of web traffic.

For months, it was an international spectator sport.

Almost every time that someone interacted with #MeToo, they were generating income for Facebook or Google or Twitter, which were the three companies that dominated advertising and political expression on the Internet.

Here's a list of the major institutional holders of Facebook, circa September 2017 AD: The Vanguard Group, BlackRock, Fidelity Investments, State Street Corporation, T. Rowe Price Associates, Capital World Investors (a subsidiary of Capital Group), Northern Trust, Morgan Stanley, Invesco, Geode Capital Management.

Together, these ten companies owned just over 31 per cent of Facebook.

Here's a list of the major institutional holders of Google, circa September 2017 AD: The Vanguard Group, BlackRock, Fidelity Investments, State Street Corporation, T. Rowe Price Associates, Capital Research Global Investors (a subsidiary of Capital Group), Capital World Investors (a subsidiary of Capital Group), Northern Trust, BNY Mellon, Wellington Management.

Together, these ten companies owned just over 31 per cent of Google.

Here's a list of the major institutional holders of Twitter, circa September 2017 AD: The Vanguard Group, ClearBridge Investments, BlackRock, Morgan Stanley, Slate Path Capital, State Street Corporation, OppenheimerFunds, Coatue Management, First Trust, Northern Trust.

Together, these ten companies owned just over 27 per cent of Twitter.

With one exception, none of these institutional holders was operated in any meaningful sense by anyone other than some old white guys in suits.

And the job of these white guys in suits was to make money for the people who owned everything.

In the case of the one institutional holder that was run by a woman, the woman in question had inherited the company from her father.

This literally was the Patriarchy.

And #MeToo had made them, and their clients, a huge amount of money.

The general consensus of opinion was that Twitter, more than any other company headquartered in and around the San Francisco Bay Area, had destroyed America.

It had turned everyone into kindergarteners, it had murdered journalism, and it had almost certainly helped Donald J. Trump get elected.

In the seven years following its initial public offering in 2011 AD, Twitter had never made a dime. It lost money for twenty-seven straight quarters.

Yet when it posted its results for the fourth quarter of 2017 AD, which was the time period encompassing the Weinstein revelations and the subsequent social fallout, Twitter revealed that in the final three months of the year, the company had made $91,000,000.

It was a #MeToo miracle!

And it couldn't have happened to a nicer group of men!

In the early days, it felt as if the organic uprising of women was going to be the main story. It was one of those rare moments of social openness where the rules are up for grabs.

Anything could happen.

But this was America.

#MeToo became the same story as every story in America: a nexus of how power and money played out amongst the Celebrity branch of American governance.

The revised story fixated on the three industries that were the locus of Donald J. Trump's power: the entertainment industry, journalism, and politics.

The organic outcry was lost amidst stories of the appalling behavior of certain men with professional careers in the public sphere. These stories tended to run the gamut: they went from unfortunate comments to groping to flat-out rape.

A handful of the stories weren't even about sexual harassment.

They were about consensual relationships with deeply unsavory people, which had been recontextualized after the #MeToo moment.

Literally every woman alive who'd engaged in the biological imperative of sex with men had undergone the routine humiliation of consensual sex with at least one deeply unsavory person.

This was the bullshit con of heterosexuality.

But most of those women, who were poor and didn't work in media, weren't given the opportunity to write opinion pieces for *Variety* about their shitty ex-boyfriends and old lovers.

Their shitty ex-boyfriends and old lovers weren't members of the Celebrity branch of American governance.

The unspoken social undercurrent of the revised story revealed itself.

#MeToo became about the way in which encounters with men had stymied the ambitions of women who had wanted to achieve upward social mobility in the industries that were the nexus of Donald J. Trump's power.

Which, look, by itself this was no small problem.

But it's a very far cry from what kicked the whole thing off, which was a story about a serial rapist who actively worked to destroy people after he raped them.

All of which creates an atmosphere that makes it very fucking hard to write a book about an island of women and not have everyone think you're allegorizing a hashtag.

The whole thing's ruined before it even started!

And, reader, trust me, I can imagine the responses to this chapter before they're typed by dullards into social media, and they all boil down to something like this: "Who the fuck does this guy think that he is?"

To which I reply in advance: on the topic of #MeToo, I have more innate moral authority than most people in America.

And this isn't because of inborn privilege.

There's a simple explanation as to why I have innate moral authority on the topic.

I'm almost certainly the only person alive who was sexually harassed in front of a crowd of 280 people by a woman who pens *New York Times* opinion pieces about sexual harassment, and I'm absolutely certain that I'm the only person alive who experienced this sexual harassment several years after winning a $1.2-million judgment in a lawsuit against an Internet stalker who libeled me as a rapist.

## Chapter Twelve

## hello from sex drenched hollywood

Smartphone saliva brought the Jaguar XJ-S to Hollywood, a neighborhood that was being victimized by the international capitalist class's money laundering.

The money laundering took the form of cruddy new apartment buildings and ugly hotels.

Hollywood was also a neighborhood that had become a hotspot of nightclubs, places where people went to dance, get high, and challenge the received sexual wisdom of the upper middle class.

Several blocks before their arrival, the women of Fairy Land knew their final destination.

They knew this because the navigation rope had wrapped itself around its target, which was the thirteen-story Fontenoy Apartments on Whitley Avenue.

From a distance of several blocks, the women of Fairy Land could see the building glowing.

The Fontenoy was an early Los Angeles folly, from back in the 1920s AD, dressed up in nouveau-riche ornamentation and a French-Norman roof.

When they arrived on Whitley Avenue, Rose Byrne parked the Jaguar in the Fontenoy's underground parking structure, right after Rose Byrne used magic to blast open the structure's automatic gate.

She took a parking spot that was reserved for someone on the tenth floor.

Celia cast a spell on the car, creating a glamor that caused human beings' eyes to malfunction.

When human beings looked at the Jaguar, they didn't see a vintage car designed by the British.

They saw a series of orange construction cones and were surprised by neither the appearance of the cones nor the implication that a parking spot, an inert piece of concrete demarcated by lines of paint, was out of order.

*Oh*, they thought. *Here's something else that's broken.*

Everyone in America possessed an unconscious, and sometimes conscious, acknowledgement that their empire was in decline.

But gone were the halcyon days when one could expect the whole thing to end through an invasion of the Mongols or the Ottomans or the Huns.

Gone were the sweet moments when barbarian hordes would pull down the walls of your capital city and murder all of your cousins.

Now an empire died of a thousand tiny wounds.

Postal carriers stopped delivering mail.

Air travel became a horror.

Infrastructure went to shit.

Trains crashed.

And parking spots went out of order.

Because the women of Fairy Land were traditionalists, they didn't ride the elevator from the basement, but rather walked out of the underground parking structure.

They emerged back on Whitley Avenue.

Several years earlier, the faceless entity that owned the Fontenoy had installed a security gate. Rose Byrne blasted it open with magic and then did the same thing with the front door, which was also locked.

In the lobby, they passed through a small room that looked like a bordello, and walked to the elevators opposite the front entrance.

Celia pressed the call button.

The doors opened.

They got into the elevator.

Ropey strands of salvia could bring Fairy Land's women to a generalized magical destination, but it could not indicate why that destination was magical or what they should do when they got there.

Given that this chapter occurs at this book's rough three-fifths mark, it's pretty obvious that Fern isn't in the Fontenoy.

Neither of the women know that.

Which is shameful ignorance and demonstrates the limits of their preternatural powers.

If the women of Fairy Land are really supranatural beings, unbound by the laws of nature and capable of casting spells that alleviate issues of plotting and characterization, you'd think that they'd have the resources to check the page number.

Anyway.

They're in the elevator and they're looking at the buttons which lead to the Fontenoy's other twelve floors. If Fern is in the building, they have no idea what floor she's occupying.

The women of Fairy Land don't have any choice.

They're going to have to explore each apartment in the building, one by one, until they can determine whether or not Fern is present within the structure.

Which she obviously isn't, if for no other reason than the fact that this chapter, like almost every chapter in this book, isn't really about anyone finding Fern. This chapter is a poorly fleshed-out fictional pretense to write about something that isn't fictitious.

This is, after all, a novel written in an era when the entire purpose of fiction has been outmoded and destroyed by vast social changes.

Another thing that the women of Fairy Land don't know is that they're in the most magical place in Los Angeles.

The Fontenoy is where the American Twenty-First Century AD was invented.

They started on the second floor, bursting into the apartment nearest the elevator.

No one was home, but Rose Byrne did have an interesting conversation with a yellow parakeet.

They burst into the next apartment, where three young men were smoking marijuana and watching television.

In anticipation of the Season Seven premiere of *Game of Thrones*, the three young men had entered into a covenant.

After the June 26th, 2016 AD finale of Season Six, each of the young men had gone to the source material and read every published volume of George R.R. Martin's magnum opus.

1,736,054 words of pure shit!

But reading the books had not slaked their thirst, and in anticipation of the approaching Season Seven premiere on July 16th, 2017 AD, the young men had agreed to spend the summer rewatching every extant episode of the televised adaptation.

As the women of Fairy Land burst into the apartment, the young men were watching the eighth episode of Season Three.

The television was displaying a scene in which the mad dwarf Tyrion Lannister is in a boudoir with his unwilling wife Sansa Stark. They've just been married and Tyrion's father has ordered Tyrion to break his bride's maidenhead.

The dwarf, in anticipation of this horror, has gotten ridiculously drunk.

With great reluctance, his bride sheds her clothing.

He stops her. If she does not want to sleep with him, he shall never force her.

Then the dwarf passes out.

This scene is of some interest because both the televised adaptation, and its source material, feature a character who's drunk himself silly and refuses to sleep with someone on moral grounds, rather than the obvious explanation of too much alcohol rendering him unfit for the congruous act.

This scene, in both book and television formats, points to the place where George R.R. Martin's *Game of Thrones* is a divergent universe from the one in which we live.

It ain't the elves.

It ain't the fucking dragons.

It ain't the kid who can see the future.

It ain't the snow zombies who function as an obvious insult to the people of Scotland.

What makes *Game of Thrones* diverge from our universe is one very special magical rule.

This is the magical rule which creates the divergent universe: no male character in *Games of Thrones* ever experiences erectile dysfunction.

The three young men were stoned enough that they all imagined someone had left the front door unlocked. They thought that the women of Fairy Land had the wrong apartment.

One of the young men chatted up Celia while Rose Byrne demanded to know about Fern.

Another of the young men made a joke about the absurdity of inquiring about ferns when clearly another green plant was the apartment's dominant spirit animal.

The women of Fairy Land didn't get the joke.

And this wasn't because the language of the joke was slightly mixed in its metaphors.

The joke was like all jokes about marijuana.

Terminally unfunny.

On it went, apartment by apartment, floor by floor.

They burst into apartment #403 and found a woman named Ashley Lopez sitting on her living-room floor.

She was practicing Transcendental Meditation, a technique in which the practitioner repeated a mantra, in the silence of their own mind, after having blown about $1,000 on a seven-day course to learn an easy trick that any old asshole can Google in about five minutes.

With her mindfulness practice disrupted, Ashley opened her eyes and saw the women standing over her.

She didn't question their presence.

It was one of those faery things, a biochemical process. The supranatural entities were emitting pheromones that calmed the human psyche.

"Can I help you?" asked Ashley Lopez.

"We are looking for my daughter," said Celia. "Have you seen her?"

"What's her name?" asked Ashley Lopez.

"Her name is Fern," said Celia.

Rose Byrne looked at the decorations on Ashley Lopez's living-room walls.

It was some witchy nonsense: a reproduction of The Tower from the Thoth tarot, the hieroglyphic monad of John Dee, a banker's cheque endorsed by Austin Osman Spare, a Stele of Revealing, a mural of Tiamat, a painting by Steffi Grant, the logo of the Builders of Adytum, and other bullshit.

Ashley Lopez was locked into a ceremonial magick groove.

Ashley still believed in things like gods and primal magic and art nouveau and the manifestations of expression that dominated human consciousness before the psychic cataclysm of World War One.

What can you do?

Everyone's got something.

Ashley Lopez was confronted by the women of Fairy Land, who were actual magic.

All of her ceremonial magick was of no use.

On those lonely evenings when Ashley Lopez crossed the Abyss and went on the Dark Pilgrimage to Chorazin, the whole thing was about psychological insight into her own self and the limits of identity.

Which was a real change from the old days.

In the old days, magick used to be goofy shit like necromancy, which was the art of raising the dead, and demonology, which was the art of making the Spirits of Hell do your bidding.

The defining aspect of demonology was the bathetic juxtaposition of its methods and its aims.

The Spirits of Hell, who were supranatural beings capable of unimaginable feats, were summoned by the demonologist and asked to perform silly little tasks like facilitating intercontinental travel, or making another person have sex with the demonologist, or causing the reputation of a demonologist's enemy to suffer grievous ruin.

By the Year of the Froward Worm, no one needed the Spirits of Hell to help them travel to Asia or get fucked or ruin an enemy.

Now people just owned smartphones.

Ashley Lopez's tenancy in the Fontenoy was foreordained by a lifetime of practicing ceremonial magick.

In addition to challenging the limits of her identity, the ceremonies had blasted open her seven chakras and made her susceptible to the unseen but very real magical currents running throughout Los Angeles.

When she signed her lease, it was like a magnet being drawn to metal.

The Fontenoy was the most magical place in Los Angeles.

Way back in 1989 AD, a young man had moved onto the ninth floor of the building.

He was, just, like you know, this guy.

His name was Matt Drudge.

He'd been raised around Washington DC, which was the capital city of the United States of America, and that proximity gave him a fixation on the currents of power.

He bummed around Hollywood for about half a decade. And this was the old Hollywood, the Hollywood of the Yucca Corridor, the Hollywood that existed prior to the infestation of the international capital class's money laundering.

It was gang territory. It was full of drug dealing. It was full of prostitution.

In 1994 AD, Drudge's father paid him a visit.

He was appalled by his son's life.

At the time, Drudge was selling T-shirts at CBS Studios in Century City, which was on the other side of the hills that hold the HOLLYWOOD sign.

The old man bestowed a gift upon his son from Circuit City on Sunset Boulevard: an IBM PC compatible computer.

This was before the release of Microsoft's Windows 95 destroyed the American West Coast, another psychic cataclysm, and oddly, one that's never been written about in any meaningful detail.

Drudge's computer had a modem, which was a stupid little device that connected to telephone lines and allowed his computer to call up other computers.

Using his modem, Matt Drudge discovered the Internet. And this was the old Internet, the Internet of Usenet and #hack on EFnet, the Internet that existed prior to the infestation of the international capital class's money laundering.

Drudge's first utterance on the Internet, ever, was three days after Christmas 1994 AD at 1:48PM.

It said:

**hello from sex drenched hollywood**

Drudge replied to himself at 3:31PM. His response said:

**we are so sex drenched here in hollywood. 65% of us city
dwellers have herpes**

And so, on a cloudy Wednesday afternoon, on the ninth floor
of the Fontenoy, the Twenty-First Century AD was born.

Ashley Lopez had lived in the Fontenoy for five years, performing
ceremonial magick and using all kinds of magickal phrases, and she'd
never said anything with as much power as the one phrase which
had baptized a century.

She'd never said anything as important, or as ominous, as hello
from sex drenched hollywood.

No one could have known that Matt Drudge was the only authentic
genius of the Twenty-First Century AD.

He was the only person in the world who understood how the
Internet really worked.

And he had found his demon.

Not long after he'd written about 65 per cent of people in Hollywood having herpes, Drudge founded an email newsletter obsessed
with the currents of power in American life.

The newsletter was about the entertainment industry and politics,
which, by virtue of the Celebrity branch of American governance,
were the same thing.

The newsletter was called the *Drudge Report*.

It offered its readers a very gossip-inflected take on the issues
of the day.

Everything broke in 1998 AD.

*Newsweek*, which was a magazine that offered milquetoast
political and cultural reporting, decided not to run a story about
an alleged affair between the sitting President, William Jefferson
Clinton, and a twenty-two-year-old White House intern named
Monica Lewinsky.

Drudge learned about the spiked story and sent word to his mailing list.

He didn't know it, but he'd murdered the gentleman's agreement between news journalists and politicians, which was more or less a tacit acknowledgement that politicians could fuck around in private as long as Washington bureau chiefs were invited to dinner parties in Georgetown.

And Drudge had, accidentally, trashed the American idea of good governance, fostering an environment in which the Republicans would go on to impeach William Jefferson Clinton, and learn that the way to power was through publicity stunts and using the Legislative branch not to govern but rather to obstruct.

After the Lewinsky thing, Drudge's fame went nuclear, went global.

He got a short-lived TV show. He got a radio show.

His newsletter evolved into a webpage that collated links to articles on other websites, and, on occasion, featured some of Drudge's own reporting and, in times of emergency, an animated siren GIF.

The links to other websites were written by Drudge himself in an ultra-minimalist headline style. hello from sex drenched hollywood.

The webpage was three columns of black text on a white background.

There was no flash and no glut.

The design never changed.

Not once in two decades.

It was perfect in the way that Steve Jobs, a psychopath who enslaved Chinese children and made them build electronic devices which allowed American liberals to write treatises on human rights, had envisioned perfection: the absolute and seamless melding of form and function.

By the Year of the Froward Worm, Drudge's website received ten billion visits per year.

In the late 1990s AD, there was an unbelievable amount of bullshit about how the Internet was going to offer new platforms of expression that leveled the playing field, and how computers would produce an enormous flowering of creativity and new opportunities.

What no one admitted, or perhaps even realized, was that while the Internet would indeed create a million opportunities for people to express their ignorant-ass opinions on topics about which they knew nothing, those opinions would not offer any real benefit to the ignorant-ass people who offered them.

The ignorant-ass opinions would only enrich the people who owned the platforms of expression.

And the people who owned the platforms of expression were the same old shits who ruled the world.

Here was the genius of Drudge laid bare: he understood, before anyone else, that the way to make money on the Internet was by monetizing other people's content.

After Drudge shattered journalism, the international capitalist class gathered up the fragments and ground them into dust.

The noble profession transformed from attempts at a first draft of history into a quest for eyeballs on websites.

In the process, seasoned professionals lost their jobs and were replaced with cocaine-addled children from Brooklyn who worked for spare change.

The international capitalist class didn't care.

Journalism had always been a pain in their ass.

What they wanted was traffic on the websites that they'd funded.

And Drudge drove that traffic.

Even though Drudge's website consisted almost entirely of links to other websites, it provided a coherent and linear worldview. The links were like a jigsaw puzzle. If you read Drudge for a week, you could piece together who he was and what he thought.

He made sense of an era in which the world had become

incomprehensible, and when the traditional arbiters of American life had given up any hope of explaining the global situation.

His website was the Internet's unmoved mover, just about the most read news site in English, and his millions of daily readers would deluge any site that he linked.

And even more importantly, he was read by absolutely everyone who was anyone in media. He drove entire cycles with headlines that were no more than fifteen words in length.

He was literally the most powerful voice in America.

And if you think that's an exaggeration, consider this: for all of the explanations floated as to why Donald J. Trump won the Presidency with his impossible victory, no one has ever suggested the most obvious.

Which is that Donald J. Trump won the Presidency because Matt Drudge decided that Donald J. Trump should win the Presidency, and did everything he could to cast the best possible light on Trump's many missteps.

Donald J. Trump's impossible victory had come via a very small margin: 77,744 votes cast in the three states had determined the Electoral College.

0.02 per cent of the US population.

By November 6th, 2016 AD, Drudge's website received that many visitors every two and a half minutes.

If you want to know about the American Twenty-First Century AD, I recommend watching two videos.

One is available on the website of C-SPAN, which is a non-profit organization that hosts an archive of media related to the governance and affairs of public life in the United States.

The other video is on YouTube, which is an expensive attempt by Google to make copyright law irrelevant.

The first video is Matt Drudge's appearance on November 11th, 1997 AD at the Annenberg School for Communication, which was a division of the University of Southern California, an institution of higher learning that used things like a School of Communication to cloak its relationship with the military–industrial complex.

The second video is Matt Drudge's incredibly weird October 6th, 2015 AD appearance on *The Alex Jones Show*, which was a radio program hosted by the eponymous Alex Jones, a disgraceful little man who believed that poisoned water turned frogs into homosexuals, that 9/11 was an inside job, and that clouds were made of Muslims.

The USC appearance occurred several months before *Newsweek* and Lewinsky, which makes it a valuable document of Drudge before he broke the story that would define his life. It features Drudge on a panel with several high priests of journalism.

The first high priest is Michael Kinsley, who'd been on TV and written for the *New Republic*, and who was the editor of Slate.com, which was a news website funded by Microsoft with money that they'd made from ruining the West Coast.

The second high priest is Todd S. Purdum, then the Los Angeles bureau chief for the *New York Times*, which is the definitive American organ of sober judgment, good taste, and quality reporting.

By contrast, Matt Drudge was a guy with an email account.

He got his email from a company called L.A. Internet Inc.

He paid for his own Internet access.

He worked out of the ninth floor of the Fontenoy.

Everyone on the stage can't imagine that Lewinsky is coming. Both Purdum and Kinsley think that Drudge has already issued the story that will define his life.

Back on August 10th, 1997 AD, Drudge sent a report to his newsletter.

The report quoted an anonymous GOP operative who said that a Clinton aide named Sidney Blumenthal had beaten his wife.

The story was untrue.

Drudge issued a retraction.

Blumenthal sued Drudge for $30,000,000.

Prior to this incident, media coverage of Drudge had been geewhiz! articles about what he was doing, about how the Internet was really strange, and about how strange it was that Drudge was a weird person doing something strange on the Internet.

The minute after the Blumenthal thing, the knives were out.

You can see it in the video of the USC panel.

Kinsley and Purdum suggest that Drudge's methods are abhorrent, they tell him that he's a flash in the pan, they say that he's irresponsible, they repeatedly insult him to his face.

The smugness is unbearable.

It's actually shocking.

Drudge, meanwhile, defends himself to the best of his abilities and talks about his ideas of what the Internet is going to do to journalism, which is create a nation of citizens who operate the news, unfiltered and without editorial interference, and unrestrained by the social mores of the upper middle class.

When he speaks, he sounds slightly naïve and a little self-righteous.

But think about this: he's a guy who makes about $3,000 a month and he's being sued for $30,000,000 by a Presidential aide. And he's on a stage where he is, by any conventional metric, seriously outclassed by his fellow panelists.

When Drudge speaks, it's clear that he's attempting to be understood.

He's a person asking to be taken seriously.

His exchanges with his fellow panelists are, effectively, Patient Zero diagnosing his own disease, and its symptoms, to aging doctors who don't read the new research.

And they hate him.

The loathing is palpable.

During the last ten minutes of the video, there's an audience Q&A.

The only question is asked by a future psychotic named Andrew Breitbart.

Breitbart would go on to be Matt Drudge's assistant, handling the afternoon shift of the *Drudge Report*.

In the Q&A, Breitbart asks why the mainstream media gave Hunter S. Thompson free reign to lie and distort the truth while not allowing Drudge any latitude in his own reporting. Breitbart suggests that this lack of latitude derives from Drudge's conservative-leaning politics.

One doesn't like to praise the devil, but this isn't the stupidest path of inquiry.

But here's the real significance: Breitbart is the only person, throughout the entire event, who doesn't insult Drudge or treat him like a child who's been caught stealing cookies.

Breitbart went on to found the Breitbart News Network, a website which by the Year of the Froward Worm had become the dominant voice of the Far Right in America.

When Breitbart died in 2012 AD, presumably from a toxic mix of being both a drug freak and a huge fucking asshole, a guy named Steve Bannon ended up in control of the Breitbart News Network.

In August of 2016 AD, he became Chief Executive Officer of Donald J. Trump's Presidential campaign.

When Trump assumed the Presidency, Bannon went to the White House.

When Blumenthal sued Drudge, Drudge didn't have any resources to mount a legal defense. He was on the wrong side of the Democrats. He was on the wrong side of the White House.

And this was before Lewinsky!

The only people who helped him, and assumed the cost of his legal liabilities, were people on the Far Right.

They did his case mostly pro bono with occasional donations from supporters.

The video of Drudge on *The Alex Jones Show* is something else.

Before Google made a gesture towards political theater by declaring Alex Jones to be persona non grata, he filmed every episode of his radio show and put the videos on YouTube. The Drudge was no different.

Because of this, as the episode is being recorded, Drudge refuses to emerge from the shadows. He lets Jones interview him, but the image remains fixed on Jones.

Matt Drudge, the only genius of the new century, has hijacked another forum.

For the first, and only, time in the history of *The Alex Jones Show*, Alex Jones shuts the fuck up.

Drudge talks about many of the same ideas that he expresses in the USC video, but now he's less nervous, and now he's embittered.

If, back in 1997 AD, he was Matt Drudge, who was just, like you know, this guy, now he's MATT DRUDGE, GOD OF ALL NEW MEDIA.

He's still talking about citizen reporting, but he's dispirited by the rise of the corporate groupthink and the way that it's influenced the homogeneity of the news. In a moment of sounding uncomfortably like the present author, he denounces social media.

He boasts of his independence from everyone.

And then it gets depressing.

Drudge sings the praises of Alex Jones. He sees the radio host as a lonely man who wages war against that corporate homogeneity, which is true from a certain perspective, but which ignores the true insanity of Alex Jones, a person who believes that the late singer-songwriter Jeff Buckley was a robot built by Muslims.

At first, it feels like maybe Drudge is being polite.

But then he starts throwing out his own crazy ideas.

He suggests there's a cover-up of Hillary Clinton's lovers, with the implication being that there's scores of women who've had the former Secretary of State's tongue in their birth canals.

He says that Clinton is old and sick and that there's a cover-up about her impending death.

He claims there are 80 million illegal immigrants living in the US.

Things are different than back in 1997 AD.

The coherent worldview has changed and encompassed some very dubious thoughts.

There's an edge in this interview that's nowhere to be seen in the early days.

This is a person who knows that he'll never be understood.

While Michael Kinsley sneered at Drudge for an hour in 1997 AD, he was wrapped in a delusion about the nature of his job. He thought that he was a person who offered the world a valuable service, but actually, all he did was lure people into looking at advertisements.

In the video, he can't imagine that, within about twelve years, it'll turn out that the Internet is better at advertising than newspapers, and that his colleagues in journalism, all the hallowed practitioners of the art, are going to be chasing Patient Zero's vision of the future, reducing institutions of sober judgment into op-ed factories that, try as hard as they might, will never be able to compete with the sheer entertainment psychosis of a seventeen-year-old denouncing Jews on YouTube.

Another thing that he can't imagine: by the Year of the Froward Worm, anonymous and unsupported allegations on the Internet will be the backbone of his entire industry.

And the last thing that Kinsley can't imagine is that he's insulting the one person who could have helped.

Drudge was, and is, the only person who understands the Internet.

And he was insulted so badly that he sought refuge with the scum of the world, and he took all of that genius and all of its attendant power, and he befriended the people who were nice to him.

That's how history works.

That's how politics work.

You figure out how to get along with people you find unpalatable. You figure out how to make a decent argument that convinces people who don't agree with you. You don't throw away people because you think they're powerless and worthless.

Or you end up like Michael Kinsley.

Totally forgotten and left behind.

Just a smug asshole no one remembers in a video that no one watches.

Here's a pro-tip for the Democrats.

If you want to win Presidential elections, there's a very simple thing that you can do.

It's too late to harness Matt Drudge's unbelievable influence over the national dialogue.

He's an autodidact and you insulted him.

You can't make friends now.

But you could always kill him.

Call out the Clinton death squads!

# Chapter Thirteen

## Routine Humiliations

To understand how I ended up being sexually harassed in front of 280 people by a woman who pens *New York Times* opinion pieces on the topic of sexual harassment, you have to understand what my career was like before the success of my novel *I Hate the Internet*.

It was non-existent.

I'd published a novella called *ATTA*, which was a psychedelic biography of the lead 9/11 hijacker.

It had moved a surprising amount of copies for a short work published on an independent press, and generated a great deal of secondary academic writing, but for a variety of reasons, no one noticed that any of this had happened.

After *ATTA* came out, I worked on another book, which would eventually turn into *The Future Won't Be Long*. I wasted two years trying to get the thing published.

None of it came to anything.

When I wrote *ATTA*, I was living in Los Angeles.

By the time that it was published in 2011 AD, I had moved to San Francisco.

In 2014 AD, I moved from San Francisco and ended up back in Los Angeles.

While I lived in San Francisco, the only positive thing that had happened, career wise, was that I ended up doing a writer's residency in rural Denmark.

This was in the summer of 2013 AD.

While I was at the residency, I met the Danish writer Dorthe Nors.

In addition to being a truly lovely person, Dorthe also happens to be one of the best writers in the world. Her books *Minna Needs Rehearsal Space* and *Mirror, Shoulder, Signal* are fucking intellectual masterpieces.

But she's a woman, which means that while she's become very successful, her work is always reviewed in a specific way: no one pays attention to the intellect and everyone looks for the moral instruction.

Dorthe and I became friends.

She was on the cusp of becoming a literary superstar.

In 2017 AD, she was nominated for a Man Booker International. No one deserved the award more.

In the unique case of Dorthe, I suspend my disdain for awards.

Dorthe doesn't just deserve the Man Booker International.

She deserves every award.

She should win the Nobel Prize in Literature.

She should win Motor Trend's Car of the Year.

Bad Sex in Fiction!

As Dorthe was transforming into a superstar, she helped me out in whatever ways that she could. This is how I ended up getting an email in the summer of 2014 AD from a guy named Adrian Todd Zuniga.

Adrian Todd Zuniga is the founder and the host of a thing called Literary Death Match.

He'd met Dorthe somewhere in Europe, at one of the ten billion literary festivals that extend invitations to Dorthe.

She told him that he should have me participate in Literary Death Match.

So he reached out.

I said yes.

Saying yes to Literary Death Match was a moral compromise of the highest order.

To understand why, I need to explain the thing.

Literary Death Match works like this: four writers are given the opportunity to read their work.

Unlike normal readings, Literary Death Match happens in two rounds.

In each round, two writers perform their work, and then their work is critiqued by three judges. These judges are often celebrities.

The judges choose one writer as the victor of each round, and then the two victors face off against one another in a final round which involves a humiliating game.

Whoever demonstrates the greatest capacity for making a fool of themselves is the winner of Literary Death Match.

This is awful shit. It's the clusterfuck of debasement that has overtaken writing.

Everyone pretends that they're on the same side, everyone pretends that they're friends, and everyone makes awful pronouncements about the seriousness of their work while maintaining their aw shucks relatability, and sometimes writers are rewarded for their pomposity with badly rendered line drawings of their faces on bookshop walls.

And sometimes, if the writer is a good little boy, people will reward his pomposity with the gift of a tote bag.

Most of these tote bags have an aphorism or a logo printed on their sides.

The aphorisms and logos are always very positive about publishing.

I've never bought a tote bag in my life.

But I've still got about twenty hanging in my kitchen.

One of them says BOOKS.

I knew what Literary Death Match was.

I abhorred it.

And I still said yes.

That's how desperate I was.

Summer of 2014 AD was particularly bad.

I'd finished writing the manuscript for *I Hate the Internet* and two things had become apparent: (1) it was the most significant piece of work that I'd done and (2) absolutely no one would publish it.

When I was offered Literary Death Match, these two things had left me beyond debased.

I was thinking, honestly, that if I won the thing, it'd at least give me another meaningless credential to put in query emails to agents who would refuse to represent my manuscript.

The iteration of Literary Death Match to which I'd been invited occurred on July 10th, 2014 AD, and it was held at Largo at Coronet on La Cienaga Boulevard.

Largo is one of those venues that people who aren't from Los Angeles can't possibly understand. It's where the Celebrity branch of American governance entertains itself in a 280-seat venue.

If your response to the existential horror of Donald J. Trump is a desire to have your liberal pieties reinforced with a joke about *Star Trek*, then you should fly to Los Angeles and go to Largo.

The comedian Patton Oswalt will be waiting with your chuckles.

The other writers who were performing at Literary Death Match were Aimee Bender, Jay Martel, and Annabelle Gurwitch.

Jay Martel was the producer of *Key & Peele*, which was a popular sketch comedy show in which two African-American actors who'd grown up as members of the middle classes performed skits based around the hilarity inherent in the accents of poor African-Americans.

Annabelle Gurwitch was an actress who'd found some success as a writer of books about her sex drive as she approached the age of fifty.

Aimee Bender was a literary writer. She taught creative writing at the University of Southern California, and was director of that university's Creative Writing PhD program.

I've never read her work, but my friend Dean Smith was in the audience at Largo with his boyfriend Mike Kitchell, and Dean Smith said that he'd read Aimee Bender's book *The Particular Sadness of Lemon Cake*.

The judges at Literary Death Match were Amber Tamblyn, Jody Hill, and Dana Gould.

Amber Tamblyn was an actor and a poet with several volumes of published poetry. She'd done a lot of good in the world, having convinced people to give money to the poet Diane di Prima when Diane di Prima had serious healthcare issues and needed help with the costs.

At the time of Literary Death Match, Amber Tamblyn was just coming off a starring role in Season Eleven of the sitcom *Two and a Half Men*, which was the highest-rated television show in America.

Jody Hill was a director and writer of films and television. Through the terrible magic of Los Angeles, we'd met about eight years earlier, but neither of us could remember where.

Dana Gould was a stand-up comedian and a former writer for *The Simpsons*.

To state the bleedingly obvious: I was the freak.

Everyone else at Literary Death Match had significant amounts of money and significant amounts of success, and with the exception of Aimee Bender, all of them were representatives from the Celebrity branch of American governance.

I was poor and I wrote psychedelic biographies of Islamic-themed terrorists.

Thanks, Dorthe!

The first round of Literary Death Match was Aimee Bender versus Jay Martel.

I was in Largo's green room with Annabelle Gurwitch.

She was charming.

When Aimee Bender and Jay Martel stopped reading, the judges chimed in and offered opinions on their work. The judges ended up going with Aimee Bender.

I should say that I had never been to a Literary Death Match.

So I had no idea what the judges' critiques would be like.

I certainly wasn't expecting what I saw during the first round, which was a rah-rah all-in-together-now malice masked by a layer of bonhomie.

If you want to imagine an analogue, think about Celebrity Roasts, which are spectacles where a celebrity will attend an event that honors the celebrity by having other celebrities say cruel things about the honored celebrity.

Literary Death Match wasn't anywhere as cruel as a Celebrity Roast.

But it was the same atmosphere.

Somewhere in the middle of this, when Amber Tamblyn was talking, she mentioned that she was drunk.

The next round happened.

Annabelle Gurwitch and I had decided in the green room that she'd read first.

She did.

And then I read.

My appearance at Literary Death Match occurred after years of countless San Francisco literary readings. If I'd learned anything, it was how to work an audience.

I fucking killed.

And then it was time to hear from the judges.

Annabelle Gurwitch and I sat in chairs. Stage right.

The judges were seated stage left.

We watched as our performances were dissected with the

jokey malice of a Celebrity Roast. In front of an audience of 280 people.

You'll forgive me, but I can't remember a word of what anyone said about Annabelle Gurwitch.

And you'll forgive me when I say that I can barely remember what Jody Hill and Dana Gould said about me, although I do remember that one of them talked about how innovative it was that I read my piece off an iPad.

It wasn't an iPad.

It was an Android tablet.

The last judge to comment on my piece was Amber Tamblyn.

She'd been taking notes throughout the event, and she began by reading one of her notes. This is what her note said, give or take: "This guy is wearing white pants. That's hot."

She was a person who was infinitely more successful than me, with infinitely more money. She was on America's highest rated television show. She was published by serious New York presses. And she was in a position of actual, literal judgment on my merit as a writer, and that judgment, if positive, could affect the success of my work and my future.

And she was drunk and making sexualized comments.

In front of an audience of 280 laughing people.

And all I could do was sit there, take it, and pretend to laugh. While my friends watched.

By any conceivable metric used during #MeToo, this was sexual harassment.

But, seriously, who fucking cares?

Amber Tamblyn wasn't even the worst.

One time, I was assaulted by a rabid fan outside of the Echo Park Film Center, and another time, I received unsolicited emails from a beloved elder statesman of the literary scene fantasizing about sucking my cock.

He remains a friend.

And I know that as a society we've descended into revenge narratives in which a lesser figure remembers some stray incident from the past and uses it to attack someone who's significantly more famous.

Speak bitterness!

This is our entertainment.

And I realize how uncomfortably close this chapter reads to those narratives.

But that's not what this is.

Because here is an everlasting truth: if you get Diane di Prima money, you should be allowed to sexually harass the living shit out of everyone in the world.

If I were to give advice to anyone who wants to enter the public sphere, this is what I would say: don't.

If this theoretical person insisted on entering the public sphere, I would say: recognize the binary presentation inherent in mass media. A public figure can either be good or evil. There are no shades of gray.

So recognize this binary and do yourself a favor: do not cloak yourself in virtue.

Cloak yourself in vice.

Being cloaked in virtue creates an impossible situation: the presentation of self as infallible.

And you will fail.

And when you do, the mass media will be waiting, and the public will feast on your corpse. Nothing tastes better than false virtue.

But cloaking yourself in vice?

There's nowhere to go but up.

The early days will be difficult, but if you can last four years, you will be an unshakable fixture.

Who knows?

Do this long enough and you might become President of the United States of America!

If the Queen of England trips over a dog, it's a national scandal.

When Liam Gallagher kicks an old man down the stairs, no one even blinks.

That's Liam being Liam.

But when our kid hugs a jaundiced paraplegic?

All of that said, it remains a very peculiar experience to be sexually harassed by someone who pens opinion pieces for the *New York Times* on the social scourge of sexual harassment.

If there's one aspect of every opinion piece on the social scourge of sexual harassment, it's that they all contain an implicit core: that there are ways to make the world a better place.

Which, of course, there are.

But when the tools used to make a better world are owned by the Patriarchy, the best outcome you're going to end up with is a discussion about the social mores in the workplaces of the haute bourgeoisie.

And, remember, that's the best case.

Here's one much worse: that, in the end, everyone's life is still dominated by the whims of the very rich and the social mores of the slightly rich. And that this new reality is exploited by the people who understand that appearances are more important than reality.

All of which is to say that by fixating on sex, the discussion around sexual harassment misses the key element.

Which is the harassment.

The people who end up in positions of power end up in those positions because they are very, very good at humiliation.

That's their skill.

That's how they end up as CEOs.

Everyone who has ever had a job has been humiliated by their boss.

This is the nature of the thing.

And, yes, it sucks that the men who end up in power are so fucking crude that the only way they can imagine humiliating women is with sex.

But every single boss who's humiliating his women underlings is also humiliating his male underlings.

This is who we, as a society, put into power.

Remind me: how many obsequious movies and books and articles have been written about Steve Jobs?

In the end, having a job, even a job like writing, is about interfacing with money, and the biggest lie of our society is that the individual currencies of money are units that measure value.

Money doesn't measure value.

Money is the measure of humiliation.

What would you do for a dollar?

What would you do for ten dollars?

What would you do for a million dollars?

What would you do for a billion dollars?

So of course Amber Tamblyn would sexually harass me at Literary Death Match.

Why wouldn't she?

She'd been put into a position of power at an event predicated on the perpetual humiliation of writers.

# Chapter Fourteen

## When Y Meets X

After the Fontenoy was a bust, Celia and Rose Byrne spent weeks and weeks exploring magical strands of smartphone navigation, which gave the women a decent internal map of Los Angeles and its surrounding environs.

One ropey strand of salvia took them to the Self-Realization Fellowship Lake Shrine, where they wandered around a lake decorated with religious kitsch.

Another strand took them to the site of Jack Parson's hermitage in Pasadena, where L. Ron Hubbard learned about ceremonial magick and imbued himself with the ideological basis of what would become Scientology.

Another strand, and by far the longest, took them out of Los Angeles and all the way to 274 Coast Boulevard in La Jolla, where, during World War Two, Anna Kavan had spent several months hard drinking and going ga-ga for an architect while looking at ridiculous California coastal splendor.

Another took them to 6026 Barton Ave, the address at which Samson de Brier held his cultural salons, where the former Francis Fuller had made the deal for *Handspun Roses* several decades before Celia wiped out any memory of the film or its director.

Another took them to a lecture at the Philosophical Research Society on Los Feliz Boulevard, which had the virtue of being very close to the house on the hill.

Another took them to the Bellagio gate of Bel Air, where buses from the San Fernando Valley dropped off the permanent servant class of Latino Americans to perform domestic duties in the homes of the Celebrity branch of American governance.

Another took them to a one-room structure behind 7508 Sunset Boulevard, where the members of Guns N' Roses had lived in depravity.

And there were other places, arbitrarily chosen by authorial whims: the former St. Francis Hotel, and the shack on North Genovese where Marjorie Cameron spent the final years of her life, and the site of the former Motel Hell on Hollywood Boulevard, and the former Security Pacific National Bank Building on Hollywood Boulevard, where in the early 1980s AD a tribe of street freaks called the Night People took up residence while the bank still operated out of the bottom floor.

And there were others too.

Countless others.

But nowhere did they find Fern.


Meanwhile, the women of Fairy Land spent their evenings in bars.

They sampled places like Frank N Hanks and the HMS Bounty before settling on Tenants of Trees as their regular haunt.

Tenants of Trees was a Silverlake bar that was home to a fairly pleasant outdoor patio.

It was a human meat market filled with the sexual desperation of people who'd made the mistake of following their dreams and moving to Los Angeles.

Celia used the meat market to engage in reckless sex with some of the city's more pathetic men.


One night, Celia and Rose Byrne were sitting in an open-air room off the patio.

"I have seen too much of this mortal world," said Rose Byrne.

Rose Byrne was wearing a T-shirt that said: CRIMSON GLORY.

Celia was wearing a T-shirt that said: KING DIAMOND.

"Another drink, I think," said Celia.

Celia had cast a spell on Tenants of Trees which gave them an open and bottomless tab.

Celia made her way to the bar, passing a man and woman involved in a meat-market transaction. The transaction was comprised of monosyllables.

"That's, you know, so dumb," said the woman.

"Shit, isn't it," said the man.

"Right, don't you think?" asked the woman.

"Fuck," said the man.

"What you, like, do, I've done," said the woman.

Celia sat on a stool at the center of the bar.

The bartender, a young woman with full-sleeve tattoos, was serving other customers. She didn't see Celia.

A man on the stool to Celia's left turned his body in her direction.

"Whenever I espy a woman in licensed tour apparel, I am stricken with a fevered and paralyzing round of myxomatosis," said the man.

"I beg your pardon?" asked Celia.

"King Diamond, madame," said the man. "Your shirt. Is this not a reproduction of the *Abigail* artwork?"

"I suppose," said Celia.

Celia had no idea about King Diamond, the eponymous vocalist of the heavy metal band King Diamond, or the band itself, or the band's 1987 AD concept album *Abigail*.

As with every other day, magic had chosen her outfit.

Through the coincidental power endemic to fiction, the man was also not wearing an outfit of his choice.

He was wearing a pair of banana-yellow shorts with a fringe trim.

And, like Celia, he was also wearing a T-shirt.

Unlike Celia, his T-shirt did not advertise a heavy metal band from the 1980s AD.

His T-shirt said this:

# I SUPPORT
## SCIENCE
## HUMAN RIGHTS
## PUBLIC EDUCATION
## AFFORDABLE HEALTH CARE
### IMMIGRANTS AND REFUGEES
**FREEDOM OF SPEECH, THE PRESS, AND RELIGION**
CHOICE, CIVIL RIGHTS, GUN CONTROL, FAIR WAGES

## WITH LIBERTY AND JUSTICE FOR ALL!

The man's T-shirt was very long.

That morning, with his body smarting from the previous night's Abu Ghraib-themed BDSM/taqiyya session, HRH had done a Skype interview.

The journalist was from Portland, Oregon. The interview subject was the Klaus Mann Center, a homeless shelter in Portland that HRH had opened in 2007 AD. The shelter had a specific focus on LGBTQIA+ youth.

"I believe," said HRH into a laptop that displayed the computerized face of the interviewer, "that it is our duty to protect the least fortunate of society."

"It's very unusual, though, isn't it?" asked the interview.

"I should hope that this belief is universally held," said HRH.

"You're a Saudi prince," said the interviewer.

"The royal flesh is my own," said HRH. "Yet do not forget, I am a citizen of St. Kitts and Nevis."

"I was only curious if things like the Klaus Mann Center made family reunions awkward," said the journalist.

"Whenever is a reunion of family not a-drip with awkwardness?" asked HRH.

"One last question. Why name a shelter in America after a German writer?"

"I had wished to christen the enterprise after Annemarie Schwarzenbach," said HRH. "An advisor warned me against both the length of her name and its linguistic closeness to that of film star and former California governor Arnold Schwarzenegger. In her stead, I opted for that friend of her bosom, Klaus Mann, a man whom I rate as a personal hero. He was tortured by his father. When the Nazis willed themselves to power, Klaus fled into exile, and beyond the snug confines of the Weimar Republic, he found that his fey lust for the bodies of other men caused great pain. He committed suicide. Yet I consider his life a triumph. Through the torrents of suffering, he authored several brilliant books and one unvarnished masterpiece. He inspires us all."

After the interview, HRH went to a board meeting at the Venice Beach offices of Snapchat.

Snapchat was a smartphone app that had achieved a long-standing dream of corporate America: cornering the ever elusive market of child pornography.

Following a tip received at an orgy full of unattractive men and female sex workers, all of whom were in the thrall of MDMA, HRH had gotten in on the Series A funding of Snapchat.

Snapchat was a late-period capitalist innovation: a corporation either worth nothing or everything, and one with such a complex relationship to money that it was impossible to judge the company's failure or success.

The Series A funding had earned HRH a seat on the board.

HRH arrived wearing a suit that'd been tailored in London by Gieves & Hawkes.

By the end of the board meeting, the suit was so stained that HRH had to borrow clothes from an employee of Snapchat.

"There is a curious lacuna in *Abigail*, and one that is never revealed through the stylized vocals of King Diamond," said HRH to Celia. "Speak not of the ludicrous sequel. We are not barbarians, madame. We consider texts unburdened by *a priori* knowledge. As King Diamond sings, we meet the ghost of Count de LaFey, and also his unfaithful wife, and their descendant Jonathan and his wife Miriam. One almost need not even mention Abigail herself. The stillborn child of de LaFey's wife, conceived in the sullen pits of adultery. Although the main thrust of the album concerns itself with Abigail's attempts to possess Miriam, represented as the symbolic transition from eighteen to nine, I remain struck by our ignorance of Abigail's father. Her sire is the one player never identified. I wonder, madame, have you any theories as to the identity of this unfortunate progenitor?"

"I beg your pardon?" asked Celia.

"Is this swine bothering you?" asked Rose Byrne.

From her bench in the open-air room, Rose Byrne had been keeping an eye on Celia.

At first, she wasn't concerned when she saw Celia talking with HRH.

She'd seen Celia speaking with a legion of meat-market men.

But then she noticed HRH's face pushing too close to Celia.

Celia was inching backwards on her stool.

Rose Byrne decided to intervene.

Her broadsword was in a scabbard.

The scabbard was hanging from her battle belt.

Throughout their journeys across Los Angeles, the broadsword had occasioned enough comment that Celia had cast a spell making the weapon invisible to mortals.

But it was always there.

HRH turned to Rose Byrne.

HRH looked Rose Byrne up and down.

"If there is any one thing that I am able to recognize within an instant, it is a servant," HRH said to Celia.

"Her name is Rose Byrne," said Celia.

"Wonderful!" cried HRH. "A dwarf with a broadsword! Straight from the pages of John Ronald Reuel! Madame, you offer no end of surprises! Where did you find such a creature? I must have her! Another blinkered specimen for my menagerie of the damned! How much must I offer to purchase this beauty?"

"We have no use for money," said Celia.

"I am not for sale," said Rose Byrne.

"Sir, I know not how it is that you see the broadsword," said Celia. "I suggest that you leave us in peace. Rose Byrne is disagreeable and her weapon was sharpened this very morn."

"You issue threats, madame?" asked HRH.

"A statement of reality," said Celia.

"Are you as unpleasant as she claims?" HRH asked Rose Byrne. "Your apple face betrays no wrath. I see only dwarven mirth. Sing me a song of the misty mountains cold!"

"I am a whirlwind," said Rose Byrne.

"If I fluster your companion any further, you will use this sword on my person?" asked HRH. "You will murder my body in Tenants of Trees?"

"Without a doubt," said Rose Byrne. "Your head will roll on the tiles."

"Wonderful!" cried HRH. "Wonderful!"

HRH jumped off his bar stool.

HRH kneeled on the ground before Rose Byrne.

HRH bent his head.

"Come now, you broken creature of Khazad-dûm! Here is my neck! Make swift with your cut. Pretend that I am the bastard offspring of Charles the First and the Great God Pan! I will be the martyr of the people! Chop, chop, cut, cut, make your haste!"

Rose Byrne's previous murders in Tenant of Trees had required a great deal of magic.

Many lives had been erased.

Celia saw no need for the bother.

She cast a spell to transport HRH out of Tenant of Trees.

But the spell fizzled.

Rose Byrne stood over HRH.

Rose Byrne ached with the ideated reality of a serial killer.

She moved her hand to her broadsword.

But she could not remove it from its scabbard.

HRH rose from the ground.

"As I imagined," HRH said to Rose Byrne. "One more disappointment in the litany that is life."

HRH sat to Celia's left.

"Sir," said Celia. "Who are you that you stayed her hand?"

"I am the alpha and the omega," said HRH.

"I beg your pardon?" asked Celia.

"I will use a metaphor that I hope gives clarity," said HRH. "Think of yourself as a being of rare luck. You sit in the presence of a superhero. Throughout the livelong day I am a mild-mannered financial wizard and neoliberal philanthropist. By night, I venture forth and make the world sane. I am like nothing you have ever met. Wait until you read my press coverage. As with the faint hopes of a penile inadequate, it is measured not in length but thickness!"

Celia stood.

"Come, Rose," said Celia. "Enough of this."

They walked out of Tenant of Trees.

HRH turned to the woman sitting at his left.

She twenty-five years old.

She was an aspiring actress.

She was from Kissimmee, Florida.

She had moved to Los Angeles to follow her dreams.

Her body was filled with the following psychoactive agents: Paxil, Lexapro, and a microdose of LSD.

"My dear," said HRH to the aspiring actress, "I wonder if you have ever perused the speeches of Cesar Chavez?"

# Chapter Fifteen

# Until the Wheels Fall Off and Burn

By the way, all of the women in Fairy Land, and the Fairy Knight too, had Afro-textured hair and skin loaded with eumelanin in the stratum basale of their epidermis.

When the women of Fairy Land wandered around Los Angeles in their vintage metal T-shirts, this is what people thought: *Hey, there are some Black girls.*

This was followed by another thought: *Wait, Black girls like Megadeth? How is that possible?*

And this wasn't because the people of Los Angeles were essentializing, which was a crude mental process by which inherent characteristics were attributed to an arbitrary and socially constructed grouping of humans.

The people of Los Angeles weren't having this thought because they were racist and believed it unlikely that Black girls would enjoy the sounds of Megadeth.

The people of Los Angeles were having this thought because they were shocked at the bad taste of anyone in a Megadeth T-shirt.

Megadeth were awful.

No one's accusing you, reader, of having read this book with a mental image of lily-white faeries as its main characters.

But let's be honest.

All of this book's other readers have done exactly that.

It's a cruel narrative trick that relies on ingrained cultural assumptions about mythological beings, character names with Celtic origin, and the underlying biases of fantasy literature.

But it's not as if there weren't a few clues back in Chapter Four.

Prince Thomas of the Kingdom of Purpoole clearly refers to Celia's skin as "dusky."

Also, Prince Thomas suggests that Celia's a queen of Clerkenwell and a sister of Luce.

And, as everyone knows, Black Luce or Negro Lucy was a woman of Sub-Saharan African descent who ran a brothel in Clerkenwell during the last decade of the Sixteenth Century AD and the first decade of the Seventeenth Century AD.

It's not you, reader.

It's everyone else.

But that's racial prejudice, isn't it?

And yes, reader, I understand the peril into which I've thrust myself by suggesting that Richard Johnson's made-up characters possess imaginary physical characteristics which group them into an arbitrary social construct.

Nothing could be more controversial.

Someone might get upset!

On the Internet!

Where important things happen!

No one likes to talk about it, but we live in a world where a significant proportion of the population believes that Batman is real.

Batman is a comic-book character.

Here is his origin story: he was born super rich, and his rich parents were murdered in an alley while Batman watched, and then when Batman's trust fund matured, he used the money to enact a systemized campaign of violence against the poor.

Batman goes out every night and makes the world sane.

Most of Batman's true believers don't believe in the physical reality of Batman.

It isn't that kind of belief.

It's religious.

But then again, there are always the ones who think they can talk with gods.

In 2014 AD, there was a news story about a pair of twelve-year-old girls who stabbed another twelve-year-old girl. When the girls were apprehended, they were asked why they had tried to murder their BFF. The girls told the cops that they were killing for Slender Man.

Slender Man was an imaginary supranatural character that had been created by someone on the Internet.

Slender Man wore a bad suit and he hung out with children and he inspired tedious academic papers by bottomfeeders.

When the girls were asked why Slender Man wanted them to kill, they said that Slender Man would reward their human sacrifice with a resplendent palace in Hell, where they would rule for eternity amongst the damned.

The bottomfeeders who wrote academic papers about Slender Man weren't that different from the girls who stabbed their BFF.

They were looking for tenure at state-funded universities, which meant that they too were seeking a resplendent palace in Hell, where they too would rule for eternity amongst the damned.

The media played the stabbing for its obvious shock.

Given the character's origins, which were heavily documented and easily verifiable, how could anyone think that Slender Man was real?

Psychological examinations revealed that one of the assailants was in regular telepathic communication with Mr. Spock from *Star Trek*, all four of the Teenage Mutant Ninja Turtles, and Lord Voldemort from the *Harry Potter* books.

The *Harry Potter* books were a series of fantasy novels about an English boarding school, wherein the most fantastical thing that happened was the complete absence of buggery and same-sex handjobs.

Mr. Spock from *Star Trek*?
Why not?
Lord Voldemort?
All right.
But the *Teenage Mutant Ninja Turtles*?
Unless she'd somehow encountered self-published black-and-white comic books from the 1980s AD, the twelve-year-old was presumably receiving communications from the most commonly known versions of these intellectual properties.

And the commonly known versions were characterized by nothing more than their irrepressible hunger for pizza and their use of an American dialect of English that sounded like the media stereotype of California surfers.

They said shit like: "Cowabunga, dude and dudettes! I can't wait to gnosh on some gnarly pizza and get, like, weirded out! Mondo nutsiness! Time to boogie!"

Imagine that horror beamed into your fucking head.

The right question wasn't why someone would believe in the reality of Slender Man.

This was the right question: *Why wouldn't they?*

America was full of millions of people who posted to the Internet, daily, about the importance of Batman, and insisted on interpreting prevailing social trends through the prism of Batman.

These people believed in Batman, they knew that Batman was real, and they invested Batman with religious faith.

Batman was a new god.

Batman had risen from the rankest nether regions of pop culture, nurtured on the Internet after September 11th, 2001 AD, which was when a bunch of Muslims facefucked the collective psyche of mankind and transformed reality into a shitty disaster movie from the mid-1990s AD.

Life became a cartoon.

A new pantheon was required.

And there was Batman.

And there was Mr. Spock.

And there were the Teenage Mutant Ninja Turtles.

And there was Harry fucking Potter, still unbuggered, still longing for the strong and nurturing caress of a same-sex handjob.

All of these intellectual properties were no different than Slender Man.

They were just some crap that someone had made up.

And they all had definite, and well-documented, points of origin.

And this is why writers run into terrible peril when they write about supranatural characters that directly, or accidentally, touch upon hot-button issues like race or gender.

The problem is never race or gender.

That's only the smokescreen.

The problem is the supranatural creatures.

The writer risks profaning a new religion.

Like all religious people, the new religion's adherents are completely insane.

But they're not so insane that they're willing to make a direct argument about their religion.

You can't say that Batman is real.

Not in public.

Not yet.

So they grasp at the obvious.

And like any zealots, they demand obsequious gestures as retribution for the profane.

One obsequious gesture that emerged around the Year of the Froward Worm was the employment of what were termed sensitivity readers.

Authors hired sensitivity readers, who were apparently of marginalized backgrounds, to read through the authors' manuscripts and identify issues of bias or grotesque cultural misrepresentation.

Basically, it was a writer hiring someone from the Internet to tell the writer why they were wrong before other Internet people could tell the writer why they were wrong.

Imaginary narratives about fantasy worlds were being fact-checked!

By people who were about ten minutes away from making a sacrifice to Slender Man!

Like most efforts of the liberal intelligentsia to maintain plausible deniability about one's culpability in the global order of exploitation, the concept of the sensitivity reader dripped with unexamined racism.

It essentialized to an extreme degree, suggesting that there were inalienable qualities specific to arbitrary social constructs, and furthermore, that any one individual could comprehend, and identify, biases against millions of people based on nothing more than the accident of their birth.

Even the name was insane: it suggested that people from arbitrary social constructs had an innate sensitivity that differentiated them from other human beings, and that this sensitivity was based in a unique moral superiority.

And it is this thought—that the arbitrary circumstances of birth give the ability to comment on a slim range of human suffering—which has animated a central motif of the book that you are reading.

The motif in question is the idea that the purpose of the

Presidency of the United States of America is the transformation of Muslims into aching piles of ash and steaming puddles of blood.

As the towelheaded son of a dirty fucking immigrant camelfucker, I've focused on the most personally applicable aspect of the American War Machine and transformed it into a reccurring joke.

Yet, reader, does not this approach suffer from the sin of narrowness?

It's not as if the American War Machine has limited itself to the execution of Muslims in the Middle East and North African region.

It's not as if the American War Machine only fucks up the relatives of people who self-identify on the Internet as #MENA.

Ever since 9/11, the American War Machine has unleashed total chaos upon the world.

By the Year of the Froward Worm, seventy-two sovereign states were involved in its conflicts.

That's 39 per cent of the world's countries.

By the Year of the Froward Worm, about 13,486,400 refugees came from five countries: Syria, Afghanistan, South Sudan, Myanmar, and Somalia.

All five of these places had been touched by the American War Machine.

Five had been fucked with by the Central Intelligence Agency, the major intelligence agency of the American War Machine.

Four had hosted members of the American War Machine's military.

Three had been bombed by the American War Machine.

Two had hosted major American War Machine military operations.

One had hosted the longest war in the history of the American War Machine.

As I write this, America wages a secret war in Sub-Saharan Africa.

According to the best available information, this secret war is taking place in the following twenty countries: Mauritania, Senegal, Mali, Liberia, Burkina Faso, Ghana, Nigeria, Chad, Cameroon, the Central African Republic, Gabon, the Democratic Republic of Congo, Burundi, Tanzania, Uganda, Kenya, Somalia, Ethiopia, Djibouti, and Botswana.

The secret war is conducted under an American combatant command named AFRICOM.

Much like the multinational conglomerate that owns Penguin Random House, AFRICOM is headquartered in Germany.

If I had to guess, I'd suggest that about 0.5 per cent of the American population knows that AFRICOM exists.

Even that estimate is wild in its optimism, as it would mean that around 1.6 million people in the United States know their country is waging a secret war against Sub-Saharan Africa.

And based on the evidence, I find this to be impossible.

Here is that evidence: if fifty people freak out on Twitter about issues of racial misrepresentation in a cultural product about supranatural creatures, it generates coverage in the house organs of the American liberal intelligentsia.

Oh, the articles they'll write!
There is fun to be done!
There are points to be scored!
There are games to be won!

Fifty people is nothing.

Which means that the threshold for generating media interest is very low.

So if 1.6 million people know about the secret war in Sub-Saharan Africa, wouldn't this topic receive endless media coverage?

Insert your own joke here.

# Chapter Sixteen

## Drink of Me, Eat of Me

At the end of September in the Year of the Froward Worm, the women of Fairy Land left the house on the hill and followed the last strand.

Saliva-based navigation was responsive to changes in traffic patterns, and while the shortest route to their destination would have been to take Los Feliz Boulevard to the 5 onto the 10 and then come in through 4th Street, a traffic accident had made the 5 a complete horror show.

The saliva-based navigation directed the women on to Vermont to the 101 to the 110 and had them come in through 6th Street.

Because their destination was in Skid Row, and because they were on 6th Street, Rose Byrne drove the Jaguar XJ-S through the most abject scene of American cruelty.

What you have to realize about America is that America was a mug's game, it was a bullshit con, and nothing proved how fucked the country was more than Los Angeles's homeless population.

Official estimates in the Year of the Froward Worm, based on nothing, were 58,000 people.

Unofficial?

More like 100,000.

More people than had won Donald J. Trump his Electoral College victory!

And even that number might be low.

It was impossible to say.

There'd always been homeless people in Los Angeles, but the first decade of the Twenty-First Century AD hosted two events which pushed the situation into overdrive.

The first event was when nineteen Muslims attacked the United States with airplanes on September 11th, 2001 AD.

This provided the pretext for a series of unending wars in the Middle East.

Lots of Americans, like the former Adam Leroux, went over to foreign countries and killed a huge number of Muslims, and had the process fuck up their heads and bodies.

And unlike depictions of PTSD in cultural products made by Hollywood professionals, the consequences of this damage were more severe than flashback montages after someone mistook a traffic sign for a Shi'ite.

The other event was in 2007/8 AD, when predatory banking practices had collapsed the economy and obliterated the homes and wealth of a disproportionate number of African-American and Latino peoples.

So there were a bunch of former soldiers, who'd been given a glimpse of humanity at its worst, and as a result had been rendered unfit for society.

And there were a bunch of people without any money or homes.

And don't forget: the weather in Los Angeles was tolerable in every month of the year, which was untrue of almost every other place in the country.

And also don't forget: the Twentieth Century AD was about the ruthless exploitation of peoples' natural weaknesses for mind-altering chemicals, and this exploitation had been legitimized by every rung of society.

Despite best efforts by the money laundering of the international capitalist class, the neighborhood of Skid Row had not changed that much, and because the Jaguar XJ-S was on 6th Street, the women of Fairy Land had a perfect view.

The streets were lined with canvas tents and human bodies.

There were about fifty tents on each side of every block.

The women passed SROs, which were single-room-occupancy hotels that catered to the homeless. The women passed missions, which were Christian charities that attempted to feed and clothe the homeless. The women passed the Skid Row building of the Los Angeles Police Department, which was a state-funded apparatus that, amongst other tasks, kicked the shit out of homeless people.

What none of this conveys, really, is the squalor.

And, hey, it's mildly fucked up to write about the most destitute people in the country and say that they were living in filth.

It's not as if they don't know.

But at the same time, it's a fact.

The filth was off the charts.

There was trash and piss and shit and it was everywhere and it had been there for so long that it had changed the color of the sidewalks and the streets.

There's a way that you, reader, can measure the ways in which the American government had failed its most vulnerable citizens.

Google!

Google was a company that'd made more money off advertisements than any other company in the history of the world, but it had been founded by people who were embarrassed by a business model dependent upon advertising lawn chairs, car insurance, and Viagra.

To deflect the embarrassment, the company cloaked itself in an aura of innovation and some old bullshit about the expansion of human knowledge.

Google maintained this façade by providing web and mobile services to the masses.

The most beloved of these services was the near daily alteration of the company's logo as it appeared on the company's website.

Almost every day, the Google logo transformed into cutesy, diminutive cartoons of people who'd done something with their lives other than sell advertisements.

These cartoons were called Google Doodles.

They encompassed the whole spectrum of achievement, with a special focus on scientific achievement and the lives of minorities. In its own way, this was a perfect distillation of politics in the San Francisco Bay Area.

Whenever they appeared, the Google Doodles were beloved and celebrated in meaningless little articles on meaningless little websites.

They were not met with the obvious emotion, which would be total fucking outrage at a massive multinational corporation co-opting a wide range of human experience into an advertisement for that very same corporation.

Here was the perversity of Twenty-First-Century AD life: Native-American women had a statistically better chance of being caricatured in a Google Doodle than they did of being hired into a leadership position at Google.

And no one cared.

People were delighted!

They were being honored!

By a corporation!

But look, reader, before you assume your bien-pensant righteousness about the tech industry, let me point out that it's not as if publishing is any better.

Of the *New Yorker*'s forty-seven issues published in the Year of the Froward Worm, ten featured a cutesy illustration of a Black woman on the cover.

By my count, and this may be low because it's impossible to verify everyone's identity, the *New Yorker* published fourteen pieces by Black women.

If you assume an average contributor count of thirteen people per issue, then that's 611 contributors across the year, which comes out to exactly 2.29 per cent of the magazine's 2017 AD contributions being authored by Black women.

And ten out of forty-seven is 21.28 per cent.


Anyway.

In 2007 AD, Google introduced Google Street View.

Google Street View was a massive invasion of privacy.

It worked like this: Google bought cameras that could take a full 360-degree image.

Google strapped these cameras atop cars, and then hired people to drive these cars around America, while the camera took photographs every five feet. Then, using GPS geolocation, Google matched the images taken by the cameras to virtual locations on Google Maps.

You could put an address into Google Maps and see that location's real-world appearance at the exact moment when Google committed a privacy violation.

In 2014 AD, a timeline feature was introduced, which allowed the user to view the full history of Google's privacy violations.

In some places, this didn't mean anything, because Google had only sent a car out once.

In major cities, like Los Angeles, you could use the Street View timeline to look at a dense archive of imagery.

Reader, here is a game that you can play.

Go to Google Maps and search for "5th Street & Crocker Los Angeles."

Go to Street View.

Google will display its most recent invasion of privacy.

If you're savvy, you'll be able to figure out how to use the timeline.

If you aren't, ask a friend.

Go to the earliest image on the timeline, which should be from 2007 AD.

What you will see is an intersection in Skid Row.

While not in the best shape, it is not overrun with human misery.

Now move forward through the timeline.

Watch as the years pass by and watch as the human misery accumulates. Watch as the tents rise up. Watch as the suffering mounts. Watch as the bullshit con of America fails its most vulnerable citizens. Watch as liberal democracy dies.

And, yes, reader, it is sad.

And, yes, it is a shame.

But here we are.

You and me.

Or as they say in Turkish: *sen ve ben bebek.*

And we're still doing nothing.

Worse than HRH!

But doing nothing is better than Google, a corporation which has decided that, facing a social cataclysm, the appropriate course of action is to violate the privacy of the homeless and then post the evidence on the Internet.

The ropey smartphone navigation directed Rose Byrne to turn left from 6th onto Stanford Avenue.

The women saw their destination before they arrived.

The strand of magical saliva was wrapped around a two-story building surrounded by single-story warehouses.

The single-story warehouses were full of companies involved in the importing, exporting, and wholesaling of seafood.

But the women didn't need navigational saliva to tell them where they were going.

There was a line of disheveled people coming out of the two-story building.

Rose Byrne found a parking spot in front of the TUNA EXPRESS CO.

The women climbed out of the Jaguar and walked over to the building wrapped in smartphone navigation.

Celia's body was resonating with a green feeling.

Fern was in the building.

And if this were a book written by someone who still had the ability to build suspense or cared about meaningful plot resolution, there'd be about three-to-four thousand words about how Celia went in the building and found Fern and discovered what Fern was doing in Los Angeles.

And it would be so dramatic.

Your heart would be in my hands.

But this book isn't being written by that kind of someone.

I'm burnt out.

Donald J. Trump was elected to the Presidency of the United States!

So there's really no point.

Stop hoping that books will save you.

Stop pretending.

Everyone else has.

You aren't getting your three-to-four thousand words.

You're getting about four hundred and fifty.

The women of Fairy Land went into the building and found Fern on the top floor.

She was bringing homeless people into a backroom.

There was a tense reunion.

Celia demanded that Fern come home.

Fern refused.

Celia asked Fern what was so important about staying in Los Angeles.

Fern brought Celia into the backroom.

Fern showed Celia what the homeless people were doing in the backroom.

They were drinking the blood of the Fairy Knight, who was sitting in a plastic chair and had a tube coming out of a vein in his left arm.

The homeless guzzled his blood from the tube.

Fern said that she had found her brother nine months earlier.

He was hopelessly insane and haunting the boardwalk at Venice Beach.

Fern used magic to bring the Fairy Knight out of his insanity.

He awoke into sanity and said that he had been wandering the world for centuries.

The Fairy Knight said that while he was insane, he had converted to Christianity.

It'd happened in Avignon.

But then he'd gone so mad that he'd forgotten about everything.

Now that he was sane, he wanted to emulate one of the most basic Christian ideas, which was to give of himself to the poor.

As a magical being, his blood could serve as endless succor and would flow without end.

He wanted Fern to serve his magical blood to the homeless.

Fern cast some spells.

Fern found the building on Stanford Avenue.

The Fairy Knight opened shop.

The Fairy Knight gave succor to the most rejected people in America.

His blood nourished the poor and healed the sick.

Fern wanted to be with the Fairy Knight.

She wasn't going home.

She didn't care if the women of Fairy Land had to live without any charm in their lives.

Everyone else in the world lived without charmed lives.

If the worst thing that happened to the women of Fairy Land was a loss of charm in their lives, then they were doing better than the rest of the planet.

She too had converted to Christianity.

It had happened long before she rescued the Fairy Knight.
And now her brother's blood had given her life meaning.

# Chapter Seventeen

## How It All Went Down

Celia sent Rose Byrne back to Fairy Land.

There was much protestation, but the Queen is the Queen.

That's it.

Rose Byrne's gone from the book.

Celia spent the next few months in Los Angeles.

She cast a spell that taught her how to drive, and because she had a decent internal map from her forays into saliva navigation, she found her way around the city.

Sometimes she went to Hollywood Boulevard and strolled atop the Walk of Fame, dodging the tourists, and doing a supranatural trick where she saw the whole history, the layers of time superimposed on one another, going back to the beginning, to the Hadean.

And other times she went to Stanford Avenue and talked with her children as the homeless drank the blood of her son.

Her children proselytized to their mother.

They told her about Jesus Christ and his redemptive powers that would give mortals life after death and wash away their sins.

Celia's children kept talking about Heaven and the crucifixion and eternal life and the Epistles of Paul.

They wanted Celia to convert to Christianity.

Celia couldn't get on that trip.

Celia could smell the bullshit.

One Sunday morning, Celia went for a walk.

She took the precarious route down Glendower Ave, which had been built for the rich and thus didn't have usable sidewalks, and went to Vermont Ave.

She walked past gigantic Moreton Bay figs.

The trees reminded her of Fairy Land.

She traveled west on Los Feliz Boulevard and then south for several blocks on Edgemont, passing into a significantly poorer area with the crossing of every east–west boulevard.

At the corner of Fountain, she heard singing.

The voices were coming from a white building on the northwest corner.

The sound reminded Celia of the Ceremony of the Grunting Skyrock, a recent addition to Fairy Land's festival calendar.

The Ceremony of the Grunting Skyrock had been instituted in the Year of the Pleasurable Caravan, which roughly corresponded to 1000 AD, 390 AH, and 4760 AM.

In the Year of the Unmemorable Salt, which directly preceded the Year of the Pleasurable Caravan, a rock had fallen from the sky and smashed into Fairy Land.

Somehow the magic of Fairy Land had prevented any property damage, but the meteorite did leave one hell of a hole.

The women of Fairy Land kept the meteorite in its hole until someone realized that a giant rock from the sky was as good excuse as any to throw a party.

The Ceremony of the Grunting Skyrock involved a lot of choral singing.

For reasons that were always mysterious, the songs that the women sang were filthy tavern ballads about sex and human beings who couldn't stop pissing their own pants.

One of the songs, which was old Turkic-Roma magic, went like this:

*Bu kimin donu*
*Kaynanamın donu*
*Ben yıkamam onu*
*Bok kokuyor donu*

Despite their lyrical subjects, the songs sounded beautiful. When a hundred voices rise up as one, all individual imperfections disappear into a flawless unity.

And that's what Celia heard coming out of the white building.

Celia went into the white building. It turned out to be the HOPE International Bible Fellowship, housed in what had once been the Fountain Avenue Baptist Church.

The building wasn't much changed from when it opened in 1929 AD. It was the same shape and it still had people sitting in its pews and they were still listening to bullshit about how to worship Jesus Christ.

Celia took a seat in a back pew, next to a small woman.

The Queen of Fairy Land watched as the humans went through the motions, none of which made any sense, and she sat through the sermon, which she couldn't quite understand.

This wasn't because Celia didn't have a firm theological basis in Bible study.

Celia couldn't follow the sermon because it relied on two conflicting cultural shorthands that were presented as if they were in harmony.

Christian sermons in American life were always more about America than Christianity, and America was the ideological enemy of Christianity.

When the service was over and the Christians had stopped singing and shaking hands, Celia wondered what the hell she'd just seen.

The woman sitting beside Celia noticed the Fairy Queen's confusion.

"You are new here?" asked the woman.

"Is this a church?" asked Celia. "I have read about churches but I have never been inside a church."

"Yes, this is a church," said the woman.

"My children have become Christians," said Celia. "My son and my daughter."

"My children," said the woman, "they are not so good about church. You are lucky."

"Am I?" asked Celia.

"Yes," said the woman. "I wish my children they were thinking about Jesus."

"My children will not stop," said Celia.

"Beautiful," said the woman.

"I am not certain," said Celia. "It has been very painful."

The woman reached into her purse. She pulled out a book. She put the book in Celia's hands.

"Read this," said the woman. "You will make sense of your children."

Celia looked down at the book.

On its black cover, there were gold foil letters that said:

# HOLY BIBLE
## King James Version

The pre-Internet library of Fairy Land had never included a copy of the Bible.

Not in any of its forms or translations.

This was an oversight, particularly as the Bible was one of

the three most influential literary works ever published. The other two were القرآن and the seven volumes of J.K. Rowling's *Harry Potter*.

The *King James Version* of the Bible was a 1611 AD English translation of the Christian Bible, which was originally put together in the Fourth Century AD, and was comprised of two parts, the Old Testament and the New Testament.

The Old Testament was a collection of documents that'd emerged from the Jewish faith.

There existed another version of the texts, used by Jewish people in a very different way than Christians, called the תַּנַ״ךְ.

There were a lot of stories in the Old Testament, but the underlying Christian interpretation suggested that it was a book about YHWH, a divinity who had created the world and all of the living beings on the planet, and then spent thousands of years torturing his creations.

The New Testament was primarily about the life of Jesus Christ, his disciples, and the implications of his message as it carried through the world.

Despite having never read the Christian Bible, Celia was the one person on Earth who had an innate critical apparatus for comprehending the disjunction between the Old and New Testaments.

She'd spent about four hundred years reading and thinking about *Tom a Lincoln*, which was another book split into two parts.

Of this structure, Richard S.M. Hirsch writes: "[Richard Johnson] … had early on decided … to organize his matter in two parts, in this case showing heroic exploits in Part I, and the moral retribution for them in Part II."

In other words, Part I of *Tom a Lincoln* was about a father who did some weird shit, and Part II was about the father's son paying the price for that weird shit.

Which was the Christian Bible in a nutshell.

Celia brought the *King James* back to the house on the hill.

She read.

It took several weeks.

The *King James* wasn't *Game of Thrones* long, but it was pretty close.

The Old Testament was ancient, and other than the *Song of Solomon*, which induced at least one meat-market visit to Tenants of Trees, reading it felt like being back in Fairy Land, like inhabiting a universe of unclear moral rules, where the brutality of magic could break your spirit on nothing more than a whim.

The New Testament was different.

Celia couldn't grasp the epistles.

*The Revelation of St. John the Divine* was a bore.

Even *Acts of the Apostles* was difficult.

But she understood the gospels, which were four narratives about Jesus Christ and his life.

And because Celia'd developed that critical faculty, she could weed out an author's made-up bullshit from the reality upon which he'd built his narrative.

For centuries, she'd been doing this with *Tom a Lincoln*, seeing where the fictional account of herself differed from the reality, and comparing the Red-Rose Knight's pillow talk about his childhood with Richard Johnson's early chapters.

Here was Celia's conclusion: Jesus was weird as fuck.

This was the actual Jesus, Jesus without the Christ, not the totemic icon used as justification for a thousand awful wars and for millions of deaths.

This was not the Jesus of Fern and the Fairy Knight.

This was not Jesus of the Church or the churches.

This was not the Jesus of the mean-spirited American, the smiling face that blessed slavery and indigenous genocide, the impetus behind KILL A QUEER FOR CHRIST.

This was the real Jesus.

Until his advent, the ancient world had never placed any intellectual premium on kindness or mercy.

Even good people like Diogenes of Sinope or Epicurus had the habit of talking about virtue as a thing that could be developed by the self for the self. If people wrote or thought about sacrifice, it was in the service of the state or the dominant group.

Never in service of the powerless.

And then Jesus arrived from Bumfuck Shitsville, which, despite its proximity to Sepphoris, is what Nazareth was, and he spoke Aramaic with a hick Galilean accent, and he was a carpenter's son, and he hung around with the filth of society. Sex workers, illiterate fisherman, lepers, literary agents, and tax collectors.

He was nobody.

And he talked funny.

And what he said, the core message, delivered in that hick accent, was this: *stop being a total fucking dick.*

If someone hits your face, offer them the other cheek.

Forgive those who trespass against you.

Serve others before serving yourself.

The poor shall inherit the Earth.

Throw away your possessions.

Mercy is the greatest good.

Don't cast the first stone.

Worry not over money.

Embrace the sick.

These ideas have been repeated so many times that they've become platitudes, bumper-sticker morality for the users of Twitter and depressed women of Instagram.

They're like anything in an era of mass production.

Reduced into meaninglessness, transformed into marketable product.

T-shirts.

Words divorced from ideas.

Sharp edges smoothed down.

Yet the intent remains. Jesus had asked his followers to follow a moral code that violated every known precept of human nature.

Consider, by contrast, the trilogy of plays by Aeschylus known as the *Oresteia*.

The *Oresteia* goes like this: Agamemnon, from the House of Atreus and King of Mycenae, returns home after being away for over a decade. He's been in Troy, where he practiced the art of ethnic cleansing.

Before Agamemnon left for war, the goddess Artemis ordered him to sacrifice his daughter.

So he did.

He killed his daughter and sailed off to be a hero.

While Agamemnon spent ten years practicing ethnic cleansing across the Aegean Sea, his wife Clytemnestra stewed over the murder of her daughter. She took a lover named Aegisthus.

When her husband returns to Mycenae, Clytemnestra and Aegisthus murder Agamemnon and then assume the crown.

Years later, the son of Clytemnestra and Agamemnon, a guy named Orestes, comes to Mycenae. On orders from the god Apollo, he murders his mother and Aegisthus.

Unfortunately, there are these mythological things called the Erinyes.

The Erinyes, or the Furies, are the living embodiment of vengeance. They torment anyone who breaks the basic rules of society.

One of these rules: don't fuck with hospitality customs.

Another: don't kill your mother.

The Furies chase Orestes all over Greece, until one night, they fall asleep and Apollo spirits Orestes away to Athens, where the matricide begs help from the goddess Athena.

Athena puts Orestes on trial in Athens. He gets prosecuted, he has to defend himself.

The trial ends with a split jury. Athena casts the final vote in favor of Orestes, which frees him, and which also pisses the Furies off.

They scream and shout about the sorrow they're going to wreak upon the world as revenge for the insult. They spit and they foam.

Athena, meanwhile, is the face of reason and calm. She soothes the Furies, slowly, suggesting a better function for them in the world. Why rage when you can help mankind and be worshipped? Who wants all that grief when life can be easy?

The Furies agree and undergo a metaphysical transformation.

They become the Kindly Ones.

They've been tamed by Athena, the personification of Wisdom.

The *Oresteia* is an allegorical representation of a major event in human history. It's a stand-in for the establishment of civil justice. It's about how societies maintain order in the face of outrageous crimes.

The theme is so universal that all you have to do is engage with any website for about five minutes before you find yourself in the middle of the same debate.

The *Oresteia* offers a comprehensible vision that works on shared assumptions of how human beings operate.

You might not be able to claim blood for blood, but the court system still allows you a claim of retribution. Wrongs are made right and the world is put into order.

There will be justice.

But not vengeance.

If Jesus had been advising Orestes, this is what he would have said: *Forgive your mother for killing your father. Ask her to kill you next. If she refuses, bring her into your home and feed and clothe her. Love her. And expect no reward for doing as I command you. There is nothing you stand to gain by this mercy other than mercy itself.*

One must have as much sympathy for the perpetrator of a crime as for the crime's victim.

This is an inhuman standard.

Even Celia, who wasn't human, couldn't wrap her head around it.

Taken to its furthest logical extreme, the implication is that people don't have to follow the scripts of their lives.

You are more than your base urges.

You don't have to be as terrible as everyone else.

You don't have to burn with pointless judgment.

There is another way.

And it is guided by absolute mercy and radical compassion.

This crazy hick showed up in sophisticated ol' Jerusalem, where everyone posted on social media about the decline of society.

And he spoke of love and forgiveness and mercy and brotherhood.

And he told the people of Jerusalem that they didn't have to follow the scripts of their lives.

So they killed him.

199,900 years of shitting in the living room.

He was crucified, given the lowest of all deaths.

"Ow, that really hurts," said Jesus when the Roman legionnaire Casca Longinus thrust his spear into Jesus' side.

"Give a fuck, me," said Casca Longinus. "Haddaway and shite, you poof."

Then Jesus died.

And maybe he came back to life.

Who fucking knows?

Anything's possible in a world so supranatural that Donald J. Trump ends up in control of 6,800 nuclear warheads.

## Chapter Eighteen

# Bleak House

To understand how I ended up winning a $1.2-million judgment in a lawsuit against an Internet stalker who libeled me as a rapist, we have to go back to the early dim days of when I first decided to be a writer.

This was back around 2007 AD, when I was newly arrived in the city of Los Angeles.

I went west after the collapse of a romantic relationship that had lasted seven years, and I had moved to Los Angeles with the unconscious desire to be one of the people who come to California to die.

Much to my surprise, it turned out that moving to Los Angeles wouldn't kill you.

So I had to do something.

Being a writer seemed as bad a fate as any.

In the first decade of the Twenty-First Century AD, there was a vogue called blogging.

Blogging happened when people operated websites and used those websites to publish their own inane commentary on the issues of the day.

There was a sense, then, that one could somehow launch blogging into a career as a writer.

Don't ask me to explain this.

I did the same thing as every other pathetic would-be writer in the first decade of the Twenty-First Century AD.

I started my own blog.

I offered inane commentary on pointless bullshit.

My blog attracted a small but dedicated readership. I'm sure that the daily writing probably helped in some way, but fuck me if I can tell you how.

One member of that small but dedicated readership would end up becoming a huge problem.

At the time, I didn't know their real name, but they'd left several comments on my blog, and they'd always use the same pseudonym: "Oyster the Clown."

The comments were about me being a big ol' homo.

In June of 2008 AD, the same person had sent me an email.

It made no sense.

This was the full extent of the communication between me and Oyster the Clown.

By 2009 AD, I'd stopped writing on the blog.

The website was still there, with its senseless opinions getting no younger, but I couldn't be bothered.

I was doing a million other things, including figuring out how to get books published.

If my career as a writer felt non-existent when I was sexually harassed by Amber Tamblyn, then in 2009 AD I was something below that.

My career wasn't even a career.

It was a stupid little idea on which I'd wasted too much time when I could have been doing things that actually made money.

Literally no one knew me as a writer.

There was nothing to know.

I should also mention that this happened before I lived in San Francisco.

I had yet to be exposed to the mendacity of the people who make money off the Internet.

My faith in humanity was not yet murdered.

I was much softer.

Over Thanksgiving of 2009 AD, while I was celebrating the genocide of the indigenous peoples of the Americas, someone went on the website of *Vice* and left comments on about fifty articles.

*Vice* was a media platform that specialized in gross-out journalism and videos in which a sneering idiot from Brooklyn would visit a war-torn locale and contextualize the havoc in terms that could be understood by American children.

The comments said two things.

"Jarett Kobek is a rapist" or "Jarett Kobek is a pedophile."

*Hello*, said I to myself, *you're neither a rapist nor a pedophile! Why, these comments on the Internet are simply not true!*

Because I am good with computers, I was able to figure out that these comments had been posted from Woodland Hills, California, which was about twenty miles from my apartment in Los Angeles.

I was also able to figure out that they had been posted by Oyster the Clown.

This was not a happy moment.

It's difficult to be libeled as a rapist and a pedophile on the Internet and not feel as if the sky is collapsing on your head.

It is an awful thing to experience.

*Someone is out to get you*, said I to myself.

At the time, reader, I didn't know it but I was encountering the very strange and new experience of someone writing Jarett Kobek fanfiction.

Generally speaking, fanfiction is written whenever someone decides that they want to tell a story about an intellectual property to which they have no legal rights.

A good example would be when a Batman true believer wants to offer up a prayer and types a little story about Batman kicking the shit out of The Joker.

Or snogging The Riddler.

Or whatever.

These stories tend to go into the Internet.

Alas, many of them, like the Jarett Kobek fanfiction, are about pedophilia and rape!

And, reader, as we've read about someone else's Jarett Kobek fanfiction, I shall write a bit of my own.

I'll tell you a story about the failure of *The Future Won't Be Long*.

You'll have to pardon me, as this fanfiction will be short on both pedophilia and rape.

But it will employ the grotesque language of business.

Which is almost as bad.

If you believe in brands, then you must also believe that the success of any brand derives from its ability to reflect and be defined by its core values.

If, following the self-published US release of *I Hate the Internet*, you can conceive of a Jarett Kobek brand, then you must also conceive that its core value was this: *fuck you*.

Self-publishing meant that *I Hate the Internet* had erupted into the world with no permission, no rules, and disconnected from the social and class strictures dominating American writing.

And the novel's text had done something nearly impossible: it had shit on the rich not from a sense of envy but rather one of superiority.

The brand said this: *I denounce thee.*

*I denounce thee, publishing.*

*I denounce thee, civility.*

*I denounce thee, you masters of reality.*

*Fuck you.*

After *I Hate the Internet* was released and succeeded beyond his wildest ambitions, Jarett Kobek couldn't imagine any direction other than going to one of the five major publishers.

At the moment of his triumph, Jarett Kobek suffered a failure of imagination.

He flung himself at Penguin Random House with all the vigor of a dog returning to its own vomit.

He allowed himself to be published in the trade dress of a literary writer.

He revealed himself as a class pretender, as someone who believed that he could operate on the level of Jonathan Franzen, as the kind of fraud who'd take that misbegotten Treblinka money and run run run.

It was the smart decision.

But the smart decision was what it always is.

The anti-life equation.

The death of fuck you.

And, boy, did Jarett Kobek ever pay the price.

In the end, his ultimate *fuck you* was to himself.

Anyway.

*Vice* deleted the comments.

I spent the new few weeks Googling my own name, obsessively, wondering when Oyster the Clown would strike again.

But nothing happened.

Silence.

In early April of 2010 AD, I visited San Francisco, where I delivered a paper on the underground comix artist Rory Hayes at a comic-book convention.

During my visit, I received an email informing me that I'd been subscribed to the mailing list of Biggayfrathouse.com, a website dedicated to a Big Gay Frat House in San Francisco's Castro District.

The email carried the IP address of the person who subscribed me.

An IP address is the individual marker of any point of access to the Internet.

The IP address in the email resolved to a Comcast Cable account in Washington DC.

In about 1,000 words, this will be an important detail.

I Googled for my own name and discovered that a few minutes after I'd been subscribed to the mailing list of Big Gay Frat House, someone had gone to the website of CNN and posted two comments on an article about the screenwriter Diablo Cody's pregnancy.

The first comment was from someone calling themselves, "oyster."

The first comment read: "Abort it now!"

Just below, "Jarett Kobek" had commented: "I do enjoy a good fetus rape."

Things again fell silent.

On May 3rd, 2010 AD, an article that I'd written was published both in print and online.

It detailed a visit that I'd made in 2009 AD to northern Iraq, where I'd spent a small amount of time at Lalish, the central religious shrine of the Yezidi, who are a persecuted religious culture from Syria and Iraq.

Getting the article published was a total pain in the ass.

This was well before the Yezidi were genocided by the Islamic State in 2014 AD, which meant that the Yezidi were not yet a story that appealed to the editorial class.

And the ultimate thrust of what I wanted to write was an unpopular message on the verge of America's supposed withdrawal of military troops from Iraq.

The thrust was this: *We've made a huge mess and these people will pay the price.*

It took a year, but I ended up publishing with the

*NYU Alumni Magazine* on the advice of my friend Rich Byrne, who said that glossy alumni magazines tended to pay serious money.

He wasn't kidding.

I got $1,800 for a 1,500-word piece.

The editorial process was tortured, and the article was a disaster, and somehow the whole thing ended up as a holiday in other people's misery.

It functioned in the exact same way as videos on *Vice.*

Someone shows up in a crisis zone and leaves anointed with a superficial knowledge of other people's pain.

On the night of the article's publication, the situation with Oyster the Clown exploded.

Hundreds of comments were left across a wide spectrum of websites.

These were the usual: gay/rapist/pedophile.

The really dangerous stuff was the accounts opened in my name.

Facebook accounts.

Accounts on one of Google's early attempts on social media.

And most insidious of all, an account on YouTube, which contained a surprising amount of personal information in the profile data.

The YouTube account had been used to leave endless comments on videos of children.

These comments were not savory.

There was other stuff too.

I'm not going to bother to recount it here.

This went on for about a month.

New comments, new accounts.

Meanwhile, I was finishing the manuscript of *ATTA*, and I knew that it was the first significant writing that I'd done, and I further knew that its completion would necessitate getting in touch with professionals in the publishing industry.

I also knew that the first thing that professionals in the publishing industry would do, if they were considering the manuscript, was search for my name on Google.

The results would be the fake Jarett Kobek perving out on videos of children and hundreds of comments about my pedophilia.

And the job of any competent publishing-industry professional is finding an excuse to say no.

By this point, I'd wasted about two or three years on the bullshit of writing.

I didn't need anyone else's help fucking up my life.

It was too late to go back now.

Something had to be done.

At the time, I was poor as fuck.

But class in America is a weird thing.

Half of it is money.

Half of it is social access.

I had no money, but I did have social access.

I ended up talking to a friend of a friend, who was a lawyer at the Electronic Frontier Foundation.

They passed on the name of a law firm in San Francisco that routinely dealt with this shit.

"What would you do?" I asked the friend of a friend.

"Sue the fucker," said the friend of the friend.

So I did.

I sued the fucker.

My attorneys were Ridder, Costa & Johnstone of San Francisco.

And here's another way that I was poor but not poor.

I paid the attorneys with money that I got from my family.

If you ever want to sound like an insane person, cold call some attorneys and tell them that you're being impersonated on the Internet by someone who is libeling you as a rapist and a pedophile.

Imagine that conversation!

As I'd spent some time discussing the situation with friends, I knew the first question that the attorneys would ask.

"Do you have any idea who's doing this?"

"No," I said.

In that initial phone call, the lawyers said that in their experience almost all of these cases derived from romantic entanglement.

An ex-boyfriend, an ex-girlfriend, or the ex-boyfriend or ex-girlfriend's new partner.

When men were targeted, it was always the same: rapist, pedophile, homosexual.

With women, it was: slut, whore, skank.

Often accompanied by boudoir media taken in a haze of coercion or deluded innocence.

Remember: this happened back in 2010 AD.

A more innocent time!

What made the actions of my stalker so egregious were their relative rarity.

Hardly anyone was dealing with this shit.

By the Year of the Froward Worm, which roughly corresponded to 2017 AD, 1438 AH, and 5777 AM, about 40 per cent of online political and social discourse was indistinguishable from the treatment I'd received at the hands of Oyster the Clown.

Seven years after my misery, and everyone was being smeared as a rapist and a pedophile!

One of the common points in the literature available to victims of stalking is the idea that the victim will go through a period of self-recrimination. They will hunt down their every ill deed and wonder which one was the cause of their current misfortune.

The literature is uniform in its rejection of the victim bearing any responsibility for their misfortune.

*It's not your fault*, says the literature.

But, in my case, I find this to be bullshit.

I went through my period of self-recrimination, and my only conclusion was that the whole thing was my fault.

I had put myself out there.

No one had asked me to write a blog.

No one had asked me to be a writer.

I had done this to myself.

This was another instance in which my situation had anticipated the political and social tactics of the Year of the Froward Worm.

People who made the mistake of putting themselves out there, with the delusion that they should have a voice in the public sphere, were sifted through a purity test in which every public utterance that they'd ever made was given ruthless scrutiny.

If you were delusional enough to be an artist or a writer, you had to anticipate that the only possible reaction your work could receive was unfathomable amounts of hatred.

Let's say that Donald J. Trump, the President, decides that he's going to ban all Muslims from entering America.

Let's say that he effects this ban by issuing an Executive Order, which was a way for the President to do whatever the fuck he wanted under the pretext of the law without having Congressional approval.

Now let's imagine some slightly clueless person with a Twitter account.

This person is enraged by Donald J. Trump's Muslim ban.

This isn't his America!

His America doesn't ban Muslims!

His America just murders them by dropping bombs on peasant villages!

This person decides that they want to criticize Donald J. Trump's Muslim ban.

The way by which this slightly clueless person enacts his criticism is with a stupid little cartoon.

He draws big fat Donald J. Trump riding a beleaguered elephant, which is the go-to caricatured symbol of the Republican party. The elephant is trampling an America flag.

A dialogue balloon comes out of big fat cartoon Donald Trump's mouth and it says, "I'm protecting America."

At the bottom of the cartoon, another dialogue balloon comes out of the elephant's mouth.

It says, "Plus he hates Ragheads. He's not crazy about Spics either."

Whose life will be ruined for at least several years?

Will it be the person who banned Muslims and ripped apart families and is literally killing people in the Middle East while ensuring that Palestinians live in misery?

Or will it be the person who attempted to criticize the person who bans Muslims, and in doing so used exaggerated rhetoric in an admittedly awkward attempt to strike at the truth?

Who will suffer?

Who will be haunted until their end of days?

The rich person or the poor person?

You'll never guess what happens.

When I wrote the first draft of this chapter, I decided that it was only sporting to give my readers an opportunity to contribute to my eventual destruction, which is now the unavoidable fate of anyone who has ever been a writer.

What I had put in this very spot, reader, were some cheap misdeeds from my past.

The unstated joke about these cheap misdeeds was that none were particularly damning.

In the end, I'm just a shy, bookish person.

Happily, between the writing of that first draft and the publication of this book, I've committed a far greater sin than anything I could have confessed from my past.

In that window of time, I wrote and published a short book in defense of XXXTentacion.

XXXTentacion was a young musician who was shot to death at the age of twenty.

He was murdered after he'd been arrested and accused of beating the living daylights out of his pregnant girlfriend.

And the shooting occurred after he'd bragged, in an interview, about a homophobia-inspired beating of a fellow inmate in Florida juvenile detention.

These two incidents had caused much morality written on deadline.

He was the person who unified everyone across the political spectrum in their disgust.

He was the new O.J. Simpson.

And I defended him.

Without ambiguity, without shame.

I had sympathy for the devil.

Without repentance, without prejudice.

So there's your raw material.

Go right ahead.

You can use almost any page of that XXXTentacion book to fuck up my career!

Rob me of the opportunity to contribute shitty opinion pieces to a dying news media!

Deprive me of the ability to be hired as faculty at a small liberal arts college where I can delude the stupid and the rich into thinking that they'll be writers!

The future is in your hands!

Slender Man commands you!

But, reader, I give you fair warning.

You might be able to fuck up my shit, but no matter how much you huff and puff, you'll never take away my tote bag that says BOOKS.

When my lawyers asked me who I thought might be responsible, I offered a crazy person's answer: I suggested that my blogging had worked as sorcery and I'd summoned up a demon that was haunting me for the crime of hubris.

The suggestion was politely ignored.

My attorneys filed suit in Los Angeles Superior Court.

They received power of subpoena.

Power of subpoena meant that they could send out demands to the Internet service providers in Woodland Hills and Washington DC.

And when the subpoenas came back, we'd have the name of my stalker.

There's a story in here that I can't tell you, because it would go back on a promise that my attorneys made to a third party, but we very quickly ended up with the name of the person responsible for all the bother.

I'd been harboring the delusion that, when the name was revealed, it would play out like Agatha Christie, and the unmasking would give me a sense of understanding and wisdom.

But that's not what happened.

It was someone that I didn't know.

At all.

Hadn't met.

Not once.

With no connection to anyone that I'd ever known.

There was no reason behind the stalking and libel.

It was random.

And I could give you my stalker's name, right now, immortalizing them in the annals of literature. There's nothing stopping me. I can't be punished for reporting on public records available in the case files of Los Angeles Superior Court.

But as I've been writing this chapter, I've reflected on how life plays out.

And how strange things have become.

Back when I was being stalked, there was no question that I was on a level playing field with my stalker.

I was no one.

He was no one.

But things have changed.

I'm an international bestseller, I've done countless radio appearances, I've been on television more times than is good for the spiritual health of any one person, I've been chased at the Frankfurt Book Fair by a swarm of book paparazzi, sat through about one hundred and fifty interviews, I've been hotboxed by Alan Moore, I've had Carl Bernstein talk to me about how his son plays guitar for Demi Lovato, I've informed Seymour Hersh about my cat's irritable bowels, and I've annoyed Zadie Smith for about forty minutes at a reception filled with billionaires, Salman Rushdie, and the Jordanian royal family.

I'm famous in Serbia.

I'm writer-famous in Germany and the United Kingdom.

The power differential has shifted.

And we must embrace mercy above all things.

When my attorneys gave me my stalker's name, I spent about a week putting together a picture of who'd been fucking with my shit.

There was a near vacuum of information, but he had a page on the Internet Movie Database, and I was able to figure out that he was a thirty-four-year-old man from Washington DC.

He was a failed screenwriter.

Unemployed and living with his parents.

And the namesake of his father.

He was a junior.

At the very moment when Junior was fucking up my shit from the family's million-dollar row house, Senior was in the United States Senate, working as an assistant to a long-serving Republican.

I was being fucked with by Republicans in Washington DC!

For the first time in my life, I felt like a true American artist.

The father had spent decades working his way up through the Republican hierarchy, until he ascended into a job with the Republican Finance Committee. At one point, ABC News had called him, "One of the Republican party's top officials."

It had all fallen apart in 1996 AD, when the RFC was hit with a sexual harassment lawsuit that specifically focused on Senior. It alleged that on a near daily basis, Senior expected to fondle his female subordinates.

The culmination came in October 1996 AD, when *20/20*, a television show, ran a report on the lawsuit and on Senior in specific.

It contained footage of Senior at a Republican holiday party, dressed like Santa Claus, leering at younger woman.

It also contained footage of Senior being confronted at the Republican National Convention by the reporter Brian Ross, asking Senior to explain why he had sexually harassed women while dressed like Santa Claus.

This was the beginning of the end.

Senior kept getting demoted to lesser and lesser positions in the Republican hierarchy until he ended up working in the Senate as an assistant.

Reader, let me say this: I'm sorry that this book has included two sexualized mentions of Santa Claus.

None of this is what I wanted.

This is what life has done to me.

In May of 2000 AD, the *Washington Times* ran a puff piece about the previous home of my stalker's parents. This was where they were living before they bought the row house.

It was the sort of rubbish that newspapers run whenever a rich person wants to sell their home. Stuffed with quaint, folksy detail.

My stalker's mother is quoted in the article, talking about how the home was haunted.

She tells a story about how the ghosts had fucked with a wheel of cheese.

I was being stalked by a person who'd grown up with a haunted wheel of cheese whose father had been exposed on national news for leering at women while dressed as Santa Claus.

That's life.

No one ever said it'd be easy.

It's very easy to laugh about these absurdities, but there was another way to look at the situation and quake with dread.

I had stuck my nose in a hornet's nest.

These were very rich people.

And they were very well connected.

They were consummate Republican insiders.

And I was fucking with them.

Reader, I could supply you with endless details about the intrigues of the case and how my stalker dodged being served with the lawsuit, and how his parents aided and abetted him in dodging service, and how he finally accepted service after I had my attorneys call his sister and leave a message on her work voicemail.

But I'm only going to give the basics.

Before my stalker accepted service, Senior ended up on the phone with my attorneys, and he tried to talk them out of the lawsuit.

He threatened and he blustered.

He finally claimed that Junior suffered from "nerve problems" which kept him from working, but that he'd try to get his son on board with the lawsuit.

He said that he couldn't understand why anyone would waste the resources suing his son, given that his son had no money.

I can't remember what my attorneys said in response.

Had I been asked, I would have said this: *I'm from Rhode Island.*

Rhode Island is the smallest of America's fifty states.

It has the longest official name: The State of Rhode Island and Providence Plantations.

I haven't lived in Rhode Island for nearly twenty years.

But I'm always from Rhode Island.

Whenever someone from Rhode Island is on reality television, they're always the worst of the worst of the worst. They're the people television producers cast because they know that the presence of a Rhode Islander is a shortcut to endless drama.

Rhode Island was founded in the Seventeenth Century AD by the most obnoxious people in the New World.

People like Roger Williams and Anne Hutchinson.

They had fled England because their bad personalities threw their neighbors into murderous rages. They sailed across the Atlantic and settled in bullshit Massachusetts hellholes like Salem and Boston.

And then their bad personalities promptly threw the new neighbors into murderous rages.

They were banished from Massachusetts.

And they had to go somewhere.

So they went and founded Rhode Island.

The crazy never left.

It's still there.

Think of it like this: unlike every other colony in New England, Rhode Island never had a witch trial. But we sure as fuck dug up some old corpses, cut out their hearts, and called them vampires.

If Senior had asked me why I was suing his son, this is what I would have said: *Your son made a terrible error in judgment. He thought that the limits of his own imagination were the boundaries of the universe. But he had no idea about the chaos of Rhode Island. There's a reason why it says INRI on the cross.*

After the phone call with my attorneys, Senior convinced his son to accept service.

And then they stonewalled.

Months went by.

By stonewalling, what Senior did was this: he hung his only son out to dry.

I wasn't stopping.

I was from Rhode Island.

And my attorneys were fucking sharks.

If you're ever sued, there's good strategy and there's stupid strategy, and then there's the worst strategy.

Which is to do nothing.

And that's what my stalker did.

Despite all of my attorneys' phone calls, despite the constant forwarding of documents and filings related to the case.

He did nothing.

His parents would not help him.

We kept going, kept moving the case along, and we ended up filing a default motion.

When a defendant refuses to interact with the civil courts, the plaintiff enters a motion of default. When the motion is granted, the plaintiff then enters the documents for a default judgment.

If the court accepts the plaintiff's plea for judgment, it means that the plaintiff has won the case. There is an accepted absolute veracity in the plaintiff's filings.

The defendant agrees, tacitly, that all of the plaintiff's claims are true. The defendant agrees, tacitly, that they are not contesting their responsibility.

My attorneys filed the proposed default judgment.

On February 11th, 2011 AD, Justice Daniel J. Buckley of the Los Angeles Superior Court signed off on the full requested amount.

$1,235,144.75.

One million two hundred thirty-five thousand one hundred forty-four dollars and seventy-five cents.

My attorneys had derived this figure as the ultra-extreme of what the law allowed.

I haven't tried to collect on the judgment, which has compounding 10 per cent yearly interest.

As of this writing, my stalker owes me $2,406,947.70.

By the time this book is published, the amount will be more.

And that's the last contact I ever had with my Internet stalker.

All of the comments he left about me are gone.

All of the accounts he made in my name are gone.

It's like none of it ever happened.

But given that it did, I hope you'll forgive me when I express discomfort with an entire society, and its decaying journalistic apparatus, orienting itself around the destruction of individuals based on things posted to the Internet.

# Chapter Nineteen

## Exeunt Rusticano

A magical island devoid of its charm would be like feminism in a society where all the men had been expelled or murdered. Pretty fucking pointless.

Celia did the only thing that she could.

She called in the Big Dog.

She summoned Rusticano.

He'd been off Fairy Land for three hundred years.

There had been no word in a century.

But he had lived on Fairy Land for centuries and the background radiation of its magic had made him undying.

He was somewhere on Earth.

Celia cast a spell.

Rusticano was transported straight into the house on the hill.

He arrived midsentence, in a burst of light and untamed magic.

"… und deshalb empfehle ich immer einen Tampon," he said.

In the Gray's Inn adaptation of *Tom a Lincoln*, Rusticano occupies the traditional role of an Elizabethan/Jacobean clown.

He's a lower-class brute in a fictional world where everyone else in resplendent in their finery and goes on about Fairy Queens and dragons.

Rusticano is the one who, in the middle of a speech about the redemptive blood of the Savior, can be relied upon to unleash the world's most unholy fart.

It's the simplest of things, but the device works.

The device always works.

Upper-class social mores, as constructed by the middle-class people who create cheap entertainments, are structured around a pretense that people with money and power believe themselves to be something more than dumb animals.

Enter Rusticano's fart.

What greater rebuke to the pretense of non-animal man than the trumpet-like sound of stinky methane being expelled from a clown's ass?

But that was just a play written to amuse rich kids.

There was a real Rusticano, and other than the name, he shared nothing in common with his fictional iteration.

Rusticano was a human oddity.

He was the one man who'd come to Fairy Land and escaped the hangman's noose.

After the Red-Rose Knight was killed by Orson's shit, the women of Fairy Land rounded up all of the Red-Rose Knight's men.

The men died screaming.

Every single one of the men had defended themselves with weaponry and brute force.

Except Rusticano.

In the massacre, Rose Byrne had been the chief executioner, but she didn't command the task force. Leadership fell to Celia, who stood on a chariot pulled by Fairy Land's meanest buckskin stallions.

Her warrior women followed behind like a bridal train.

When the chariot arrived at the Babbling Brook of Sorrow, where Rusticano spent his days, Rusticano did not flee. He did not pull out his sword.

He stood and faced the women.

"Hail Rusticano," cried Celia. "The time has come for your demise."

"What is my crime, lady?" asked Rusticano.

"No crime, sir," said Celia. "Only that you are a man in Fairy Land. No men shall remain on this island. Your leader is dead. Your friends are dead. You too shall join them in nevermore."

Rusticano kneeled down and picked up a rock.

The women of Fairy Land drew back their arrows and unsheathed their swords.

Rusticano tossed the rock into the Babbling Brook.

"Are you certain," he asked, "that I am a man?"

"What else would you be?" asked Celia.

"No one has ever told Rusticano what makes a man, so how can Rusticano judge for himself? Can you tell me?"

"A man is the opposite of a woman," said Celia.

"Do I not have the same arms and legs as you, do I not have the same head? Should not an opposite be in direct opposition to the thing it opposes?"

"Your body is different than ours," said Celia.

"Are your bodies so similar?" asked Rusticano. "Look at the skinny maid, holding her axe. Is her body the same as the fat one who cripples the horse? Are those differences so much less than the distance of my body from yours?"

"Too much prattle, fair Rusticano," said Celia. "Your talk will not save you."

"Lady," said Rusticano. "I am happy to die if you wish it. But I have shared your salt and lived as your guest, and I have given you my own gift, and by those sacred and ancient terms, I claim certain rights. I demand to know why I should die. Tell me, then, what makes a woman and what makes me not a woman."

"Do you bleed with the moon?" asked Celia.

"I do not," said Rusticano. "But is that what makes a woman? I vow to you here that I shall take the sword to my flesh with every full rise and let flow as much blood as you demand."

"Where are your breasts?" asked Celia.

"Again, lady," said Rusticano. "I have no breasts but I see at least three women here with chests flatter than mine. Are they not women?"

"What of that prick between your legs?" asked Celia.

"Are we so certain that it is a prick?" asked Rusticano.

"What else would it be?" asked Celia.

"I would caution against defining a thing by its appearance," said Rusticano. "How many chairs are there on this island? Each looks different from the others and yet we see them and know that they are chairs. This is because a chair is a thing for sitting upon, and as with a prick, it is defined not by its appearance but rather by its function. So tell me, lady, if this is a prick, then what is its function?"

"You piss through your prick," said Celia. "And you put it inside a woman."

"These are the two functions of a prick?" asked Rusticano. "These are what define a prick, and you say that having a prick is what defines me as a man?"

"Yes," said Celia. "I put this to you as the reason why you must die."

"And will you swear by this definition?" asked Rusticano. "Will you swear by it before the hospitality under whose banner I now march?"

"I swear it," said Celia.

"And you speak that oath with the full force of your reign?" asked Rusticano. "This definition is the law of Fairy Land?"

"It is," said Celia.

"If the two functions of the prick are to piss on the earth and make shame in a woman," said Rusticano, "then are not all women of Fairy Land halfways a man? For do not all of you piss the same as me? You may claim that your piss issues forth from a different place than my own, but Rusticano says that the piss is defined by itself in its own state of being and not its source. When someone speaks a word, do you concentrate on the teeth and the tongue? Nay, you heed the final issuance. When my piss is on the ground, does it demonstrate any difference from your own puddles? Nay, lady, I suggest that this cannot be a function that defines a prick."

"You are right," said Celia. "A prick is a prick because it goes into a woman."

"Then lady," said Rusticano, "I ask you to find a single woman here on Fairy Land in whom I've entered. I've pricked none of your island. I've pricked no woman anywhere in the world. How often did you laugh when the Red-Rose Knight made sore jests about my untried virginity? I submit to you that by your own definition what hangs here is no prick. I know not what I am, lady, but I further submit that Rusticano is no man."

Rusticano stayed on Fairy Land.

Centuries ticked off.

He was transformed into an immortal supranatural creature, but he never developed the ability to cast spells.

Rusticano was not accepted as a full member of Fairy Land's society.

He was just this person who lived in a cave near the Babbling Brook of Sorrow.

Rusticano developed a reputation.

He was someone who could talk his way through anything.

Sometimes the women of Fairy Land relied on Rusticano to solve problems.

Like when Freita Muscleback and Bianca Findlay both fell in love with Youna Shifa.

Love affairs on the island were especially fraught with peril.

If something went really wrong, everyone would be stuck dealing with the consequences for centuries.

This model of old lovers' inescapability was something that the mortal world would later duplicate in the form of Facebook.

The social media platform had doomed everyone in the mortal

world to the worst possible fate: living in a small town where they never ever lost contact with the people whom they'd fucked in high school, and worse yet, seeing the people whom they'd fucked in high school post daily updates on the topic of White Supremacy.

White Supremacy was a rhetorical device that'd been developed to describe the unfathomable social advantages that allowed the dominant social group in America to experience hereditary social wealth, primarily at the expense of people descended from African slaves who, once upon a time, literally had been that wealth.

The very expression of the concept drove a lot of people crazy.

They denied that it existed.

They stamped their feet and put their fingers in their ears.

But c'mon.

Of course White Supremacy was real.

The author knows better than anyone.

He is nothing but the product of White Supremacy.

He was raised in a single-parent household!

Child of divorce!

Rhode Island!

Traumatized by an early violent death in the family!

And his father was a Muslim!

And an immigrant from the Middle East!

And a member of the proletariat!

And an alcoholic!

#MENA!

And even with these obvious deviations, White Supremacy still carried me to the promised land of a commercial failure published with Nazi money by Penguin Random House.

Meanwhile, Byron Crawford, who is the best writer that you're not reading, was self-publishing his own books.*

---

*Technically, Byron Crawford shares the title of the Best Writer That You're Not Reading with Fiona Helmsley.

And Ernest Baker had to do the same thing with *Black American Psycho*, one of the previous five years' most interesting novels.

Published through fucking Amazon.com!

Print on demand!

So, yes, fucking obviously.

White Supremacy is real.

But the fact of its existence in no way alleviates the tedium of Facebook updates on the topic. Particularly those written by your high-school sweetheart.


On the day when Freita Muscleback and Bianca Findlay realized that they were both in love with Youna Shifa, they approached Rusticano.

Rusticano was in his cave by the Babbling Brook of Sorrow.

"What is the nature of the problem?" asked Rusticano.

"We both love Youna," said Freita. "Has anyone ever told you about Boadicea Thrumpguts?"

"The bloody story," said Rusticano. "I know it well. I wonder if the nature of your problem is not love, but rather something else. You would agree that love is predicated on an object of love? If one loves, then one must necessarily love something?"

"That is right," said Freita.

"Would you also agree that if love is predicated on an object of that love, then one cannot love nothing?"

"Yes," said Bianca. "It is impossible to love nothing."

"If the lover must necessarily love something or someone, then does the lover love the beloved based on contingent actions, or does the lover love because she recognizes a quality in the beloved that is a mirror of a greater love?"

"I am not sure that I follow, Rusticano," said Bianca.

"Do you love your mother?" asked Rusticano.

"Yes, Rusticano," said Bianca.

"On what basis do you love her?" asked Rusticano. "Is it because of an action that she performed?"

"No," said Freita. "One is born with a love of her mother."

"If this love is not contingent," said Rusticano, "then may we say that it is based not on the actions of the beloved, but rather some quality that the lover can recognize even before she speaks words?"

"You are correct," said Freita.

"Then why are you worrying over whether the actions of the beloved affect the nature of the lover's love?"

"I don't understand," said Freita.

"When your beloved is occupied with something other than yourself, such as preparing a meal or hunting a deer, do you stop loving them?"

"No," said Bianca.

"If you agree that the beloved does not impede the lover's love with the performance of tasks unrelated to the lover's love, then why should the lover's love be affected by the beloved's love of another? Do you fault your beloved when she expresses love for her sister? Does the lover's love diminish because the beloved loves a family member?"

"No," said Bianca.

"If you say that a beloved's love for another does not detract from the lover's love, then would you admit that when the lover experiences jealousy, it cannot be from any diminishing of love that is reactive to the beloved's actions?"

"Yes," said Freita.

"Rusticano would suggest that this jealousy is not above love, but rather its opposite, which is the fear of loving nothing. When your beloved loves another, and your fears rise up, you must remember that your fear is not of a fear of your own diminished love, but rather fear that you are loving nothing. But as we have proven it is impossible to love nothing, then this fear is without base and is a meaningless thing."

"You are right there, Rusticano," said Freita.

This went on for hours.

By the end of it, Freita and Bianca had agreed to share the love of Youna Shifa. It was going to be the Fairy Land version of San Francisco polyamory. The only problem was that no one had bothered to ask Youna Shifa if she loved Freita or Bianca.

She didn't.

The centuries passed.

Rusticano grew bored with the island. He asked Celia to send him to the mortal world, where he would make his way.

She agreed.

The only condition was that once Rusticano left the island, he could never return.

He departed.

Word filtered back through the usual channels.

Rusticano was in Spain.

Rusticano was in Germany.

Rusticano had opened a business.

Rusticano's business sold luggage.

Rusticano's business was evolving into fashion.

After the psychic cataclysm of World War One, there were no more reports.

At the very moment that he disappeared in a flash of untamed magic, Rusticano was sitting in a Coffee Fellows at München Hauptbahnhof's northeast corner.

He was eating an egg bagel sandwich and talking to his friend Liv Lisa Fries.

And then, like that, he was standing face-to-face with Celia in the house on the hill.

"My lady," he said. "It has been too long."

"I have need of you, Rusticano," said Celia. "The debt comes due."

"Payment in full," he said. "I am yours to command."

Celia told Rusticano about her children and their conversion to Christianity.

"What would you have me do?" asked Rusticano.

"Talk them away from their folly," said Celia. "Get them out of that building. Convince Fern to come back to Fairy Land."

Celia tried to drive Rusticano to Stanford Avenue, but Rusticano insisted that before they departed, he be allowed to drive the Jaguar around the neighborhood.

He said that he was a fan of vintage British engineering.

"How will you find your way?" asked Celia.

"Rusticano keeps a smartphone upon his person," said Rusticano. "But I require that you cast a spell and turn on its international roaming."

Celia cast the spell.

Rusticano owned a Samsung Galaxy Note 8. He'd installed LineageOS 14.1, an open source fork of CyanogenMod, which was itself an open source fork of Google's Android OS.

When Rusticano returned from his neighborhood sojourn, he carried a black duffle bag.

He did not explain the bag.

He informed Celia that she could drive them to Stanford Avenue.

They headed downtown.

"In my experience, people with religious beliefs are the least open to reason," said Rusticano. "Yet Rusticano has his ways. My only request is that you do not interfere with my deeds."

"By my leave," said Celia, "I vow that I shall not interrupt you."

"No matter the action?"

"No matter the action," said Celia.

"The nature of the problem is that they are in this building and will not leave this building?" asked Rusticano.

"They believe they are doing the work of Jesus Christ," said Celia.

"They always do," said Rusticano.

"Have you read the Bible?" asked Celia.

"Once," said Rusticano. "Many years ago."

"Jesus was weird as fuck," said Celia.

"I imagine that had he come to Fairy Land, a crucifixion would have been the least of his worries."

Celia parked the car in front of the TUNA EXPRESS CO.

They followed the line of bodies inside the building.

They went up to the second floor.

They went into the backroom.

Fern was pumping out her brother's blood into the mouths of several homeless men.

The Fairy Knight was on the table, half dazed.

"You say that you believe in Jesus Christ and do his works?" asked Rusticano of Fern.

"We do," said Fern.

"Nothing can shake you in your faith?" asked Rusticano.

"Nothing," said Fern. "We have been baptized. We are his."

"What say you, Fairy Knight?" asked Rusticano. "Are you too unshakeable in your faith?"

"Totally, completely, utterly," groaned the Fairy Knight.

Rusticano paused.

Rusticano thought.

"You may not remember," said Rusticano, "but the Red-Rose Knight was my bosom friend. I knew the man when he was still Tom a Lincoln, and I was there when we crowned his head with a laurel of roses."

"We remember," said Fern.

"I wager that I knew the man better even than your mother understood him," said Rusticano. "I never shared his bed, but I spent more time with him than any other."

"Our father would not object to our service," said Fern.

"Oh, I have no doubt that he would not," said Rusticano. "The Red-Rose Knight would offer no dissent from this practice. But do you heed Rusticano when he says that the Red-Rose Knight was the stupidest man that he ever met? Your father was a jumped-up fool who believed that he was better than Lincoln, and for his delusion, all he earned was a few years between the thighs of a fairy queen before he drank a glass of water filled with filth. I grant you that this is more than most men, but it does not change anything. Children, your father was a jackanapes, and while the royal blood of England and the royal blood of Fairy Land flows through your veins, I fear that you have not inherited any of your mother's wisdom. Do you know that the woman asked me here to dissuade you from your perverse hobby? Rusticano agreed. Rusticano thought about his best method of attack, considering every possible avenue of criticism. Then Rusticano remembered. There is only one way to deal with religious people, and there is only one way to deal with the grandchildren of King Arthur, a man who I also met, and who, if I may say so, rivaled your father for his stupidity."

Rusticano had left Lincoln with the Red-Rose Knight because he'd hated the grotesque meanness of the English. When he returned to the mortal world, to mainland Europe, he found that not much was different.

It'd been 1,000 years and there was still so much evil.

The names had changed but shits were still ruling the world.

Everything was violence. Everything was war.

The poor were still starving.

The only difference now was that Rusticano himself could not die.

And he could not return to his cave by the Babbling Brook of Sorrow.

Rusticano decided to embrace the values of the mortal world.

He married a woman named Evette, a tanner's daughter, and with her started a family.

The early years were good.

Rusticano was in love.

But it wore off.

After a decade, nothing about Evette or their children could alleviate the hollow feeling.

He didn't want to see his wife die.

He didn't want to learn that his children were not immortal.

He didn't want to pretend that a domestic life had any meaning.

Food, clothes, shelter.

Every fucking day.

Without end.

Faking his own death, Rusticano abandoned his family and made his acquaintance with those who had passed the Cash Horizon. He went to interesting parties, he hoarded money, and he had reckless sex with people who were bored out of their minds.

These antics could amuse for a moment, maybe even for a week, but in the end, everything was empty. The parties and the people were dull as dishwater.

Alcohol helped.

Alcohol always helped.

Thinking that honest labor might give his life some purpose, Rusticano took up a trade.

Rusticano founded his own company.

He had great success with handcrafted luggage. The company expanded and Rusticano experienced even greater success with fashion.

But the rewards of his business were only iterations of the same boring things.

Food, shelter, clothing, sex.

The world moved on and entered the Twentieth Century AD.

Rusticano could see the score.

He watched as liberal democracies consumed themselves with internal divisions about their relative social order, and he watched as these liberal democracies placed the petty squabbles about these internal divisions upon a foundation of ghettos and the foreign dead.

People had stopped arguing about the divine right of kings and now screamed at each other about human rights, about how terrible it was that some inequality in the internal society had made a mockery of that society's values, and then retreated into their homes and feasted on the mass-murdered flesh of animals while their militaries dropped bombs on distant locales and the mechanisms of their societies destroyed the poor with unfair labor practices.

There was no place for Rusticano's wordplay and his reason.

Not in the mortal world.

The Twentieth Century AD had only one rule: might made right.

Rusticano was immortal.

He was stronger than everyone else.

He could do anything he wanted.

Rusticano opened his black duffel bag and took out a five-gallon plastic fuel can that he'd purchased from Rite Aid at the corner of Vermont Avenue and Hollywood Boulevard.

Rusticano unscrewed the cap on the fuel can.

Rusticano splashed out five gallons of gasoline that he'd purchased from the Shell station at the opposite corner of Vermont Avenue and Hollywood Boulevard.

He did it so fast that neither Celia nor Fern nor the Fairy Knight could stop him.

The homeless people were too tripped out on the Fairy Knight's blood to realize what was going on. And anyway, they were people who America had deemed useless, so they weren't particularly surprised to be abused by a stranger.

"You may now thank me for my honesty," said Rusticano.

Rusticano used a lighter that he'd bought at Rite Aid to ignite the gasoline.

Everything burned.

As their flesh caught fire, but they did not die, both the Fairy Knight and Fern said the Lord's Prayer.

It was for nothing.

They might as well have said a prayer with a proven track record. They might as well have said this:

*Arafat Kazi got into the pit to see Guns N' Roses at the Staples Center.*

The building burned.
    Celia burned.
    Rusticano burned.
    Fern burned.
    The Fairy Knight burned.
    The homeless burned.

Undying beings came out of the charred wreckage.
    Rusticano looked at Celia.
    Celia looked at Rusticano.
    "Lady," he said. "Your children are no longer in the building. I would ask that you send me back."
    Celia cast a spell and Rusticano disappeared.
    One minute he was there.
    Then: blink.
    He was in a Coffee Fellows at the northeast corner in the München Hauptbahnhof.

Celia's magic had not accounted for the difference in time zones and the operating hours of Coffee Fellows.
    It was midnight.
    Rusticano was trapped behind locked doors.
    He threw a table through a plate glass window and walked down Prielmayerstraße towards the former Bürgerbräukeller.
    As with the Gray's Inn play, he had wrecked another narrative.
    His actions had precipitated an unsatisfying end to this book, causing its story to dissolve into a hectoring lecture about Christianity divorced from any pretext of plot.
    Exeunt Rusticano.

# Chapter Twenty

# What Rusticano Didn't Say

Rusticano was nobody's fool.

He knew that the best arguments against Christianity were surprisingly terrible, and furthermore that these arguments relied on philological research, observations about historical injustice, scientific empiricism, and the issue of theodicy, which was the fancy way of asking *Why does God let bad things happen to good people?*

When people asked *Why does God let bad things happen to good people?* what they really meant was this: "Why does God let bad things happen to me?"

It's a very Twenty-First-Century AD argument.

Cooked in a base of insipid narcissism.

The strongest of the bad arguments were the ones that relied on scientific empiricism, which pointed out the impossibility of God creating his son in human form.

And the impossibility of that human form rising from the dead.

But appeals to rationality and scientific truth, while making great sense on paper, faced a very significant problem.

The world kept getting weirder.

The everyday lives of everyday people were completely insane.

Roughly 100,000 people controlled the fates and destinies of 7,799,900,000 people, and the 7,799,900,000 let themselves be subject to the whimsies of the 100,000.

But let's be clear: the madness of everyday life was its own issue.

It didn't have any relationship to whether or not Christianity was bullshit.

Obviously, Christianity was total bullshit.

It was the most insane bullshit!

But it was impossible to make an argument against superstition and magical nonsense, and have it stick, when that argument was delivered from a society where every citizen was a magician.

And yes, reader, that includes you.

You too are a magician.

Your life is dominated by one of the oldest and most perverse forms of magic, one with less interior cohesion than the Christian faith, and you invest its empty symbolism with a level of belief that far outpaces that of any Christian.

Here are some strips of paper and bits of metal!

Watch as I transform these strips of paper and bits of metal into: (a) sex (b) food (c) clothing (d) shelter (e) transportation that allows me to acquire strips of paper and bits of money (f) intoxicants that distract me from my endless pursuit of strips of paper and bits of metal (g) leisure items that distract me from my endless pursuit of strips of paper and bits of metal (h) pointless vacations to exotic locales where I will replicate the brutish behavior that I display in my point of origin as a brief respite from my endless pursuit of strips of paper and bits of metal (i) unfair social advantages that allow my rotten children to undertake their own moronic pursuits of strips of paper and bits of metal.

Humiliate yourself for strips of paper.

Murder for the strips of paper.

Humiliate others for the strips of paper.

Worship the people who've accumulated such vast quantities of strips of paper that their strips of paper no longer have any physical existence and are now represented by binary notation.

Treat the vast accumulators like gods.

Free blowies for the moldering corpse of Steve Jobs!

Fawning profile pieces for Jay-Z!

The Presidency for billionaire socialite and real-estate developer Donald J. Trump!

Kill! Kill! Kill!

Work! Work! Work!

Die! Die! Die!

Go on.

Pretend this is not the most magical thing that has ever happened.

Historical arguments against Christianity tended to be delivered in tones of pearl-clutching horror, usually by subpar British intellectuals pimping their accent in America, a country where sounding like an Oxbridge twat conferred an unearned credibility.

Yes, the Crusades were horrible.

Yes, the Inquisition was awful.

Yes, they shouldn't have burned witches in Salem.

Yes, there is an unfathomable amount of sexually abused walking wounded.

Yes, every Christian country has oriented itself around the rich and done nothing but abuse the fuck out of its poor.

But it's not like the secular conversion of the industrialized world has alleviated any of the horror. Read the news.

Murder, rape, murder, rape, murder, rape, murder, rape, murder, rape, murder, rape, murder, rape, murder, rape, murder, rape, murder, rape, murder, rape, murder, rape, murder, rape, murder, rape, murder, rape, murder, rape, murder, rape, murder, rape, murder, rape, murder, rape, murder, rape, murder, rape, murder, rape, murder, rape, murder, rape, murder, rape, murder, rape, murder, rape, murder, rape, murder, rape, murder, rape, murder, rape, murder, rape, murder, rape, murder, rape, murder, rape, murder, rape, murder, rape, murder, rape, murder, rape, murder, rape, murder, rape, murder, rape, murder, rape, murder, rape, murder, rape, murder, rape, murder, rape, murder, rape, murder, rape, murder, rape, murder, rape, murder, rape, murder, rape, murder, rape, murder, rape, murder, rape, murder, rape, murder, rape, murder, rape, murder, rape, murder, rape, murder, rape, murder, rape, murder, rape, murder, rape, murder, rape, murder, rape, murder, rape, murder, rape, murder, rape, murder, rape, murder, rape, murder, rape, murder, rape, murder, rape, murder, rape, murder, rape, murder, rape, murder, rape, murder, rape, murder, rape, murder, rape, murder, rape, murder, rape, murder, rape, murder, rape, murder, rape, murder, rape, murder.

Despair.

All secularism has done, really, is remove a yoke from the rich. They'd always been horrible, but at least when they still paid lip service to Christian virtues, they could be shamed into philanthropy.

Now they use market forces to slide the whole thing into feudalism.

New York University built a campus with slave labor!

In the Twenty-First Century AD!

And has suffered no rebuke!

Applications are at an all-time high!

The historical arguments against Christianity are as facile as reviews on Goodreads.com, and come down to this: *Why do you organize around bad people who tell you that a Skyman wants you to be good?*

To which the rejoinder is: yes, the clergy sucks, but who cares how normal people are delivered into goodness?

As for philological research.

C'mon, get real.

None of these arguments would've worked on Fern or the Fairy Knight.

How does one supranatural creature tell two other supranatural creatures that they shouldn't believe in a fourth supranatural creature?

Rusticano couldn't make that argument.

So he made a fire.

You can't talk people out of religion.

But you can violently assault them and burn down their churches. Or spraypaint MUHAMMAD PROPHET OF BUTCHERS on their masjid.

It won't work, you won't disabuse people of their belief.

But anything's better than subjecting the world to another lecture about atheism.

# Chapter Twenty-One

## καταδυσόμεθ᾽ εἰς Ἀΐδαο δόμους

The 2016 AD Aston Martin Vanquish made its way up Sunset Boulevard.

Dmitri Huda had the night off.

HRH was in the driver's seat.

HRH turned left onto Silver Lake Boulevard.

A sex worker was in the passenger seat.

She looked out of the passenger-side window at the Silversun liquor store.

HRH followed Silver Lake Boulevard to the 2016 AD Aston Martin Vanquish's final destination, which was HRH's mid-century Los Angeles home overlooking the Silver Lake Reservoir.

HRH's personal breaking point with Beverly Hills had come in the autumn of 2015 AD, when the media turned its attention to HRH's cousin HRH Majed bin Abdullah bin Abdulaziz Al Saud.

HRH Majed had, allegedly, thrown a party over three days.

The party had, allegedly, spanned from September 21, 2015 AD to September 23, 2015 AD.

On September 25th, 2015 AD, three women, who'd been employed by HRH Majed to provide housekeeping services during the party, filed a civil lawsuit with the Superior Court of Los Angeles.

In the complaint, the women were anonymous. They were listed as JANE DOES 1 through 3.

On October 22nd, 2015 AD, the three JANE DOES filed an amended complaint.

And this second complaint caught media attention.

In the complaint, it was alleged that over the alleged three nights of alleged drug abuse, HRH Majed bin Abdullah bin Abdulaziz Al Saud had: (1) allegedly attempted to urinate on or around JANE DOES 1 through 3 while saying, allegedly, "I want to pee pee!" (2) allegedly threatened to kill JANE DOE 1, allegedly saying, "Tomorrow I will have a party with you and you will do everything I want, otherwise I will kill you" (3) allegedly jumped on top of JANE DOE 2 while she was seated and allegedly started rubbing his body against her body in a sexual manner and then, allegedly, shouted: "I am a prince and I do what I want! You are a nobody" followed by, allegedly, "You're not a woman! You're nobody! I'm a prince and I'll do what I want and nobody will do anything to me!" (4) allegedly grabbed JANE DOE 2's arm and allegedly kicked her on the knee while maintaining his grasp, allegedly leaving nail marks on her wrist and bruise marks on her thigh (5) allegedly instructed JANE DOE 3 as follows: "You're going to go upstairs. I'll be up there in two minutes and you'll do whatever I want. If not, then I'll kill you" (6) allegedly forced JANE DOE 1 and JANE DOE 2 to watch as his penis was stroked, allegedly, by a male employee who was allegedly on his knees before HRH Majed (7) allegedly forced JANE DOE 1 to watch as a different man, by request, allegedly farted in HRH Majed's face (8) allegedly told JANE DOE 1: "I will pay you to lick my entire body. If you make me feel good, you'll feel good too."

The complaint said very little of HRH Majed's subsequent arrest for alleged forced oral copulation, brought after a neighbor saw a woman smeared with blood, shouting for help, and trying to climb an eight-foot wall.

But the media reports said quite a bit.

To be fair to HRH Majed Majed bin Abdullah bin Abdulaziz Al Saud: he never faced a criminal trial stemming from his arrest at the hands of the LAPD.

The Los Angeles District Attorney's office declined to press charges.

And, through his representatives, HRH Majed denied everything stemming from both the arrest and the civil trial. A representative said: "I will not dignify these salacious allegations – which the District attorney found to be unsupported by evidence … The decision by the D.A.'s office not to file charges shows that the accuser's stories cannot be substantiated … The sheikh is very happy to put it behind him and move on with his life."

And, it must be said: the lawsuit was filed anonymously and never went to trial.

None of its claims were even proven in a court of law.

And on December 12, 2017 AD, all parties filed for dismissal.

"Can you conceive of how difficult it is for an Arabian prince to be arrested in Beverly Hills?" HRH had asked Dmitri Huda after the media descended. "Even with these false charges and obvious calumnies, how does one achieve such a miracle?"

"His father died in January," said Dmitri Huda. "Maybe he's distraught."

"I wish that my father would die in January! Or any other month! You would never find myself dismantling an equitable arrangement with law enforcement! If one cannot trust the LAPD, then one can trust nothing. The heat is on, Dmitri."

And so HRH escaped to Silver Lake.

The 2016 AD Aston Martin Vanquish pulled into HRH's driveway.

A small plastic device sent out a radio transmission that instructed a motor to open the garage door.

The 2016 AD Aston Martin Vanquish pulled into the garage.

HRH removed the crystal key from the ignition.

HRH and the sex worker walked up the stairs and into HRH's hallway.

"Is this you?" asked the sex worker, pointing to a photograph of a young HRH and Ronald Wilson Reagan, taken during the last year of the former actor's Presidency, when Alzheimer's disease had begun transforming the former actor's brain into useless mush.

"I am indeed the prepubescent so pictured," said HRH.

The sex worker walked past the photograph of HRH and Richard Milhous Nixon, taken in the early 1990s AD, just before the former President's death. In the photograph, an unfortunate wisp of a moustache was present on HRH's upper lip.

HRH walked past the photograph of himself and William Jefferson Clinton, taken in the late 1990s AD. In the photograph, HRH had become a young man.

The sex worker walked past the photograph of HRH and George Walker Bush.

HRH walked past the photograph of himself and George Herbert Walker Bush, taken only moments after HRH was photographed with George Walker Bush.

"The noblest soul ever to vomit upon the Prime Minister of Japan," said HRH.

The sex worker walked past the photograph of HRH and Donald J. Trump, taken around 2005 AD. The two men were in Bangkok. They were surrounded by pleasure girls.

"Fuck," said the sex worker. "You know him?"

"He is a friend of my father," said HRH.

"Who the fuck is your father?" asked the sex worker.

"He is called The Conqueror," said HRH.

HRH walked past the photograph of himself and James Earl Carter Jr., taken around 2006 AD, in the halcyon days when HRH laundered medical marijuana money through environmental NGOs.

The sex worker walked past the photograph of HRH and Barack Hussein Obama, taken in late 2009 AD.

First Lady Michelle Obama had invited HRH to a White House dinner after HRH funded an initiative to help celebrate Women's History Month.

HRH and the sex worker were 420-friendly.

The sex worker smoked from a waterpipe that she found in HRH's living room.

HRH vaped indica.

"Now is the time, O you budding sapling of May," said HRH. "Your clothes must take their absence from your flesh."

When the sex worker took off her clothes, HRH was surprised to see that her chest, torso, and left outer thigh were inked with a multicolored tattoo.

The tattoo depicted a monster of vaguely anthropoid outline, but with an octopus-like head whose face was a mass of tentacles, a scaly, rubbery-looking body, prodigious claws on hind and fore feet, and long, narrow wings behind.

In a textbook example of the caricature endemic to the modern tattoo artist, a few of the monster's tentacles wrapped around the sex worker's nipples, and another stretched down to her mons pubis, while a final tentacle went around the left buttock and appeared to terminate at the sex worker's rectum.

"Rare is the treasure who adorns her essential skin with the cosmic horror of H.P. Lovecraft."

"Thanks," said the sex worker.

"Tell me, which of Lovecraft's works do you rank as the finest?"

"I like 'The Thing on the Doorstep'," said the sex worker.

"O my darling, with each step you reveal new depths," said HRH. "Your perversity knows no bounds."

HRH vaped indica.

"The Thing on the Doorstep" was about a man who marries a woman only to discover that her mind has been replaced with the malevolent consciousness of the woman's father. Everything revolves around open concerns of homosexuality, incest, trans people, and flat-out bestiality with a fishwoman.

On several occasions in his dewy youth, HRH had masturbated while reading the story.

"My plan had been to roger you senseless," said HRH to the sex worker. "I was to leave you drooling and dazed like a donkey attacked by the silent killer of encephalomyelitis. Yet damn your eyes, you have revealed yourself as a beast who should not suffer the usual rounds of amorous pursuits. For you, I shall unleash the highest form of depredation. I will permit entry to my inner sanctum, to the chamber where the grandest perversity flourishes. Fear not. I possess no red room of pain. This is neither *Fifty Shades of Grey* nor *The Amityville Horror*."

The sex worker followed HRH upstairs.
HRH led the sex worker into a bedroom.
There were two DXRacer chairs, a desk, and a giant LCD display attached to an Alienware Area-51 desktop computer.
HRH sat in one of the chairs.
"Position your meat in the other receptacle," said HRH. "Join me at this terminal to infinity."
"Are you trying to make me watch porn?" asked the sex worker. "I've seen porn. But it's your money."

HRH powered on the Alienware Area-51 desktop computer.
HRH opened the Google Chrome web browser.
HRH directed the Google Chrome web browser to https://www.twitch.tv.

https://www.twitch.tv was the URL of Twitch, a subsidiary of Amazon.com, which was a website dedicated to the destruction of the publishing industry.
Amazon.com was owned by Jeff Bezos, who also owned Goodreads.com, the Internet Movie Database, Blue Origin, and the *Washington Post*, which was a newspaper with a slogan that said: "Democracy Dies in Darkness."

This motto implied that without a free press casting illumination upon the powerful, American democracy would devolve into a hollow shell.

This motto had been handpicked by Jeff Bezos.

Depending on fluctuations in the stock market, on some days Jeff Bezos was the richest man in the world.

Which meant that the motto was slightly disingenuous.

You don't get as rich as Jeff Bezos without knowing exactly how people beyond the Cash Horizon wreaked havoc upon democracy: they said what they were going to do, in public, and then they did it.

In 2003 AD, about twenty people in the United States government told the world that it was going to kill a metric fuckton of Iraqis.

The whole world cried out, in unison, and demanded that the United States government not kill a metric fuckton of Iraqis.

But the Iraqis still died by the metric fuckton.

Remind me: who gave a shit about darkness?

The second problem with the motto was that it was based on an ahistorical assumption, which was that Americans lived in a democracy.

America was never a democracy.

It was a Republic.

It had been designed as a Republic.

The country's founders were horrified by democracy.

American democracy couldn't die because American democracy had never existed.

✷ out of ✷ ✷ ✷ ✷.

The front page of Twitch's website displayed a live video stream from the Overwatch League.

Two regional teams battled each other in the game *Overwatch* while a live audience watched.

The stream was narrated by two men who'd patterned their vocal style after sports commentators.

"Dallas is going to swap things up a bit. Getting aggressive here and you have to worry a bit," said one of the commentators.

"I mean that's huge for Dallas," said the other commentator. "Because now they're going to have a player advantage. It's a six versus five. That's a big hit on the way out."

"What the hell is this?" asked the sex worker.

"Are you not a millennial, madame?" asked HRH. "Is this not your natural domain?"

The vast majority of streams on Twitch were very different than Overwatch League.

A random person played video games in their home and broadcast this over the Internet. Twitch hosted the action, providing a central place for the meeting of broadcasters, who were called streamers, and their viewers.

The video game action occupied most of any individual stream. A small box, containing live video of the user, appeared in one of the stream's corners. On the right side of the screen, the stream's viewers commented in a scrolling livechat.

Depending on which streaming software was used, and depending on which plug-ins the streamer had configured, various graphics were displayed when viewers interfaced with the platform's monetization.

In other words, the people watching videos on Twitch could give money to the people broadcasting on Twitch and these donations would show up in the stream itself.

"Over many arduous months, I have cultivated a personal fandom of several Twitch channels," said HRH. "Permit a demonstration."

HRH navigated to the Twitch channel of an unremarkable young man.

The young man was playing *Fortnite: Battle Royale*.

The sex worker watched as the young man navigated his video

game avatar across an island landscape, destroying objects and simulating genocide against the other players connected to the same *Fortnite* server.

HRH navigated to the Twitch channel of a pretty young woman who lived in Tokyo.

The woman was not playing a video game. She was interacting with the livechat. She was receiving donations whenever she impersonated a character from *Final Fantasy XV*.

HRH navigated to the Twitch channel of a young woman who was dressed as Diana from *Wonder Woman*. The woman was drinking AriZona Iced Tea and playing *South Park: The Fractured but Whole*.

HRH navigated to the Twitch channel of a man in his twenties, who was cursing wildly as he attempted to play a game called *Cuphead*.

"*Cuphead* is a crowd-funded odyssey into an ersatz replica of animation from the Great Depression," said HRH. "I have never indulged, but I am informed that it is a work of manifold difficulty."

HRH navigated to the Twitch channel of a young woman who lived in Sidcup.

The Sidcup woman was playing *The Sims 4*, a piece of software that simulated the appearance of a Twentieth-Century AD suburban life that been murdered by the international capitalist class.

The sex worker watched the Sidcup woman demonstrate the décor of a simulated house in *The Sims 4*.

The house in *The Sims 4* was very moderne Danske.

It stood in contrast to the visible décor of the woman's Sidcup home.

"This is live?" asked the sex worker.

"Twitch is where the Western world's underclasses go to demonstrate their lack of utility in the face of increasing mechanization and globalized manufacturing," said HRH. "Education has failed them. These children produce nothing but hours of live video. Each day hosts an onslaught of countless banal gigabytes. Millions of other children hang upon these performers, watching their every gesture and nuance."

"It's people playing video games?" asked the sex worker.

"What you are witnessing is the death of traditional media. Do you think these children have the capacity to thrill to the slight characterization that you discovered in Lovecraft? Do you believe that after hours of this plotless false intimacy they will return to television? Here we encounter the terminal point for millennia of narrative. Goodbye the Ferrari, Tony Kushner."

"I feel fucking old," said the sex worker. "And I'm only twenty-seven."

"Worry not. All of the Shropshire lads who salivate over MILF pornography will seek to unlock your wisdom of the ages. Forget you not, madame, that blood is a rover."

"Is this what we're doing tonight?" asked the sex worker. "Are we going to fuck or what?"

"Such crassness!" cried HRH. "Delightful! Delightful! Did I not inform you that I would demonstrate the greatest perversity? Do not think that Twitch itself constitutes the horror. There remains another dimension."

HRH scrolled down on the webpage hosting the Sidcup woman's Twitch channel.

HRH clicked the donate button.

The donate button opened another browser tab in Google Chrome.

HRH switched to this tab.

HRH filled out the form on the donate page.

HRH clicked donate.

A notification appeared on the Sidcup woman's stream.

It informed the woman and her viewers that HRH had donated £2,000.

The woman pulled off her headphones and began to cry.

"One cannot donate to any Twitch channel which experiences true popularity," said HRH. "Fellows with an audience in the hundreds of thousands will not evidence the appropriate response when presented with a mere £2,000."

The Sidcup woman screamed into her computer: "No. Oh my God. Oh my fucking God. What? No. No. No. Oh my God. No. Oh my God. No. No. No. Fuck. Fucking Hell. Oh my God, no. No. No. Fuck. No. What? What? WHAT?"

"How much money do you have?" asked the sex worker.

"The zeroes pile up like the bloated corpses of dissident intellectuals at Dachau," said HRH. "Imagine the earnings from a weapons-for-hostages scheme with the Islamic Republic of Iran and multiply that figure by a billion."

HRH leaned back in his DXRacer chair.

HRH vaped indica.

"It strikes my mind that perhaps there is a way to raise the pleasure," said HRH. "Would you care to indulge?"

HRH taught the sex worker to navigate channels on Twitch.

The sex worker navigated channels on Twitch.

The sex worker found channels belonging to sadder members of the Twitch community. People with four viewers, people who were streaming games that no one liked, people who were talking to an audience of no one.

The sex worker donated $1,000 to a bald man with a goatee who was playing the VGA remake of *Quest for Glory II: Trial by Fire.*

The sex worker donated $3,000 to a man who was playing *World of Warcraft.*

The sex worker donated $5,000 to a woman in Seoul. The woman was not playing a video game. She was watering her plants and singing along to "Lip & Hip" by 현아.

All three streamers pulled off their headphones. One started crying. All started cursing. One talked about dreams coming true.

241

"You see?" asked HRH. "One can change a life with nothing more than a donation of $3,000. Streaming video is the intellectual sweatshop of the future."

HRH told the sex worker to take it up a notch.

She donated $20,000 to a young woman dressed in *Sailor Moon* cosplay.

Her shriek was so piercing that both HRH and the sex worker had to cover their ears.

"Shall we go for the big score?" asked HRH. "Do you wish to inhale the sweet smell of success?"

"What?" asked the sex worker.

"$100,000," said HRH.

"You actually have this much?"

"The bodies of Dachau. Arms sales to the Islamic Republic of Iran," said HRH. "For one night only, my cherub, with the contours of your Cthulhoid membrane illuminated by a liquid crystal display, money is of no concern."

"Let's do it," said the sex worker.

"My one request is that I pick your victim," said HRH.

HRH navigated to the Twitch channel of a young woman who was dressed like a sexy unicorn.

The sexy unicorn wasn't playing a game. She was speaking to the people in her channel's livechat.

"Okay, SweetA, thanks for the sub," said the sexy unicorn.

"No, DuskDot, I don't own a gun," said the sexy unicorn.

"Here she is," said HRH. "I have watched this one for a great long while. Her popularity is minimal. Her desperation is great. With one click, you will change her life forever. Imagine the surprise!"

The sex worker clicked on the donate button.

The sex worker filled out the form.

The sex worker donated the money.

A notification rose up on the sexy unicorn's Twitch stream.

The sexy unicorn sat in stunned silence.

The sexy unicorn could not believe what she was seeing.

The sexy unicorn checked to see if the donation was real.

The sexy unicorn threw off her headphones.

The sexy unicorn screamed.

The sexy unicorn started dancing in her lower-middle-class bedroom.

HRH leaned back in his DXRacer chair.

HRH vaped indica.

HRH smiled.

HRH experienced the shudder of a tantric orgasm.

"Do you realize that we've just changed that girl's life?" asked the sex worker. "We totally fucking changed everything."

"I am aware," said HRH.

"I can't believe it," said the sex worker.

The sexy unicorn was still dancing.

The sexy unicorn started jumping on her bed.

"She's probably never seen that kind of money in her life," said the sex worker.

"I guarantee that it is a new experience," said HRH. "Here, madame, is the true perversity. This is from where the greatest pleasure derives. You sit there and you believe yourself enmeshed in generosity, in the glow of altruism, in the spirit of human giving, but tonight you have done nothing but practice a refined form of cruelty."

"What?" asked the sex worker.

"You have taken that child and thrust her into a higher tax bracket," said HRH. "Do you believe that a peasant can handle a sudden influx of filthy lucre? Like yourself, she too is ignorant of the difference between money and wealth. She will spend this sum on clothes, on a new car, on trinkets and baubles, and when she has drained the swamp, there awaits the taxman. She will have no hope of paying. She will travel on, haunted by ever increasing debt. Her best chance will be bankruptcy after seven years. She will murder her credit and she will have learned nothing and she will own nothing. All of this because of a random act of violence perpetuated by a stranger while she was dressed in a unicorn costume that emphasized her heaving bosom. It will be your fault. You did this to that child. You have destroyed her."

HRH vaped indica.

# Chapter Twenty-Two

# **Literary Fiction**

While Fern's body burned with gasoline, and shrieks of human agony assaulted her ears, she had a thought.

Here was her thought: *This is not how I imagined things would turn out.*

To fathom Fern's disappointment, you'll have to cast your mind back to the Year of the Salted Earth, which roughly corresponded with 1997 AD, 1417 AH, and 5757 AM.

Fern spent that year out of Fairy Land.

Her existence was a minor cultural stereotype.

She was living as a pretend artist in a St. Mark's Place apartment between Avenue A & First Avenue on the island of Manhattan, which was a borough of New York City.

Fern had been in and out of New York City for almost a decade, starting in the Year of the Unquenched Longing, which roughly corresponded to 1989 AD, 1407 AH, and 5747 AM.

It that year, Fern met a young woman named Denise. They dated for a short time, but it was fleeting. Denise had to move to Boston.

Before she left New York, Denise introduced Fern to the demi-mondes of Manhattan's East Village and the Lower East Side, two overlapping ethnic ghettos that had transformed into cesspools of petty crime and cheap drugs and were gentrifying into cesspools of international money laundering and the expensive drugs required to fuel international money laundering.

It was in the East Village, where people were wearing terrible leather jackets and even worse denim jeans, that Fern met a boy named Anthony.

Anthony was from Long Island, which was an island next to Manhattan.

The western part of Long Island encompassed Queens and Brooklyn, two of New York City's boroughs.

At its eastern end, farthest from New York City, Long Island was full of property soon to be the exclusive domain of the ultra-wealthy, where the ruling class would throw parties that commingled the Celebrity branch of American politics with the people who really ruled the world, namely its international merchant bankers.

In the space between the boroughs and the money, there was a heaping mass of vast suburbs.

Anthony was from the middle. He'd grown up in the heaping mass.


Fern met Anthony in a bar on Second Avenue.

The bar was full of ersatz punk rockers and old drunks from the Ukraine.

Their attraction was so obvious, and so apparent, that it made an audible noise.

All of the bar's drunks heard the noise.

The ersatz punk rockers heard the noise.

Because the bar was full of brains pickled in alcohol, and because its patrons were sitting in a relative darkness designed to hide the shame of their existences, neither the drunks nor the punk rockers could identify the sound's origin.

The noise sounded like this:

"What the fuck?" asked one of the ersatz punk rockers.

"Ни хуя себé!" said one of the drunks.

Then she went back to her drink.

Fern met Anthony in the Year of the Baroque Promise, which roughly corresponded to 1990 AD, 1411 AH, and 5751 AM.

After the love connection made its audible sound, Anthony talked to Fern about the Krautrock band Amon Düül II.

He said stupid shit like: "I found *Yeti* at Bleecker Bob's and I had no idea what it was. 'Archangels Thunderbird' was one of those moments, you know? It fucking changed my whole fucking life. My God, those drums, that guitar."

This was the surface babbling of a human being who knew, on the cellular level, that he stood before the firestorm which would consume years of his life.

As his mouth spoke, so too did his subatomic particulars cry out: *Fuck me fuck fuck me fuck me love me love me I am yours fuck me fuck me flesh of my flesh burn me burn me my soul is boring a hole this second hole is penetrating the hole of your face the skull of your bone look at me here I am yours and yours alone and you are mine touch me I am the one for whom you have been waiting please please please please please. Kiss me, my darling, for I too am like you, I am a kinder from Bahnhof Zoo.*

Unlike the love connection, the crying out of Anthony's subatomic particulars happened on a level of quantum physics that was inaudible to human ears.

Not even people who had passed the Cash Horizon would have heard.

But in their case, the inaudibility was irrelevant: the rich are incapable of love or its recognition.

Fern was neither human nor past the Cash Horizon.

She was from Fairy Land.

She heard every word.

They talked, they hung around the East Village, they fell into bed, they wandered through the city, and because they'd both consumed endless amounts of media, they were imbued with the photogenic qualities of New York City, and these qualities freighted their wanderings with cultural weight.

Everything was ridiculously romantic.

On their third date, Anthony and Fern were walking in Washington Square Park. They were in the park because they were headed to Jones Street. Anthony had talked Fern into seeing some folk singers at Caffe Vivaldi.

The folk singers in question were absurd historical anachronisms. They were as bad as the people who wrote novels and poetry in the Twenty-First Century AD.

One of the folk singers was a woman named Bianca.

She was in Anthony's Philosophy program at the New School for Social Research, and she was doing a doctoral dissertation on Spinoza.

"Why don't you ever talk about your family?" Anthony asked Fern as they passed the statue of Giuseppe Garibaldi.

"What do you mean?" asked Fern.

"You don't talk about your family," said Anthony. "Do you have any brothers or sisters?"

At Caffe Vivaldi, they sat through an assortment of folk singers who sang 1930s AD ballads about the coming wave of international socialism. Then Bianca got on at the microphone against the back wall.

"Hi," she said into the microphone. "My name's Bianca. I'm going to sing a few songs, but while I'm setting up I thought my friend James could do a song. James is a folk singer. He moved to New York last week. I don't think he wants to do this, but if you give him a round of applause, I'm sure he'll come up. Let's have a warm welcome for James."

Bianca handed James her guitar. He put his mouth too close to the microphone.

"Uhm, hello people," James said, popping his p, "I'm, uh, I'm pretty nervous. This is the, uh, the first time I've ever performed in New York. I've never been in the city before, not before Thursday. I'm from Columbus, Ohio. Don't judge. We all, uh, have to be from somewhere and Columbus is pretty much just as good as pretty much anywhere. Well, kinda. Uhm, you know, sometimes back in Columbus my stuff doesn't really go over. I thought I'd play a classic from 1935, maybe one you haven't heard before. Someone played it for me last night on reel-to-reel. So, uhm, can you please be gentle? Kindness never killed anyone."

Fern thought about the simplicity of music on Fairy Land. Music without filter, music as in ancient times, the voice and the instrument, a holy sound in supplication to the divine.

The purity of what humanity had lost in its era of machines and computers and cars and airplanes. The lost society, the fallen dream, the missing kindness.

James looked so innocent, begging for mercy.

*I know how he feels*, thought Fern. *Oh, please, please, please, let him be good.*

James cleared his throat. He checked the guitar's tuning.

He played his song. This is what he sang:

*Every time I fuck them men*
*I give 'em the doggone clap*
*Oh, baby, I give 'em the doggone clap*
*But that's the kind of pussy that they really like*

*You can fuck my cock*
*Suck my cock*
*Or leave my cock alone*
*Oh, baby, honey, I piss all night long*

*If you suck my pussy, baby*
*I'll suck your dick*
*I'll do it to ya, honey, till I make you shit*
*Oh, baby, honey, all night long*

Long before the Year of the Unspoken Promise, Fern'd concluded that there was nothing new to experience, that all her future years would feature repeats of previous days.

She was like a sexy vampire in a novel by Anne Rice. She was bored by eternal life.

And then, in a bar in the East Village, surrounded by Ukrainian drunks and terrible black leather jackets, she discovered something new.

Meeting Anthony was like being in San Francisco in 1965 AD prior to America's construction of received drug experiences and dosing with high-grade Owsley lysergic acid diethylamide.

Unexplored territory.

It was insane love, *l'amour fou*, sex magick, the post-coital sparkle of two souls in unison wandering through a fluorescent-lit grocery store at 11:30PM, stoned, drunk, lunacy born of a shared experience, tongue in the mouth as guns fire overhead.

More Bad Sex in Fiction!

Nomination forthcoming!

The vast suburbs of Long Island were built with a specific and exact purpose: to isolate their residents from the perceived chaos of New York City, which was conceptualized as the presence of racial minorities.

In Anthony's youth, he'd sensed vibrations beyond the vast suburbs, and grasped on an intuitive level that the very experience of the suburbs, and their pretense of isolation, were the byproducts of an economic scheme over which he, and everyone he knew, had no control.

America was a prison for the young: a person either went runaway and threw themselves on the lusts of strangers, or they integrated into the sorting mechanisms of the haute bourgeoisie and hoped that a natural gift would carry them into one of the economic scheme's higher echelons.

Anthony chose the latter.

He smoked too much pot, he read too many books, he drank too much beer.

He dated a vegetarian girl who wore Malcolm X glasses, had a Siouxsie and the Banshees poster above her bed, and owned an ill-tempered ferret named Pumpkin.

He did well in high school.

After earning an undergraduate degree at the University of Chicago, Anthony ended up in New York City, on the island of Manhattan, doing a Philosophy PhD at the New School for Social Research.

Which is where he met Fern.

During those ridiculously romantic wanderings around New York City, Fern's thoughts were haunted.

She'd met Anthony at an inopportune time.

She had to return to Fairy Land.

For two years.

And she couldn't tell the truth.

Imagine the scene: Fern explains to Anthony, who is focusing on a proposed marriage between rational materialism and strict empiricism, that she is a supranatural creature from Fairy Land and that her father was the bastard son of King Arthur and that her mother is the Regnant Queen, and that, oh yeah, all of this has been the subject of Elizabethan pulp fiction and a Jacobean play, and double oh yeah, Fern could not die and was capable of supernatural feats of magic.

She cast two spells on Anthony.

The first drenched him in the radiation of primal magic, altering his brain so that Fern's periodic disappearances wouldn't register as significant events.

Whenever the biochemistry of Anthony's brain produced a thought like: *It's fucking weird as shit that I haven't seen Fern in seventeen months*, it was replaced by another thought: *Fern's gone to Bloomingdale's.*

The other spell drenched him with a second dose of primal magical radiation and created an energy field that rerouted social inquiries.

If someone asked Anthony why they hadn't seen his girlfriend, the energy field would mess up their minds. The inquisitor would forget that they hadn't seen Fern. They'd forget her entire existence until the next time they encountered her in the flesh, at which point their brains would be stuffed with false memories of seeing Fern's nonexistent paintings at hopeless group shows around SoHo.

The spells sat on, and in, Anthony's body.

They imbued him with the bitter puissance of Fairy Land.

Fern left New York City.

The affair came in dense clusters of contact and absence: one year on, two years off. It was the ultimate long-distance relationship, minus the benefits of then-contemporary modern communication.

There were no letters, no phone calls, no nothing.

Fern disappeared and reappeared.

And the magic deluded Anthony into thinking that she'd never left.

In the Year of the Mechanized Baptism, which roughly corresponded to 1993 AD, 1413 AH, 5753 AM, Fern was back in New York City.

One night, while Fern's presence was changing the color of the bedroom, Anthony got on the telephone with his mother.

His mother had been born on Long Island.

She still lived on Long Island.

She told Anthony about his uncle's various bodily ailments, which included dementia, fecal and urinary incontinence, spontaneous bleeding, a lack of mobility, a loss of skin elasticity, and kidney disease.

Then she suggested that it was only a matter of time before her brother would return home from the state-funded institution in which he convalesced.

"He's not coming back," Anthony said to his mother. "No one gets better when they're suffering full-body failure."

"You're talking crazy," said Anthony's mother. "He's still young!"

A few weeks earlier, Anthony had left Fern on Manhattan and returned to Long Island, where he'd visited his uncle in the state-funded institution.

Anthony walked past the recreation room and found his uncle's room, where his uncle's useless machine of a body had been positioned in a chair.

The useless machine could not get up from the chair. It needed a functioning machine, in the form of a social worker, to help it stand.

This caused its own problem, because every millimeter of the useless machine was wracked with pain. When it was touched, waves of agony ran through the useless machine.

The useless machine could not talk.

The useless machine had wires coming out of its arms and a wire running through its penis into its bladder.

The useless machine was wearing socks that were stained with an instance of the useless machine's uncontrollable diarrhea.

So when Anthony's mother said that her brother was still young, Anthony started screaming.

Fern came out of the bedroom and watched as her lover's face turned red and watched her lover's mouth emit violent sounds and inadvertent spittle.

"You don't understand anything!" cried Anthony into the telephone.

"The body isn't something you can just fuck around with!" cried Anthony into the telephone.

"You've never been sick, you have no idea what it's like!" cried Anthony into the telephone.

That night, when Fern and Anthony engaged in some bad fictional sex, Anthony sobbed like an infant.

In the Year of the Mechanized Baptism, New York City played host to one of its storied events: the Whitney Biennial.

The Biennial was a display of artworks. It occurred every two years at the Whitney Museum of American Art.

Generally speaking, artworks were human-made abstract representations of three-dimensional reality.

Anthony wanted to go see a film by the Los Angeles-based artist William E. Jones.

The film was called *Massillon* and it was included in the 1993 AD Whitney Biennial. Amongst other things, the film was about Jones growing up mega-homosexual in post-industrial Ohio.

"Before we see the film," Anthony said to Fern, "we should check out the show. The whole thing costs six bucks."

Everyone who'd come into contact with the energy field residing in Anthony's body believed that Fern spent most of her time painting. Anthony himself believed this.

When Anthony extended the invitation, Fern couldn't say no.

The Whitney Biennial was a professional obligation.

They walked uptown to the Biennial, which was housed in the Whitney Museum at the corner of 75th & Madison.

On the way, Anthony and Fern found themselves trapped in an unpleasant discussion.

The topic of this unpleasant discussion was familiar.

It was a reliable source of discord.

This was the topic: Fern's unwillingness to discuss her past.

Anthony was deeply suspicious that Fern was hiding vital information.

Which, of course, she was.

But Anthony's body was awash in huge amounts of testosterone and primal magic.

He could not imagine the information that Fern was hiding. No one could!

Anthony's body had funneled his suspicion into some serious masculine bullshit. He was fixated on Fern's sexual history prior to the advent of their rutting congress.

He was convinced that she had a long history of shameful encounters.

From a certain perspective, this was true: Fern had more than her fair share of Fairy Land relationships, and she'd been visiting the mortal world since the Fourteenth Century AD.

But Anthony's thoughts were more pedestrian.

He was consumed with fleeting images of suburban fingerbanging, semen-smeared threesomes, and an excess of New York City blowjobs.

Don't forget: he was from Long Island.

"I just want to know the truth!" he shouted. "I can handle it!"


Even in the best of times, the Biennial was notorious for producing a high level of annoyance.

Everyone who visited an iteration of the Biennial left the Whitney Museum and complained about how the abstract representations of three-dimensional reality in the Biennial were the wrong abstract representations of three-dimensional reality to be displayed in a space dedicated to abstract representations of three-dimensional reality.

Unlike previous Biennials, the 1993 AD iteration had overthrown the tyranny of certain kinds of abstract representations of three-dimensional reality and replaced them with different abstract representations of three-dimensional reality.

The 1993 AD show was conceived and executed to engage with voices marginalized from the mainstream of the art world and American culture. It included people descended from the indigenous tribes of the Americas, and people descended from people brought in chains to support America's original economic scheme, and people exploring the subjugation of women.

And because it was the Year of the Mechanized Baptism, the Biennial occurred before the American capitalist class realized the inherent profitability in men who had sex with other men.

So the Biennial also included mega-homosexuals like William E. Jones.

Back in those days, William E. Jones was an excluded voice.

Now he's a faithful viewer of Reality TV!

*RuPaul's Drag Race*!

Things change!

Capitalism can eat anything!

The 1993 AD Biennial presented two particularly controversial representations of three-dimensional reality.

The first was a video of the Rodney King assault, which was shot by a plumber and depicted the Los Angeles Police Department beating the shit out of a motorist descended from people brought in chains to support America's original economic scheme.

The second were the admissions badges, which everyone had to wear if they didn't want to be kicked out of the Whitney Museum.

The badges were designed by the artist Daniel Joseph Martinez and spelled out various iterations of the following phrase: I CAN'T IMAGINE EVER WANTING TO BE WHITE.

Everyone freaked out.

They freaked out so hard that they created a physical, and conceptual, environment of malice and paranoia.

If you think this is an exaggeration, reader, then I recommend that you read contemporary reviews of the 1993 AD Whitney Biennial. If you can find anything more positive than qualified sneering and affronted guilt, then you are a much better researcher than me.

And remember: the qualified sneering and affronted guilt came from people who were sympathetic to the show.

Fern and Anthony paid their collective $12 and were given admissions badges.

Fern's admissions badge said: EVER WANTING.

Anthony's admissions badge said: IMAGINE.

They wandered through the rooms and galleries of the Whitney Museum, bombarded by abstract representations of three-dimensional reality.

When Fern and Anthony arrived at the Cindy Sherman photographs of mannequins and exaggerated plastic genitalia and reproductive organs and BDSM masks, Anthony looked into Cindy Sherman's abstract representations of three-dimensional reality.

And Cindy Sherman's abstract representations of three-dimensional reality looked into Anthony.

"Here we find the nature of knowledge," said Anthony.

"What?" asked Fern.

"We can't know anything that isn't first filtered through our senses. There is no knowledge beyond that which is observed. There is no first truth. Sherman is presenting us with a moral lesson on instructive epistemology. This is the real nature of sex. This is the desire of all men. It may arrive disguised, but this is what happened when you allowed yourself to be fucked by beasts. The constructed nature of sex, informed by the media, informed by society, informed by ten thousand years of patriarchal society. Cindy Sherman has stripped it away. Now you can see them how they saw you. This is the truth of letting yourself be fingerbanged by animals."

For centuries, people had been dragging Fern to exhibitions of abstract representation of three-dimensional reality.

She'd been stuffed full of the nonsense that people said in salons, in museums, and in galleries. She'd suffered through endless men talking about abstract representations of three-dimensional reality.

And Fern was nobody's fool.

She hadn't endured these exercises in tedium and learned nothing.

She had cottoned on to the underlying, and unjustifiable, delusion that animated every one of these discussions: the religious belief that art, rather than money, was the most influential thing imagined by human beings.

And here was the only person with whom she'd ever fallen in love and he was condescending to her with an even older bullshit than discussions about abstract depictions of three-dimensional reality, and he was disguising it as bullshit about abstract depictions of three-dimensional reality.

Fern cast another spell on Anthony.

Right there in the Whitney Museum.

Right there in the Biennial.

It was one of the weirdest spells cast by anyone from Fairy Land.

The underlying nature of art was the ability of human beings to perceive an implied whole from the presentation of its parts.

Imagine the human face abstracted to the furthest degree:

No human face has ever looked like this.

And yet your brain, reader, has interpreted it as a face.

Fern's spell was intended to scramble Anthony's ability to apprehend the whole from the presentation of its parts. When the spell took its effect, and Anthony looked at the above, he would see this:

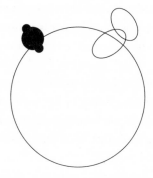

The spell was designed to wear off when they left the Whitney.

Its assumed virtue was this: it would make Anthony stop condescending to Fern about epistemology when really he was telling her she was a slut for sucking so much dick back in the suburbs.

But something went wrong.

For two years, Anthony had been saturated with the radiation of primal magic, and those two spells had sat in and on his body. They had done peculiar things to his biology.

This wasn't like messing up the mind of a landlady in Udine.

This was magic without precedent.

Anthony's biology rejected the third spell.

When Anthony's biology rejected the spell, the feedback caused an invisible magical explosion.

This explosion created a magical avatar of the 1993 AD Biennial.

In its most abstract form.

Here was the abstraction: the 1993 AD Whitney Biennial, focusing on artworks touching on issues of identity and social discord and presenting a critique of how very rich people had constructed the world, existed entirely as the largesse of very rich people.

The Museum and its Biennial were gifts from beyond the Cash Horizon.

All of the bad reviews, all of the upset, all of the guilt, all of the empowerment, all the renewed focus on marginalized voices.

It had happened because some very rich people wanted bragging rights. Through the arcane processes of those who had passed the Cash Horizon, the social capital of these bragging rights would be transformed into an actual capital.

And if you think that's an exaggeration, reader, then you could always look at the patrons listed in the catalogue of the 1993 AD Whitney Biennial.

The list is this: Emily Fisher Landau, The Greenwall Foundation, Philip Morris Inc., Sony USA Inc., Henry and Elaine Kaufman, The Lauder Foundation, Mrs. William A. Marsteller, The Andrew W. Mellon Foundation, Mrs. Donald Petrie, Primerica Foundation, The Samuel and May Rudin Foundation Inc, The Simon Foundation, and Nancy Brown Wellin.

Andrew W. Mellon was a war profiteer. He made a killing during the Spanish-American War, a conflict that was precipitated by an imaginary attack on an American sea vessel.

Primerica Foundation was the philanthropic wing of Primerica, a multi-level marketing operation that targeted lower- and middle-income Americans and got them to buy term-life insurance, as opposed to whole-life insurance, and invest the difference in mutual funds operated by Primerica subsidiaries. Multi-level marketing, by the way, was almost indistinguishable from a pyramid scheme.

Philip Morris Inc. sold a very pleasurable form of suicide.

Nancy Brown Wellin was the daughter of George Brown, who co-founded Brown & Root, which ended up as a Halliburton subsidiary.

Brown & Root supplied almost all of the logistical support for the Vietnam War, a conflict that was precipitated by an imaginary attack on an American sea vessel.

And here's a funny anecdote, apropos of nothing.

Nancy Brown Wellin was at the Armstrong Ranch on February 11, 2006 AD.

This was the day when, and the place where, then Vice President of the United States Richard B. Cheney, architect of the First and Second American Wars against Iraq, was trying to murder innocent animals and accidently shot a lawyer in the heart.

It was like gladiators before a Roman emperor.

You fight, sure, because otherwise another gladiator would kill you, but ultimately your life and your death and your fighting were interchangeable.

It was all someone else's entertainment.

You were paying obeisance to the Cash Horizon.

Then Fern's spell did something funny: it took that abstract representation of the Whitney Biennial and shot it forward through time.

The abstraction landed on the Twenty-First Century AD.

And that abstract representation infected the Internet and all human culture.

Fern doomed everyone in the Twenty-First Century AD to the worst possible fate: rehashing the Cultural Wars of the 1980s AD and 1990s AD, with all of its direct and internecine fighting, and doing it purely for the amusement and enrichment of people who had moved past the Cash Horizon.

When her spell fizzled, Fern took a good look at Anthony.

It was one of those things: when you live with someone, it's harder to notice subtle changes in their appearance.

Fern had missed it.

But now she could see.

And something was dreadfully wrong.

Fern left New York City.

In the Year of the Speckled Band, which roughly corresponded to 1995 AD, 1415 AH, and 5755 AM, Fern returned to New York City and moved back into Anthony's apartment on St. Mark's Place.

Anthony was not well.

It could not be ignored.

Anthony himself seemed unaware of the change.

Anthony kept plugging away at his PhD.

Anthony contributed to a handful of minor academic papers trapped in an arduous process of backbiting peer review.

Anthony kept teaching classes at Eugene Lang College, the undergraduate division of the New School for Social Research.

But his every step was tormented.

Fern cast spells trying to remove the primal magic and its radiation, but these too were repulsed by Anthony's biological transformation.

Fern left New York City.

In the Year of the Salted Earth, which roughly corresponded with 1997 AD, 1417 AH, and 5757 AM, Fern came back to New York City.

Anthony's apartment was empty of Anthony.

His possessions were there.

Anthony was not.

There was an eviction notice taped to the apartment's front door.

Fern cast a spell that handled the pressing issue of outstanding and future rent.

Then she tried to find her boyfriend.

It took some high-grade magic, and a ride on the Long Island Rail Road with a transfer at Jamaica station, but Fern found Anthony in the same state-run institution where his uncle's useless machine had run out of fuel.

Anthony had his own room.

The useless machine of his body had sprouted wires that were attached to other machines that monitored, and influenced, his weakening vital signs.

Sometimes he was lucid. Sometimes his useless machine would stop processing data.

Fern touched his face.

Anthony woke up. His milky eyes focused on Fern.

"I wondered when you'd show up," he said. "How was Bloomingdale's?"

Anthony's mother was in and out of the room.

His siblings were in and out of the room.

Fern never left.

She cast a spell which made her invisible to Anthony's family and the state-funded institution's staff.

When Anthony slipped back into consciousness, he and Fern would speak.

"Oh God," said his mother. "Now he's talking to himself!"

Fern tried to remedy Anthony with magic, but his body repulsed the spells.

She stayed in the room and watched as her boyfriend died.

She knew that she was the one who had assassinated him.

A day before Anthony died, he told Fern that he'd managed to complete his PhD dissertation.

"A lot of Maimonides," he said. "More than I would have thought fucking possible."

"And it was accepted?"

"I'm a doctor now," said Anthony. "Not that it helps."

When the end came, it was gentle, except for a brief moment in which Anthony began speaking with the dead.

"I see her there," said Anthony, his useless machine arm lifting itself and pointing to the empty doorway. "Why are you here, Edith?

Keep away! Keep away! You never understood. Everything you said was a lie. Every word. Keep away! Keep away!"

Anthony's family thought that Anthony was talking to himself.

Fern looked at the doorway with the eyes of Fairy Land.

And for a moment, a luminescent human form was present.

It was a woman dressed in costume from Eighteenth-Century AD America. She was carrying a bouquet of flowers in her right hand and a scythe in her left. A fake beard was plastered on her brow.

One minute Anthony was there.

The next he was gone.

His mother wept.

Fern couldn't figure out how this woman had given birth to Anthony.

She couldn't understand how any of his family shared his lineal biology.

The things that they'd argued over while he lay in his sick bed.

Money, property, romances.

He was a man who'd dedicated his life to escaping the suburban isolation of Long Island. He'd thrown himself into the world. He had not left his home in shame or fear, but with the spirit of a conqueror, with the thirst of someone who wanted to know everything.

*He is me*, thought Fern. *I am him.*

She too was from an island.

She too had chafed at the isolationism.

She too had fled everything.

Fern returned to their apartment.

She found a xeroxed copy of Anthony's PhD dissertation.

She read it.

All 263 pages.

She had absolutely no idea what the hell it said.

She walked to Fifth Avenue and went into the Graduate Faculty building of the New School for Social Research.

Before its acquisition by the university, the building had housed a department store.

It still felt like a space dedicated to shopping.

Fern took an escalator to the second floor and wandered past an abstract representation of three-dimensional reality. The abstract representation was a painting that depicted the Bacchae.

Fern found Anthony's advisor.

He was in his office.

By human standards, he was on the threshold of being ancient.

By Fern's standards, he looked like a baby.

"Can I help you?" he asked.

"I am Anthony's girlfriend," she said.

"It's a shame," said Anthony's advisor.

"Yes," said Fern. "It is."

There was a long silence.

"I read his dissertation," said Fern.

"Did you?" asked the advisor.

"I did not understand a word," said Fern.

"I'm afraid that we don't write for the layman," said the advisor.

Fern left the New School for Social Research and went south down Fifth Avenue, and through Washington Square, and through the West Village until she found herself on Jones Street.

She stood before Caffe Vivaldi.

She went inside.

Folk singers were performing.

The historical anachronicity of Caffe Vivaldi had increased after seven years of globalization.

Fern sat down. She ordered a cappuccino.

She realized that one of the folk singers performing historical anachronisms had also performed historical anachronisms on the night of Fern's third date with Anthony.

In the Year of the Baroque Promise.

The same person.

Doing the same thing.

Singing the same songs.

James wasn't there.

He'd taken his filthy mouth back to Columbus.

The advisor'd said that Anthony's dissertation was one of the best that he'd ever read, that Anthony was a star pupil, that Anthony had conquered everything he'd set out to conquer, that if Anthony had lived he would have made an immeasurable mark on the field, and even if Fern couldn't understand Anthony's abstract depiction of three-dimensional reality, she should take pride in it. The advisor was working on posthumous publication. The advisor would write an introduction that served as an in memoriam.

One of the folk singers sang a song by the Carter Family. It was called "Can't Feel at Home."

Part of it went like this:

*Over in glory land there is no dying there*
*The saints are shouting victory, there's singing everywhere*
*I hear the voice of them that I have heard before*
*And I can't feel at home in this world anymore*

You could be like Anthony and go out into the wide world and chase the only thing that was worth chasing, which was neither money nor power, nor love or comfort, but knowledge.

Escape the suburbs, rise through the social ranks, read more philosophy than is good for anyone, achieve a practical application in 263 pages.

*How does the world work?*

The thought was trapped like methane in tar, rising up, until she heard the folksinger, until she'd spoken to the advisor, until she'd read the dissertation and understood nothing.

*Oh I have a loving mother over in glory land*
*I don't expect to stop until I shake her hand*
*And I can't feel at home in this world anymore*

You could figure out how the world worked.
Anthony had.
You could develop a working model of how everything fit together.
Anthony had.
And it would mean nothing.
Knowledge was not power.
One person learning how the world worked had zero impact on how the world worked.

The boy who escaped his island only to be poisoned by the girl who'd escaped hers.
Years of fleeing Long Island.
Centuries of visiting the mortal world.
And he died six miles from the house in which he'd been raised.
The folk singer did one more verse:

*Heaven's expecting me, that's one I know*
*I fixed it up with Jesus a long time ago*
*He will take me through though I am weak and poor*
*And I can't feel at home in this world anymore*

Fern left New York City.

# Chapter Twenty-Three

# The Full Throat of Christian Virtue

Back in the Twentieth Century AD, there was a genre of writing called Science Fiction.

The writers of Science Fiction speculated about many possible futures.

A great deal of these possible futures involved robots, which were machines that emulated the bodies and practices of humans.

In some books of Science Fiction, the robots were friendly.

In some books of Science Fiction, the robots were mean.

In some books of Science Fiction, the robots replaced the humans.

In some books of Science Fiction, the robots were designed for pleasure.

But the writers of Science Fiction got the robots wrong.

In the whole history of Science Fiction, across all those tedious narratives bound in paper, not a single writer predicted the actual world in which we live.

No one ever suggested that the robots would be total fucking jerks controlled by Russia, or that the robots would use social media platforms to inflame emotions around the hot-button issues facing the 1993 AD Whitney Biennial, and that this use of social media would be part of a campaign to ensure that liberal democracy ate itself from within, and that in using these social media platforms, the robots would enrich a transnational class of oligarchs.

And no one ever suggested that the robots' use of social media would be quoted in articles written by actual journalists.

And no one ever suggested that these robots, in their mean spirit, would be indistinguishable from a plurality of the actual humans who used social media.

And, yes, reader, I know what happens to any writer who makes the mistake of mentioning Russia: instant Twitter accusations of working for the Russian government!

Let me state for the record that I don't work for Vladimir Putin, who is the President of the Russian Federation, or the FSB, who are the state security agency of the Russian Federation.

But I would!

Do you think I want to write hack bullshit about Fairy Land?

Buy me, Vladimir Vladimirovich, buy me!

If you want to understand the Hell in which we live, I suggest taking a look at changes in the American publishing industry throughout the Twentieth Century AD and Twenty-First Century AD.

At the beginning of the Twentieth Century AD, publishing was a father-and-son business. People had a press, they published writers they liked, and hopefully it worked out.

In the 1960s AD, the industry faced existential challenges of distribution, cost, and the sudden realization that the people no longer had to read trash for their numbing dose of daily entertainment.

These challenges resulted in in a wave of consolidation and mergers.

Where there had been, say, a hundred publishers, there were now about thirty.

The mergers continued throughout the 1970s AD, decelerated for a little while, and then kicked off again during the 1980s AD.

The latter decade introduced a new element: the presence of multinational conglomerates.

After the Democratic President William Jefferson Clinton signed the Telecommunications Act of 1996 AD, which deregulated rules of ownership, there was a wave of mega-media mergers that extended well beyond publishing.

Long before this happened, most of the United States' major publishers had been bought up by mega-corporations. In the new mergers, publishing was an afterthought. It was garnish on the meal.

By the mid-2010s AD, this was the state of the publishing industry: there were five major publishers, all owned by mega-companies, with three of the five owned by corporations not based in the United States.

The Big Five were Penguin Random House, Hachette, HarperCollins, Simon & Schuster, and Macmillan.

Macmillan was owned by Holtzbrinck Publishing Group, which was based in Germany.

Penguin Random House was owned by Bertelsmann, which was based in Germany, and which I've insulted enough to ensure that I'll be banished from American publishing for the foreseeable future.

Hachette was owned by Lagardère, which was based in France and was, for most of its history, powered by the manufacture and sales of weapons.

Simon & Schuster was owned by CBS, which was based in the United States.

HarperCollins was owned by Rupert Murdoch, and about whom I will soon say enough bad things to ensure that I'm banished from American publishing for the rest of eternity.

Technically, *The Future Won't Be Long* wasn't published by Penguin Random House.

Technically, it was published by Viking, which once upon a time had been the Viking Press before it was eaten by Penguin Books and became Viking Penguin, and before Viking Penguin was eaten by

Penguin Putnam, and before Penguin Putnam was rebranded as the Penguin Group and was eaten by Penguin Random House.

Reader, if you follow this metaphor of consumption to its logical end, you may imagine my failed novel as the excrement that follows such a hearty meal.

If there's one media outlet that has dominated the tone and tenor of American life since some Muslims facefucked life into a shitty disaster movie, it's Fox News, which is a network found on cable television.

Generally speaking, Fox News offers news from a Far Right perspective, and is consumed by an ongoing advocacy that Muslims should be reduced to a heaping pile of agonized screaming ash.

If you're in any liberal American home, and you want to invoke a series of paleoconservative values while implying your moral superiority to the people who hold them, all you have to do is wave your arms around as if you've been stung by a bee and shout this: "FOX NEWS! FOX NEWS! FOX NEWS!"

Everyone will know what you mean.

They'll know that you mean this: "Republicans want to burn gay people alive and put Black people in cages and fuck up everything that I believe! But that stops here! After the digestifs!"

I shop in a grocery store designed for the haute bourgeoisie.

The prices are ridiculous.

Other than the organic produce, every product in my local grocery has, somewhere on its packaging, a goofy narrative about the company that manufactures the product.

In my neighborhood, it is impossible to go to the local grocery store and buy mustard without encountering a whimsical tale about rural people from Northern California and Oregon and how their quirky values are reflected in the ingredients of their products.

These quirky values are why it costs $3 for a vegan cookie.

The narratives go something like this:

Twenty years ago, my wife Betty and I were in our kitchen, talking about the taste of the mustard that our parents bought. All of the store brands weren't anything like what we remembered, and they were made with pre-processed ingredients and contained preservatives. These chemicals might have allowed for a longer shelf life, but they reduced flavor, and even worse, no one knew what they did to people's health. "I wish someone would go back to old-fashioned values," I said. "Why won't someone make a mustard that tastes great and is good for people?"

Then Betty asked a question that changed our lives.

"Why don't we do it?"

I have watched hundreds of people read these narratives.

And as I have watched people read these narratives, the thought has occurred to me that people are more conscientious about their mustard than they are about the media they consume.

Reader, I have written a narrative in the voice of the man who owns HarperCollins and Fox News.

To acclimate you to its message, I've written this narrative in the style of stories that one finds printed on jars of organic mustard:

### MEET RUPERT

Hi, I'm Rupert Murdoch. I'm having a cuppa in my country home in Mayfair, part of a little town that the lads like to call London. You probably don't know much about my story, but ooh, crikey, I reckon it's a real ripper.

Over sixty years ago, when I inherited an Australian newspaper from my father, I knew that people didn't want a landscape chocka with media outlets producing a true spectrum of thought. The world was crying out for an oligarchical structure of media ownership, where a handful of companies controlled everything and created a false dichotomy of public opinion.

I took my father's little newspaper and used it to gain an iron control over Australia's media landscape, and I funneled the obscene profits into a slow campaign against other countries. My first target was the English. Those old bogans couldn't resist my crass strategy of big tits paired with disgusting opinions for the ill-educated masses.

I moved on to America and did the very same thing. It was ace. The molls in the American government were some real wantons, and they deregulated their media landscape so that me and a few other big'un blokes could consolidate control over almost every outlet in the country. Television, film, newspapers, and publishing. Those Americans were bang up for it. What a bunch of naughty slags.

Maybe you'll recognize one of my profitable divisions. It's called Fox News. It does a cracking job of getting the olds upset about global warming and Christmas.

I also own HarperCollins, and one of the things that Harper-Collins does is publish books by American liberals. Strewth, it's a great deal! I use Fox News to make money off rightward turns of public opinion, and then I make money off the reaction to those rightward turns of public opinion by publishing books which the ideological opponents of Fox News quote like gospel scripture.

When I'm chopping logs for my old wood stove in Mayfair, I like to ask myself whether the liberal writers on HarperCollins, who are enmeshed in the media and entertainment industries, are so stupid that they don't know they're taking money from me, or if they're so cynical and motivated by their own atomized interests that they don't care. I never do make up my mind. Who can decide with that lot of saddos?

Remember when the feminist Internet sheilas were deadset about that Paki comedian fella Aziz Ansari rooting a young moll? That was a real laugh. Aziz was in a few of my movies. *Epic*,

*Ice Age: Continental Drift*, and *What's Your Number?* I jolly well paid for his holiday in the sun. Remember the original article that told the world about Aziz's rooting? It was published on a website called Babe.net. Guess who's an investor?

Do you recall when the benders at the *Guardian* unleashed a real corker and said that *Empire*, a hip-hop-themed television drama, was 'audaciously honest on Black issues'? Crikey, do you care to hazard a guess who produced *Empire*? Want to guess who owned the network? Guess who made the real money off the advertisements and sales into foreign territories? That *Guardian* article was a shock! They made me sound a bloody golly!

I'm getting on in years, but I think I've done pretty well. Maybe some sook dags say I play the larrikin, but I run a family businesses. Ooh, crikey, I hope I've stayed true to my values. I know that when my time comes and I go meet the Great Sky Cunt, I've raised a right crop of young'uns who'll steer my works in the right direction.

If people from the Right Wing want to gain moral instruction, they go watch Fox News, and Rupert Murdoch makes money off the advertisements that are aired on the network.

If people from the so-called American Left want to gain moral instruction, they go buy a book published by a Certified Liberal who is being published by HarperCollins, and Rupert Murdoch makes money off the sale.

The purpose of anyone expressing a public opinion in American life, or consuming one, is this: to make money for about 1,500 people.

And don't think I'm singling out Rupert Murdoch.

Other than the phone hacking, anything you could say about Murdoch was true of 1,499 other individuals.

For instance: the American cable network which served as the ideological counterweight to Fox News.

It was called MSNBC. It stole Fox News's playbook and changed the cheap conservative opinions into cheap liberal ones.

Millions of people watched it every night, convinced that they were being given the inside scoop on how the Trump Presidency would crumble.

Because MSNBC wasn't a jar of mustard, it didn't come with a short narrative about its values, so maybe you can't blame its viewers for being ignorant of who was manufacturing their opinion.

But still.

The letters N-B-C appear in MSNBC.

And as everyone remembers, NBC was the broadcast network that aired fourteen seasons of *The Apprentice*.

*The Apprentice* starred Donald J. Trump, and it was on that show where he honed the skills of televised humiliation and abuse which he would use to win the Presidency.

His last episode aired on February 16th, 2015 AD.

He declared his candidacy for the Presidency on June 16th, 2015 AD.

Comcast Corporation, which owns NBC, made big money off Donald J. Trump before he won the Presidency.

And then they made money after.

And, look, I can't judge any writer who gets paid by Rupert Murdoch.

I took money from Penguin Random House, and if I hadn't had a huge commercial failure, I'd be no different than anyone else.

I'd still be there, just another haute bourgeoisie aspirant chasing my small piece of the global media landscape.

I'd be hoping to crawl through the window before they locked it from the inside.

And to put an even finer point on it: through media coverage which generated advertising revenues, *I Hate the Internet* made money for Rupert Murdoch.

I didn't even sign a contract with the devil and I still work for him.

Now here I am, disgruntled, and I'm like those Science Fiction writers of the Twentieth Century AD.

I see the future.

If you look at the corporate history of publishing, it's been the reallocation of assets from smaller pools of capital into larger pools of capital.

Within twenty years, at least one major American publisher will be majority owned by a conglomerate from either China or the Middle East.

Probably Qatar.

Maybe Saudi Arabia.

And then your moral instruction will come from writers who are cashing cheques signed by repressive regimes with long histories of human rights abuses.

Your opinions will come from writers who will be no different than New York University.

They will be founts of knowledge and they will be economically powered by hegemonies built with slave labor.

And you'll still be more concerned about who made your mustard.

None of this would be of any consequence.

Regardless of what is printed on tote bags, in normal circumstances books have no impact on the governing of any society.

And neither does television.

Popular entertainment is meaningless.

In a sane world, I'd be using the example of publishing to illustrate the increasing consolidation of wealth and money in the hands of a transnational global oligarchy, and bitching about how this excludes freaks from achievement in the arts.

But something terrible happened in 2016 AD: the ghosts of one million dead Iraqis cried out for a just revenge against their killers.

And the world listened.

And so a rogue member of the Celebrity branch of American governance took over the Presidency.

And Penguin Random House publishes his books.

And so does Simon & Schuster.

And so does Macmillan.

And so does HarperCollins.

But not Hachette.
　　There's still hope!
　　Ignore the arms dealing of its corporate parent!

Except:

> La Librairie Hachette craignait, à juste titre, que les résistants n'appliquent à la lettre le programme du Conseil National de la Résistance (CNR) et ne nationalisent cet exceptionnel outil que les nazis admiraient et dont ils avaient envisagé de faire la base d'une énorme entreprise européenne placée sous leur contrôle … Obligés de céder, ils firent tout pour maintenir leurs positions au plus haut niveau dans la reconfiguration du capital envisagée. À la Libération, pour être sûrs que nul ne songerait à les accabler, ils firent réécrire une partie de leurs archives, en ajoutant par exemple qu'au cours d'une entrevue, Laval s'était montré glacial alors que, dans les faits, il avait été d'un commerce agréable, ou d'autres remarques que l'historien éprouve les plus grandes difficultés à repérer quand il consulte aujourd'hui ces documents savamment élagués en 1945.*

Imagine a litter of three-month-old kittens. They are locked in a box. No light penetrates the box. There is a steady supply of oxygen. There is no food or water.

---

*Mollier, Jean-Yves. "L'édition française dans la tourmente de la Seconde Guerre mondiale." *Vingtième Siècle. Revue d'histoire* 2011/4 (n° 112).

The kittens are kept in the box beyond the point of starvation and dehydration.

They shriek and they moan, and they rend each other with their claws.

They kill each other.

The dead are eaten by the living.

One kitten will survive the rest, nourished on the corpses of its siblings, but its suffering will be the longest and, in its final days, it will die the worst death, lacking even the analgesic numbness that comes with inflicting pain on another living being.

Because they are dumb animals trapped in the immediacy of a terrible situation, none of the kittens will ask the right question.

None of the kittens will ask: "Who locked me in this box?"

The defense mechanisms that you've been given as a member of a Western liberal democracy will not save you and they will not save your children.

It will take several decades, but your future, and theirs, is digitally inflected feudalism.

There's a slow train coming.

Everyone knows it.

Your life, and your body, will have only one purpose.

You will make money for monsters beyond the Cash Horizon.

You will be the slave of HRH.

And because you will not kill the rich or mandate a wave of socialism, the best idea that you'll have will be to exercise your franchise at the ballot box, where you will choose a candidate who'll sell you down the river at the first flash of cash.

And your second-best idea will be to go out in public and fight with another poor person while a third poor person captures the action on a smartphone that they will turn into a monetarily profitable video for Facebook, Twitter, and Google.

And your third-best idea will be to become a cynical asshole who lies for money and writes thinkpieces to manipulate the emotions of naïve morons on the Internet.

And your fourth-best idea will be to become one of the naïve morons, and you will make money for your global overlords by pretending into devices built by slaves that the worst thing in the world is whenever a honky gas station attendant insults someone from Honduras.

And your worst idea will be to keep your head down and try to make a reasonably decent life while buying more shit and imagining that you have a special relationship with sports teams, the Celebrity branch of American governance, and intellectual property in which you have no economic stake.

None of this will save you.

If there are still historians in the future, and that's a big if, and their histories are not sanitized at the behest of centralized organizations, my guess is that the Twenty-First Century AD will be seen as the time when all the reasonably decent ideas developed by the Left were co-opted and conquered by the Right.

Identity politics, performance art, fluidity with mass media, total freedom of speech, post-modernism.

The mistake was in thinking that these tactics were the specific province of one ideology.

But a gun doesn't care who it shoots.

When those historians of the future write about 9/11, which was when some Muslims facefucked reality into a shitty disaster movie, it will be seen as the beginning of a moment that ended with the election of Donald J. Trump and the inauguration of the Hyperreal.

9/11 was avoidable, but its psychic message wasn't: the destinies that Americans believed were their birthrights, and the birthrights of their children, were not inevitable.

Those destinies were the accidental byproduct of an unparalleled prosperity boom.

And that boom ended about fifty years ago.

And to fill the hole, the American people embraced the one sector that never dies, the one industry that never goes away, the one stain that spreads forever.

They went to war.

Against the world.

Against each other.

Donald J. Trump was the natural consequence of an entire society that adopted unending slaughter as its central function.

If you believe that this is simply an American issue, you're wrong.

A few months before Trump's election, America's biggest partner in the war against Iraq, the United Kingdom, also heard the crying out of a million dead Iraqis.

And a majority of its citizens attempted suicide by withdrawing from the European Union.

And because no one ever mentions it: most of the European countries that have seen a Far Right resurgence were part of the so-called Coalition of the Willing.

The Coalition of the Willing was a shitty euphemism that President George Walker Bush used to describe the countries that his administration had beguiled or bullied into America's second war against Iraq.

And I know, reader, that causality isn't causation.

But still.

I remember.

And I hear the wailing ghosts of a million dead Iraqis.

And those future historians will also say this: when confronted by the total co-option of their tactics, and facing their greatest existential threat, American liberals doubled down on the very tactics that had been co-opted by their ideological enemies.

They fought over a corpse.

As a member of the Hyperreal, one message has resounded since the day of your birth: the discrediting of Christianity from refined intellectual opinion.

Christianity has been discredited for a very specific reason.

At its core, it exists in opposition to money.

And refined intellectual opinion is just another commodity.

Try some, buy some.

It's all just filthy lucre for Penguin Random House.

On those long and empty nights when I hear the voices of a million dead Iraqis, sometimes the ghosts speak in full paragraphs.

Sometimes they say this: *Jarett, our terrible vengeance has recon-figured your entire society into a shitty iteration of the Church.*

*We have restored the concept of original sin and we have forced your liberal intelligentsia to genuflect before it. We have ensured that they will do this in the form of vacuous statements regarding White Privilege issued between tweets about consequence-free hallucinogenic use, dank memes, and bespoke doggie daycare.*

*We have elevated a faux-Left who write books for Rupert Murdoch, and we have ensured that your society is doomed to rehash the battles of the 1993 AD Whitney Biennial with all the efficacy and power of the Byzantine scholars who debated how many angels could fit on the head of a pin while the Ottomans were sacking Constantinople in 1453 AD.*

*And, yes, Jarett, we find it very helpful that you've pointed out the apocryphal nature of this story about your ancestors and Byzantine scholars.*

*We thank you for both your honesty and your needless pedantry.*

*If you hadn't noticed, we're using the heightened language of rhetoric to make a greater point than mere factual happenstance.*

*Besides, your taxes paid for our blood.*

*So give us a break.*

*We have transformed your fellow citizens of the Hyperreal into a laity with no control over the debate or the direction of their society. We have ensured that all they can do is offer useless peasants' revolts into cyberspace while enriching their feudal overlords and strengthening the ostracism of their fellows. We have created the world's greatest device of excommunication in the form of the Internet.*

*And, yes, Jarett, we have heard your objection to the archaic use of the word "cyberspace."*

*The paucity of books in Arabic translation ensured that a bootleg edition of William Gibson's* Neuromancer *did not appear on the streets of Baghdad until February 2003, just prior to your country's invasion of Iraq. Its cover artwork was a heavily pixelated-and-dithered Internet JPG of a painting by Rowena Morrill.*

*As such, we apologize to you for our lack of a fresher reference point and for failing to use* au courant *terminology to describe your vast and unending apparatus of state surveillance, social shame, and pointless judgment.*

*We note that in your fathomless need to play the pedant, you have emailed William Gibson and asked him whether or not an Arabic translation of* Neuromancer *appeared in Baghdad. We further note William Gibson's response, in which he wrote that to his best knowledge there is no Arabic translation of the book.*

*To this end, we refute William Gibson and assert again that a bootleg version of* Neuromancer *appeared in Baghdad in February of 2003, arriving on the same shelves as the novels of Saddam Hussein. We dare you, and William Gibson, to prove that this did not occur.*

*We have ensured that your feudal overlords benefit from the Church. They are the ones who make money off inflections of dogma about the 1993 AD Whitney Biennial. They own the device of excommunication. The hierarchal social pyramid of the classroom textbook has returned.*

*You are near its bottom, but because you made the curious life choice to be an entertainer, you are not quite a serf. You are a jongleur. The third-oldest profession. Keep singing your songs. See how much effect it has on the world.*

*We will tell you about the delusion that animates your stories. You were born at the tail end of the only fifty years in history when life got noticeably better. You grew up in an historical anomaly and you have mistaken the contours of this anomaly for The Way Things Work.*

*The other 4,950 years of recorded history were bitter slogs through the wretched lives of miserable people suffering beneath unfair systems of governance. The weight of those years is against you, Jarett. What kind of idiot would assume that five anomalous decades are a better predictor of the future than the other 4,950?*

*Let's not pretend. Only people in about twenty countries had better lives during those fifty years. If you haven't killed them yet, perhaps you should inquire with the people of Iraq about whether or not they experienced a significant increase in their quality of life while suffering beneath an oppressive system of oil feudalism propped up by British Petroleum.*

*Our greatest vengeance, Jarett, is that we have recreated the Church and removed from it any hope of the Christian virtues. Your entire society has reconstituted itself around a cruel medieval structure and stripped away that structure's slim benefits.*

*Your Twenty-First Century AD is about everything interesting from your Twentieth Century AD being transformed into a very shitty religion ruled over by a high clergy of the haute bourgeoisie. They pray to monsters. Their faint wish is to somehow avoid their feudal destinies. But they too will fall.*

*Everything will be top and bottom.*

*There will be no middle.*

*Now you live in a world where there is no hope, no charity, and no fraternity.*

*Please enjoy Batman.*

*Please enjoy Harry Potter, even if he is an unfulfilled ghulat al-latah.*

*Please enjoy the Presidency of Donald J. Trump.*

*Please enjoy Brexit.*

*Please enjoy the rise of the Far Right.*

*Good luck with the future.*

*You will most certainly need it.*

*PS: We also apologize for the instance last spring when we expressed surprise that your given name isn't spelled with two Rs and one T.*

*But you killed us, Jarret.*

*You did it with drone warfare.*
*You did it with a child's toy.*
*You did it with a radio-controlled airplane.*
*Get over yourself.*

So what the fuck, reader, why not?

If for no reason other than the bloody-minded perversity of the damned, you might as well embrace the most discredited idea in Western life.

You might as well ride dirty with Jesus.

And his ultimate message.

It's not like anything else is working.

You are more than your base impulses.

You don't have to follow the script of your life.

Don't be a dick.

The only things that they can't monetize are individual acts of kindness.

It occurs to me that I never explained how Arafat Kazi talked his way into the pit.

He found the box office manager.

Arafat Kazi said that he'd bought a ticket.

But that the ticket wouldn't scan.

And then he apologized.

And apologized again.

And again.

And again.

Think about it from the perspective of the box office manager: presumably this was a person who'd spent a great deal of his life talking to people who wanted free admission.

Surely, he was hardened against grifters and schemers.

But none of those people were dressed like circus performers.

They were not holy fools clad in motley.

And none of them apologized for the bother.

And none of those people got a free ticket.

And that's why I'm a Christian.

# Chapter Twenty-Four

## The Man Who Said Bo! to a Goose

After Rusticano, there was nothing else for it.

Celia went back to Fairy Land.

Fern went with her.

The Fairy Knight was left in the mortal world, doomed to wander for an uncertain term, but with the promise that his mother and sister would keep in touch.

Fern's return to Fairy Land occasioned much joy.

Magical charm returned to the island.

The lesbianism was explosive.

What could Fern do?

The experiment had failed.

Life had not turned out how she wanted.

Everything that she'd hoped would carry her through had turned out hollow.

In the end, all that remained was where she'd grown up.

Welcome to true adulthood, Fern.

And, sometimes, Fairy Land was visited by the fractured shimmering astral projections of people tripping on dimethyltryptamine.

As always, the women of Fairy Land believed that these astral projections were remnants of The People Who Came Before.

The astral projections tried communicating with the women.

But their voices came out like Morse code sent over a telegraph wire.

Dot, dash, dot, dash, dash, dot, dot.

One spirit appeared with greater frequency than the others.

Its form had become better defined, more human.

With each of its appearances, the spirit inched closer to speech.

Its words had begun to sound like English.

Like this: *lrhsssrsssslrlrllrlrrlrllrrsssssllsssslrsssssrrsssssrlrlrssssslrllssssrl-rlssssrlrlsssrrrlll.*

One night, as Fern walked past the Warbling Yews of Nevermore, she came upon this spirit.

It looked like a man.

It spoke like a man.

"Madame," the spirit said to Fern, "I perhaps wonder if your elvish brain can be run through its robust Mandelbrotian paces."

Fern stared at the spirit.

She'd heard the story of The People Who Came Before.

Who hadn't?

They'd been the original inhabitants of Fairy Land.

And they'd grown so weary of life that they made a bargain with a creature calling itself Eru Ilúvatar.

In exchange for the blessing of eternal peace, The People Who Came Before had traded away their narcissistic senses of selves.

They'd lost all that my/me/mine bullshit.

They'd lost the curse of language.

And then they'd disappeared.

Fern was freaked the fuck out.

It wasn't that one of The People Who Came Before was speaking.

With magic, none of the rules are ever set in place.

Weird shit happens all the time.

Fern was freaked the fuck out because she couldn't imagine how, by any possible quirk of magic, one of The People Who Came Before would materialize in Fairy Land while wearing a T-shirt that said this:

# *WHY BE RACIST, SEXIST, HOMOPHOBIC, OR TRANSPHOBIC WHEN YOU COULD JUST BE QUIET?*

"Oh most noble spirit," said Fern. "Do you speak now from the Great Beyond?"

"If, in your greeny estimation," said the fractured astral projection, "the Great Beyond is the ketamine-flecked restroom of the local hotspot and private events space known as KABIN, then, yes, this hearty voice shouts from the Great Beyond."

"The restroom of KABIN," said Fern. "What are you doing?"

"I indulge in brief respite. I am in attendance at a fundraiser hosted by 2020 Democratic Presidential hopeful Senator Kamala Harris," said HRH. "Former Attorney General! Top Cop! Straight from the sewer milieu of San Francisco single-party politics! Law and order for the chaos of Trump's America! The iron fist of the prison–industrial complex sheathed in a red velvet glove!"

"You are in America," said Fern. "What part of America?"

"The District of Columbia," said HRH. "Yet my time in your world is as fleeting as the sanity of an unprepared pop sensation thrust into the charnel house of post-industrial fame. Will you not answer my question, madame, in the quick, while still we share our brief moments? I have traveled across time and space. If nothing else, I am a seeker!"

"What is the question?" asked Fern.

"For fifteen years, I have pondered one thought," said the projection of HRH. "My brain is as tormented as a hardened platoon of Achaeans struck down by the arrows of Apollo."

"What is your question?" asked Fern.

"How can one resolve the idiocy of Varg Vikernes," asked HRH, "with his undeniable aesthetic success? When I listen to his recorded works, it causes a great grotesque feeling in the interior self. I am experiencing the horrors of racism. Yet I thrill to the music. I must resolve this dilemma! Can you cut the knot, madame?"

Through all of the coincidental nonsense of fiction, Fern knew what HRH was asking.

She knew all about Varg Vikernes.

This was because of Anthony.

Her dead boyfriend had co-authored a posthumously published academic paper on Norwegian Black Metal.

This paper had appeared in 22:4 of *Popular Music and Society*.

Anthony's co-authorship had been, mostly, a favor to a fellow doctoral student named Jacob.

Jacob had been browsing compact discs at Generation Records on Thompson Street when he'd stumbled across the Fierce Recordings reissue of Darkthrone's *Transilvanian Hunger*.

This was back in The Year of the Speckled Band, which roughly corresponded to 1995 AD, 1415 AH, and 5755 AM.

When he first held the compact disc and its jewel case, Jacob had no idea what the hell was in his hands.

But the ultracontrast black-and-white cover art convinced him into an impulse buy.

Jacob went home and listened to *Transilvanian Hunger*.

He used the Internet, then in its pre-Google days, to search on Darkthrone and *Transilvanian Hunger*.

Jacob used a search engine called AltaVista.

AltaVista helped Jacob find out that Darkthrone was one of the foremost bands in the second wave of a subgenre called Black Metal.

AltaVista also helped Jacob find out that the words printed on the album's back insert—NORSK ARISK BLACK METAL—translated to NORWEGIAN ARYAN BLACK METAL.

Jacob had that old familiar feeling.

Heavy Metal, of which Black Metal was a subgenre, was like all rock music in the Twentieth Century AD: totally indebted, and dependent upon, the influence of African-American blues and R&B.

But there had been a trend in Heavy Metal.

Its practitioners had gazed towards the structures and presumed virtuosity of Classical Music.

Heavy Metal was a genre that pulled away from the African-American influence and sought inspiration amongst received conceptions of European tradition.

Jacob saw Black Metal as the furthest possible extension of this trend.

*Transilvanian Hunger* was an album defined by its abject rejection, ideologically and aesthetically, of the African-American influence.

By virtue of this approach, and its resulting sound, the album was something totally new in quasi-popular music.

That old familiar feeling arrived whenever Jacob stumbled into the cheap wordplay that animates minor academic papers.

In an instant, he came up with a title: "Why are Black People Absent from Black Metal?: National identity, artistic convention and racist ideology in a new subgenre of heavy metal music."

Jacob got to work.
And he involved Anthony.

Jacob returned to Generation Records in search of more Norwegian Black Metal.
The early Internet had recommended several bands.
One name in particular kept popping up: Burzum.

Burzum was a one-man outfit.
Burzum's one man was Varg Vikernes.
In 1995 AD, while Fern was in New York City and worried about the effects of her magic on Anthony's health, she had spent a great deal of time listening to Burzum.
Anthony called it research.
But the truth was that he really liked Burzum.
And so did Fern.

Years after Anthony's death, Fern had ended up at a waterfront penthouse party in the Karşıyaka district of İzmir, Turkey.
The party was full of soft Turkish college boys who hadn't yet done their mandatory military service.
Or had parents rich enough, and well connected enough, to buy their sons out of mandatory military service.

On the penthouse's television, a pirated download was playing.
The pirated download was an iterative copy of the 2008 AD documentary film *Until the Light Takes Us*.
*Until the Light Takes Us* was about Norwegian Black Metal, and it had been named after the English translation of a Burzum album.
The Burzum album was called *Hvis lyset tar oss*.

It had been released in 1994 AD.

The party wasn't much more than soft Turkish boys giggling as they looked at pornographic videos on each other's smartphones.

So Fern had no real choice.

She watched *Until the Light Takes Us.*

It all came back.

Anthony in 1995 AD.

New York City.

Black Metal.

And as she watched *Until the Light Takes Us,* Fern saw the story of Varg Vikernes.

How he'd come from Bergen, how he'd gotten involved with the Oslo Black Metal scene based out of the record store Helvete, how he'd dedicated himself and his music to a racist doctrine of vaguely Satanic neo-paganism, how he'd started burning down old wooden churches as a protest of the Semitic Christian invasion of Norway, how he'd murdered Euronymous, who was the owner of Helvete and founding member of the band Mayhem, and how Euronymous himself was no piece of work, having stumbled upon the corpse of Mayhem's lead vocalist after Mayhem's lead vocalist had blown his head open with a shotgun, and how Euronymous photographed the body and later made necklaces from the body's skull fragments.

Varg Vikernes was the star of *Until the Light Takes Us,* unfathomably pompous, unchallenged, serving out his sentence for the murder of Euronymous, spouting neo-Nazi Norsk ideology from within prison walls, adopting the same insufferable persona that he'd developed for the Norwegian press of the early 1990s AD.

As she watched, Fern remembered how Burzum had soothed Anthony in his creeping pain.

She remembered Anthony telling her that Varg Vikernes was

the key to the whole Norwegian Black Metal scene: he had released his own albums as Burzum, but he'd also played bass on Mayhem's *De Mysteriis Dom Sathanas* and written the lyrics to one side of *Transilvanian Hunger*.

And yet Varg Vikernes was a total fucking idiot.

He was just a crap Nazi with an Odin fetish.

And after being released from prison, he'd done the same thing as every crackpot with his glory days behind him: he'd started a YouTube channel.

But the albums that he'd recorded before prison?

Absolutely fucking brilliant.

So when the fractured astral projection of HRH confronted Fern with his inquiry about Varg Vikernes, Fern could answer his question.

Ever since that penthouse party in Karşıyaka, she'd been wondering how Varg Vikernes's brief period of aesthetic genius could emerge from the body of an idiot.

"It's my guess," said Fern to the astral projection of HRH, "that generating art, and experiencing it, has no connection to the possession of intelligence. There have been millennia of humans writing words and making music and printing posters that insult politicians. Nothing has changed. Still you wallow in your filth. Still you elevate pigs above you. Only a fool would seek intellect amongst human aestheticians. Better if you look for inspiration amongst your plumbers."

"Madame," said HRH, "when next I relieve the vital center, with your words alone shall I shake, rattle, and roll."

HRH felt his spirit begin to return to his body.

"Yet my short time is not up! As you have expressed some interest in America, may I repay your kindness? Do you wish to know the secret of this great depraved land?"

"Amuse me, mortal," said Fern.

"America is a land in which one can be employed by Boeing or Lockheed Martin or General Dynamics," said HRH, "and in that employment be hired and paid for only one purpose. The sales and development of weaponry dedicated to the eradication of Muslim flesh. The more Mohammedians that one kills, the greater the rewards. Endless wealth! A rise in society! Invitations to the best galas! Come and find me in the golden hour of cocktail reception at the Saudi embassy. The drinks are, alas, without alcohol, but I am waiting and watching for you."

The astral projection of HRH began to shimmer.

"Pray, madame, do not think that the blessed war industry would exclude you on the basis of your fairer sex. Four of the five major American defense contractors are headed by women CEOs resolute in their dedication to massacre. When America bathes in the splattered excreta of Musulmans, the country is nothing but liberté, égalité, and sororité. Yes, madame, you also could build those bombs and you too could work towards the complete obliteration of the Saracens. Not one eyebrow raised! The world will be yours! I myself have had the pleasure of a healthy conversation with Marillyn Hewson following her triumphant acceptance of an Edison Achievement Award. She was touched to the core when informed that both my father and myself are shareholders who follow her good works. Extinguish enough lives and they will reward you with a profile piece in the *Style* section of the *New York Times*. Beau Brummell for the Blackwater generation! The pantsuits and pumps that power the putrefaction parade!"

The astral projection of HRH started to disappear.

"I take my leave," said HRH. "I must make quickest haste! America will not scold or shame you for the mass manufacture of weapons with no possible function other than wholesale slaughter. Feel free to murder tens of thousands. Carte blanche! More filthy lucre for The Conqueror!"

HRH disappeared.

His voice came in a final paragraph:

"Yet if you wish to maintain your position as a resoundingly fêted killer of the distant peasantry, then there is one mistake that you must never make. Never consume Zolpidem and power up your smartphone. For if you do, madame, perhaps you will discover the truest meaning of *in vino veritas*. What if, in your drugged haze, you log on to Twitter and refer to your victims with an unfortunate slur? The social and corporate structure of America longs for tsunamis of Mohammedian blood. Yet the human resources department will have zero tolerance for the scourge of online Islamophobia. Kill them all, O my elfen dearest, but never call them Ragheads! In America, the entire society will scrape and bow before your bloody conquest. But no one will ever thank you for your honesty."